CAT'S PAW

WWW.STRIDENTPUBLISHING.CO.UK

Published by
Strident Publishing Ltd
22 Strathwhillan Drive
The Orchard, Hairmyres
East Kilbride G75 8GT

Tel: +44 (0)1355 220588
info@stridentpublishing.co.uk
www.stridentpublishing.co.uk

A catalogue record for this book is available from the British Library.

ISBN 978-1905537-29-7

Typeset in Bembo by Lawrence Mann
Illustrations & Cover by lawrencemann.co.uk

FOR OSCAR

A teenage boy walks down a street as if he owns it. He's already mugged a man in a public phone box and is feeling a foot taller than usual. He plants a stolen cigarette between his lips and snaps a flame from a steel lighter. Through the first bloom of smoke – aah – he spies a new victim. A stylish woman with short, straw-coloured hair, stopping to look in her handbag. The boy breaks into a trot and the bag is his before she can cry out. A shove to unbalance her and then he's off, sprinting towards the next alley. It's as practised as brushing his teeth.

He turns the corner to find the woman standing there.

'Mine, I think.' She takes the bag. He tries to grab it back. The woman whips it out of his reach. She's slender, about his height, might be thirty. Her features are sharp, her eyes green. The boy lunges and lunges for the handbag that's always an inch from his grasp. As if she's playing with him.

It's not a good idea to make this kid angry. He throws a punch. She catches it.

'When did you last scrub your nails?' She studies his fingers. 'Today's youth is going to the dogs, it really is. And *that* is a filthy habit.'

Suddenly there's only half a cigarette in his mouth. The smoking tip rolls into the gutter. The boy steps back. He has a flick knife in his pocket. Something tells him to leave it there. He makes one last attempt to save his pride.

'Nearly got it that time!' The woman twirls the handbag on her outstretched wrist. Then she swings it at his face. He has just enough wit left to duck.

'Pretty fast.' She nods, grudging. 'You know I nearly didn't hear you coming? Such a shame you're flushing your life down the toilet.'

'Let– let me go,' stammers the boy.

'I'm not touching you.' A spark of humour lights her eyes. 'You're curious. Reckless. And – I'm guessing – alone. Like me. But I have friends in high places. You might like to meet them. Or you can carry on with what you're doing. Falling.'

'I don't–' His mouth has dried up. 'Who are you?'

The blonde woman smiles. 'My name is Felicity.'

A PAW PRINT

At last Ben gave up and admitted he was lost. Here was the bus shelter with the cracked pane of glass that he had passed twice already. Here was the corner where he'd stood ten minutes ago, frowning at the road signs. He was lost. But he knew exactly where he was.

A car splashed past and he dodged the sheet of spray instinctively. He had walked these streets ever since he *could* walk, and he knew every puddle. He knew where he was. How could he be lost?

He was supposed to be strolling home from school. Now it dawned on him that he'd been wandering in circles. Whichever way he turned, he strayed back to this wretched crossroads. He had a good idea why. On his right lay Crusoe Crescent, which led to Riversmead Drive, which was where Tiffany lived.

Ben sighed and took the turning. It was either this or traipse round Stoke Newington till it got dark. Some mischievous imp was steering him towards Tiffany's door, no doubt to make him apologise for those stupid things he said yesterday. He needed a peace offering, fast. In his pocket he found the last of a tube of Rolos. That would do nicely.

Miaow. The faint cry came from somewhere off to his left. He stopped, suddenly tense, as if a teacher had picked on him. It was silly but, in spite of everything, cats still made him uncomfortable.

The few friends who knew Ben – really knew him, in the way that most did not – found this hilarious. He didn't blame them. After all, when he concentrated in just such a way, Ben himself could see in dim light, like a cat. If he tried, he could hear high and faint sounds like a cat. Tricks he had learned in his pashki class could let him stalk like a cat, jump like a cat and climb like a cat. He could seem, fleetingly, to have whiskers like a cat. All this was true. Yet Ben Gallagher wondered if he would ever simply *like* a cat.

The mew repeated. A cry of loneliness, or pain. He had an awkward thought. Tiffany's cat, Rufus, surely roamed around here. What if the daft thing had got hurt or trapped? She'd never forgive him for ignoring it. *Miaowwow.* It was coming from Moll Walk, a gloomy alley.

'Here, boy,' he crooned. No, wait, that was dogs. How did you call a cat? Did it matter, since they ignored you anyway? 'Cat! Hey, cat.'

Cutting between houses and a high brick wall, the alley drew him into shadow. Broken glass crackled underfoot. He could see the light at the far end, crossed by cars. He listened but heard no more cries. Turning to leave, he happened to smell the air. Oh... wow.

Only a year ago, it had been a bland weed he never would have noticed. Now it caressed his nostrils like the scent of chocolate mints. Something around here reeked of catnip. Delicious wafts of it were pouring over the wall. Was it growing in a garden on the other side?

Curiosity plus catnip – talk about a fatal combination. He made sure he was alone in the alley and bent his knees, just a little. Then his hands were clinging to the top of a wall that was tall enough to keep burglars out. With a scrape of rubber soles he scrambled to the summit. The trouble with being able to jump ten feet straight up was that there were so many excuses to do it.

Aha, what was this? On the far side wasn't a garden but a yard. He could see the back of a pub, probably the White Lion. No plants, no flowerpots, only a gleaming Harley motorbike parked by a row of wheely-bins. He sniffed again. The aroma of catnip was dizzying. He moved his knee and saw a splash of white paint on the top of the wall. No, not a splash – a paw print. A white cat's paw. The smell was rising off the bricks.

He suddenly felt very exposed up here.

'Oi!'

Ben wobbled. A stocky man barged out through the pub's kitchen door.

'What you up to?'

'Er,' said Ben. 'Have you seen a cat?'

The man glared with bright blue eyes. Ben guessed he was the landlord. His messy, grey-flecked hair and stubble gave him the air of a faded rock star. 'Have I seen a cat? Is that a trick question?'

'No. I heard it –'

'How did you get on my wall?'

'Forget it,' sighed Ben. 'I'm going.'

'Don't tell me to forget it.' The man drew himself up to his full disappointing height. 'I know your sort. Don't let me catch you again or there'll be hell to pay.'

'Yeah, get a haircut,' said Ben. He dropped back into the alley, in a pashki stance that cushioned the fall. There was no chance of the guy chasing after him, but he hurried out of Moll Walk all the same. The encounter had left him uneasy. The magic-mint smell lingered on his clothes and the sense of being watched was slow to lift. Giving Tiffany's road a miss, Ben walked quickly, glancing behind him, all the way home.

Home. That word was causing him problems. For three months, the place where he slept, ate and got ready for school had been Dad's flat on the Hillcourt Estate. Ben tended to call it *the flat* rather than *home.* It was odd waking up each morning knowing Mum wasn't in the next room.

She was no longer in London. Various little things, such as watching her home being smashed by a crane, had ended her love of the city. Compensation, when it came, had let her move into a bungalow in a nearby town, where she'd found a new job managing a café. Hertford felt like the countryside after Hackney. Lucy Gallagher had been so thrilled that she assumed Ben would be too.

'But it's miles from my school,' he had protested.

'This may surprise you, Benjamin, but they have schools out there too. Along with electricity and flushing toilets.' She laughed. Ben shifted farther up the sofa. They were in the cramped bed-sit that she had rented rather than stay at Dad's place.

'Change schools, you mean?'

'Wait till you see your new one. No spray-paint on the gates. Playing fields with grass!'

Ben listened glumly. His school might never top any league tables, but it was his. Some of his friends he had known since nursery. Yet, if it made Mum happy, he'd move schools tomorrow. That wasn't the issue. The Cat Kin was the issue. He couldn't risk losing touch with the only people who shared his secret. Least of all Tiffany.

He tried to forget the weeks of arguments that followed. He told himself he had no choice. In the end, he'd won. His prize was a bed in Dad's spare room, whole milk at breakfast instead of horrid skimmed, permission to play CDs at volume 10. Watching horror films, jousting with Dad on the home-made pinball machine. Home. And though it was arranged that he would go and stay with Mum for most of each long holiday, Ben was already missing her more than he would have dreamed possible.

Things looked better on a Friday, though. Fridays ended with double art. Even if he didn't have Mum's gift for craft, the smell of paints or the squish of modrock between his fingers made it feel like she was standing nearby. Then, after school, he would meet up with the lads at Highbury arcade to eat kebabs and thrash everyone at pinball – just as Dad might have done. On Fridays his parents didn't feel so far apart.

Ben left the arcade and took the northbound Tube. The train was strewn with wasted free newspapers, their headlines shouting about the recent robberies that had been plaguing the Underground. Ben ate Pringles. Muggers were nothing compared to what he had to worry about. The pashki class was meeting in an hour and he still hadn't made peace with Tiffany. When he thought about what he'd said to her, he wanted to shut his head in a door.

He strolled out into the ticket hall at Finsbury Park station. All he had to do was say sorry, he decided, and they would make it up. That was what friends did. In relief he flicked his last crisp at his mouth. He missed. A shove knocked him hard against a photo booth and he heard a shout.

'Hey! What the– Stop!'

Rubbing his shoulder, Ben saw a tall woman with bobbed hair, her hands raised helplessly. Three boys were sprinting down the passage towards the platforms. Swinging from the arm of the middle boy was a brown handbag.

No-one else in the packed ticket hall paid any attention. Ben went to the woman, who made a fist.

'I'm warning you…'

'Are you all right?' he asked. She seemed to twig that this hoodie was harmless.

'Heck. That was a Christmas present.' The tall woman bit her lip. She looked pale. Then she turned paler. 'My pen! My pen was in that bag!'

'Oh,' said Ben. 'Was it expensive?'

She shook her head, exasperated. 'No, no, my *insulin* pen!'

'Insulin?'

'It's a needle.' Her eyes were wide and scared. 'I'm diabetic. And I need it, I need it now…'

Now he understood – his geography teacher carried a similar syringe round his neck and had to use it after every meal. The bag-snatchers were already out of sight, racing for the trains. Luckily his inner cat never stopped to think. While he was still wondering what to do, he found himself halfway down the passage and still accelerating. At the northbound staircase a lightning hunch made him shoot out a hand to grab the banister, slinging his weight into the turn. He flew down twelve steps without touching one, skipped round a bunch of dawdling young men, and in one more leap cleared the second stair-block, plunging eight feet to the concrete.

He had not set his Mau body loose like this for a while, and it felt good. The travellers he passed had scarcely time to gasp before he landed on the concourse between platforms. A Victoria line train stood waiting, the perfect escape route for any pickpocket. He sprang on board. Then a glimpse out of the window pulled him up short. Those three boys were running off down the platform. They hadn't got on this train at all.

He jumped out just as the doors closed. Following the bag-snatchers at a distance, he watched them chase alongside the departing train, slowing when they neared the end of the platform. Now what? They'd passed every exit and had nowhere to go except back past him. Warily he sized them up. The one with the stolen handbag was the smallest. The boy on his right was built well for basketball, all shins and elbows. The third was the sort of kid that Ben used to steer clear of. He moved with a dangerous swagger and his raw, muscled arms were heavily tatooed. As different as they were, they had one curious thing in common. All three wore black bandanas tied around their heads.

The tunnel swallowed the train's tail lights. The youths jumped down onto the tracks and ran into the darkness in its wake. They merged with the gloom and disappeared.

Ben stopped dead. He rubbed his eyes. Those crazy kids had fled down a Tube tunnel. They might as well have climbed into a loaded cannon. The thought of going after them was blasted from his mind.

But what about that sick woman?

But nothing. Her bag was in a tunnel and that was

that. The end. Someone else would have to help her. It was a busy enough station.

There was nothing for it but to turn and walk away. He stayed where he was. Black headbands. They'd all worn black headbands and the same style of clothes. Hadn't there been warnings about some gang raiding the Tube? He wished he had looked at those newspapers instead of just wiping his feet on them.

A mouse pattered through the crawlspace below the rails. A line of verse pattered through his head. *I heed no words nor walls.* Why, exactly, couldn't he follow them? What actually stood in his way? He looked back. The platform was mostly deserted. An indicator board announced the next train in four minutes. Call it five. Time enough to have a peek inside.

He lowered his toes over the platform edge and onto the railway sleepers. Before anyone could notice him he slipped into the tunnel. On a black screen in his mind he imagined a blue cat's eye: Ptep, the head catra, the source of a cat's sense of balance. Ben stalked along the strip between the rails, placing each foot as a jeweller sets gems. Eth walking – the skill that cats used to cross shelves of china ornaments and leave nearly all of them unbroken. He had never needed it more. Two of these four rails could zap him with hundreds of volts.

No, no, this was stupid, this was suicide, this was utterly crazy. His inner voice frantically protested and his inner cat pretended not to hear. He picked up speed, moving deeper in.

Ahead the gloom thickened, studded by weak lamps. Dealing with darkness was second nature by now. Green Mandira, the face catra, blinked into life, and Ben focused it until the cavern lengthened in washed-out colours, its rounded walls ribbed like the gullet of a great snake. Wind sighed in his face and he nearly panicked, thinking a train was coming. No, wrong direction. It must have been air overflow from the southbound line.

Where had those kids gone? The tunnel stretched into darkness. To get out of sight they'd have to be running, and even Ben couldn't do that without risking electrocution. Were there maintenance hatches, hidden side-passages? It struck him that, despite riding so often on the Tube, he had barely any notion of what was down here.

The fearful voice inside him wouldn't shut up. Rather, it grew louder. A train would soon be bearing down on this very spot. How long had it been? Two minutes, three? Turn back, the voice yelled, turn back *right now*. Still he hesitated. An odd shape lay on the track. It could almost be a person, slumped across the rails. He stepped closer and saw with a thumping heart that it was.

The smallest of the boys lay on his front, one arm twisted under him. He looked younger than Ben, twelve at most. His bandana was pulled over his face like a bandit mask, the eye-holes showing lifeless eyelids. He was no longer touching the electric rail that had, presumably, struck him down. It looked as if his friends had simply grabbed the handbag and left him here, where the coming train would cut him in half. Ben knelt to listen at the boy's mouth and caught a whisper of breath. He was still alive.

'Can you hear me?'

Pain exploded in Ben's head. Something had hit him so hard that he saw stars, stars that dazzled every catra. Ben himself was all but knocked out, but the Mau body inside him reacted like a stung wildcat, planting both his hands on the ground and lashing out with both feet. Someone was pinned to the wall behind him, winded so instantly that they didn't even grunt. Ben staggered upright just as a bare, tattooed arm hooked round his neck.

Ben pulled at the arm in vain. As it tightened it squeezed the strength from his limbs. There had to be a pashki move to get him out of this. His head felt swollen with pressure and yet light, floaty. A roar filled his ears. The noise of a train. Oh no, *the train*...

Then it was strange. He fancied he was still in his seat on the Tube. The carriage was empty apart from him. He stared through the dark window. They were stuck in a tunnel. The lights had gone out. He was delayed. It bothered him. By now he should be walking back to Dad's flat, on his way h–

'Home,' croaked Ben. His voice sounded different. It was pitch dark. He felt as if he had woken from sleep. Time was missing. His head and neck ached and he was cold.

He was sitting on hard ground. Trying to get up

he found his arms would not move. A light flared, hurting his head.

'Told you he was alive.' It was a deep voice, but a boy's, not a man's. 'You're a worry-weasel, Hannah.'

The light bobbed farther away, tracing the outline of a rangy boy holding a small torch. Beyond him crouched two smaller figures. Crouched where, though? This didn't feel like the tunnel anymore. More like a poky room. Again he tried to move.

'Your arms are tied,' said the tall boy.

Ben opened his mouth. The boy mockingly said it for him.

'*Where am I?* You're in the Hermitage, and you're trespassing. Next question. *What are you going to do to me?* Dunno. That's up to him.'

'Him?' Ben strained at the cords that chafed his wrists. 'Who's *him?*'

The boy bent close, angling the torch into his own face. Red hair burned above the black cloth of his mask.

'Mad Ferret,' he whispered.

The torch went out, leaving Ben in a smouldering dark that no effort of his eyes could penetrate.

HERDING CATS

A young dancer, wearing black, kneeling on the floor of the bleak church hall. That was how she would look to anyone who walked in. But Tiffany Maine was alone in the building. She knew that because hers was the only breath she could hear.

She sat on her heels, fingertips resting on the herringbone pattern of wooden tiles, her arms parallel pillars. She repressed a shiver.

'I heed no words nor walls.'

Her voice rang off the grubby plaster walls, which were papered with crayon pictures. The Sunday School also used this place, thankfully never at the same time. Tiffany tried to concentrate.

'Through darkness… I walk in day.'

The only light in here came from neighbouring street lamps that turned the arched windows orange. Sour smells troubled the air. Perhaps one of the Sunday School kiddies had had a little accident. A drawing of a hippo flapped in a draught and she forgot the last line of the chant. *And I… I do not fear…*

Tiffany liked to get here early. Just ten minutes to change into her pashki kit and prepare for the lesson.

They were *her* lessons now, and she wanted them to be right. Also, it was her only chance to snatch a moment alone. Even though such moments tended to dredge up her most dreadful memories, she was learning to be glad of this too. Better to face them, stare the terrors down, than to leave them lurking in the depths of her mind, where they could leap on her without warning. She drew a steady breath.

'And I do not fear the tyrant–'

'Hi, hi, hi!' The door crashed shut on its weak hinge. 'Hiya, Tiffany!'

The main lights flicked on, hiding the shadows. Tiffany twisted round to wave at Susie Liu. 'You made it, then.'

'Yes. I am sorry about last week.' Susie dug sportswear out of a holdall. 'Sometimes my gymnastics coach can only do Fridays. I'm *sure* I packed my kit. Uh-oh. Mother can't have left my swimming towel in here, since *Tuesday*...' From the dank towel Susie untangled a black unitard emblazoned with cat whiskers. Wrinkling her nose she vanished behind the hessian noticeboard they used as a changing cubicle.

Tiffany said nothing. Susie had started gymnastics a few months ago, excited to think that the skills she learned at pashki would make her a champion. In reality it wasn't so simple. Astonished by her vault and beam displays, the thrilled coach had bustled her onto the asymmetric bars, where she nearly snapped both elbows. There were lots of problems like that. Human and feline gymnastics were too different, and you mixed them at your peril. Annoying Tiffany was perilous too. Susie had now missed two Cat Kin meetings in a row.

She wasn't the only regular absentee. Yusuf made excuses about football practice now he was on the school A-team. He came about once a fortnight. Then of course there was Olly.

Susie reappeared, reeking of chlorine, and they warmed up with the Chasing the Bird stretch-and-lunge. Daniel arrived ahead of Cecile, with another crash of the door that made Tiffany wince. She carried on with the warm-up, leading them through the basic stretches, Long Reach, Scratching Tree, Arch on Guard. Now and again she glanced at the door. Ben was never this late.

So that was it. He wasn't coming. She pushed her calf muscles to the point of pain as she recalled their quarrel on Wednesday evening. Yes, she'd said some hurtful things, but then so had he. How dare he be sulking? She'd had an apology all ready.

It would be wrong to blame her parents. After those awful few days last year, they could hardly behave otherwise. Mum and Dad had given her up for lost. They had pleaded on television for her safe return, while in their imaginations she had been murdered a hundred times. When Tiffany was returned to them, apparently unhurt, they were bound to go completely crackers.

At first this was lovely, a fairytale. Tiffany felt like Cinderella and Aladdin rolled into one. She was treated as a princess, granted breakfast in bed, pampered to within an inch of her life. Every day brought gifts, outings, makeovers, designer-label clothes. It took time to notice that she had something in common with Rapunzel too, and it wasn't her celebrity-salon hair.

Mum and Dad had locked her in a tower. Sort of. If she wanted to go out, even to Avril's house two streets away, they drove her. When she was at school, at a friend's, or seeing a film, her parents would phone, supposedly to check she was enjoying herself. She was under orders never to turn her mobile off, not even in cinemas. Once she left it behind and Mum had actually, honestly, rung the police. After the first six weeks of this, Tiffany felt six years younger. Dad tried to hold her hand when they crossed the road. Soon Mum would be checking her food for small bones.

Still, since anything beat being ignored, she tried to enjoy it. Which was why the oddest, saddest and most unfair thing took her quite by surprise. Ben noticed it first.

'Is your home phone on the blink?' he had asked her, way back in November. He'd left a few messages that she never got. Soon afterwards he remarked, 'I suppose your school is still burying you with homework,' which puzzled her because she'd had it easy leading up to Christmas. It emerged that Ben had stopped by her house, only to be told that she was studying. Then there was the time Ben said 'Hi!' to her father in the supermarket. Peter Maine veered off into the frozen section.

'You're imagining things,' Tiffany protested. 'My mum and dad think you're a hero. Why would they start treating you funny?' Why indeed. Yes, in their first rush of joy at having her back, they had hailed Ben as her rescuer. He was the bright lad who placed a vital call to a helpline (they didn't know he had done rather more than that). And there was the problem. Every time they looked at him, they relived those hellish hours. And surely they wondered. Tiffany's made-up story of her kidnapping had never quite hung together. Was there more that they didn't know? Could this boy have been somehow at fault? Might their daughter have been safer if she had never known Ben Gallagher? Annoyingly: yes.

Soon it was as obvious as a tiger at the table. On Wednesday evening Tiffany came downstairs to find Mum on the doorstep, telling Ben she wasn't in. Ben glared at them both and stalked off into the mist. Tiffany caught him up in Crusoe Crescent.

'I can take a hint,' said Ben.

'She didn't mean it,' said Tiffany.

'You don't want me to come round any more?'

'Yes! I mean, no! I mean–'

'Any idea why they hate me so much?'

'They don't–' It went on like this for a while. Presently Tiffany saw Mum skulking nearby.

'Huh.' Ben had noticed too. 'I'm glad my parents

aren't like yours.'

'They just worry a lot. They care.'

'You're fifty metres from your front door.' He lowered his voice. 'On Christmas Eve you climbed with me up the church steeple to look down on all the lights. When the midnight bells rang we nearly fell off. I'll go and tell your mum about that.'

'Don't you dare.'

'Tiffany, I can't believe you'd let them do this.'

Nor could she. Every day she felt a part of her soul pining, staring out as if through a locked cat-flap. But then, she wasn't her parents' cat. 'I'm their daughter,' said Tiffany.

'After all the trouble I went through to save you from that cage,' Ben hissed, 'you're letting mummy and daddy keep you in another one.' His face flushed – he had visibly bitten his tongue. And Tiffany was spitting mad.

'After all *you* went through?' she cried. 'You have *no idea*–' She saw Mum hurrying their way and froze her with a look. 'Ben, you can't imagine what it was like in there. What it's like for me still. Do you ever faint at school? Do you have to sleep with the ear of your old *teddy bear* stuffed in your mouth, to stop the noise when you wake in the night? No. Because it's all about *you*, isn't it? It's what *you* suffered. Well, I hope for your sake you never suffer like that.'

In rushed Mum, the referee.

'Enough now. Sweetheart, you're making yourself upset.' She pulled Tiffany by the arm. Ben might have been invisible.

'So,' Ben spluttered, 'so tell me. Tell me what it was like. I'm about the only person you can!'

'Ben,' said Tiffany's mother, 'goodbye.'

As she was led away, Tiffany wheeled round. 'And you'd better hope it never does happen to you,' she sobbed. 'Because if it does, you – you won't get any help from me.'

She had a foreboding, at the time, that these were the last words she would ever say to him. Which of course was silly.

'Picture the row of tall posts in your mind. You are standing on the first.'

Kneeling in the Sitting Cat pose, Tiffany watched the others tiptoe with closed eyes around the hall. They should all have been experts at Eth-walking by now. It worried her that most of them seemed to have got worse.

'You *must* step precisely on the top.' The more she strove to sound commanding, the more Daniel's face creased with locked-in laughter. Without Ben here they didn't seem to take her so seriously. 'When I tell you, step to the next imaginary post!'

The door of the church hall crashed. Cecile bumped Susie and they fell in a heap of giggles.

'Hey, fellow freaks!' Olly burst in, damp hair plastered across his forehead.

Tiffany folded her arms. In the silence Susie

muttered, 'Watch out, Sanders.'

'What?' Olly slung down a kitbag. 'I'm not late again?'

'A bit,' said Daniel.

Half an hour, actually. Tiffany decided to let it pass.

'Sorry,' said Olly. 'Time completely lost track of me.'

Tiffany leapt to her feet.

'Oh, so it's time's fault, is it?' she cried. 'Silly old Father Time, did he forget to wind your brain up this morning?'

'Oooh!' said Susie. 'Easy, tiger.'

'I'm just making a point.'

'He did say sorry,' Daniel put in.

'Yeah.' Cecile frowned. 'You're starting to sound like Mrs Powell. And not in a good way.'

Tiffany opened her mouth, then shut it again. When she mumbled, 'Okay, join in when you're ready, Olly,' she heard her own, duller voice.

Under the tick of the plastic wall-clock she took them through some easy routines. So far this lesson had barely brushed the cobwebs from her bones. Privately she noted that Susie's movements, though elegant, had grown decidedly un-catlike, and that Olly was cheating with bent knees. Something else was wrong, too. She was the only one here who had bothered to print her face with cat markings. Under the tabby paint, she blushed.

Their hour was almost done. In a last-ditch effort to liven things up, she got them doing Ten Hooks. This was the side of pashki that was most like a martial art.

To watch two skilled opponents was to see a ballet of battle, like a cross between capoeira and an alley-cat fight. Daniel at least was keen. A bit too keen.

'You kicked my head!' Olly yelped. 'Didn't anyone tell you it's pretend?'

'It's not pretend,' Daniel corrected. 'It's non-contact.'

'Which means you don't kick my head.'

'Sorry.' Daniel sucked his teeth. 'But that would have been nifty in a real fight. What's the move called again?'

'Jafri zafri,' said Tiffany. 'Arabic or something. It's too difficult, I don't think even I do it right. It was one of the Ten Hooks attacks I found on the web.'

'The web? You mean someone else out there knows pashki too?'

'I suppose.' The sadness, never far away, pricked her again.

Susie waved, already changed. 'Same time next week, hopefully!'

'Money,' said Tiffany. 'Remember?'

She had not asked her parents to hire the hall. It was enough that they let her out one evening a week. Daniel and Cecile dropped three pounds apiece into her shortbread tin.

'Er.' Olly grinned helplessly. 'Six pounds next time?'

Susie turned her purse inside-out. 'I'll pay you at school, I swear.'

Or I will swear, thought Tiffany. 'You never forgot the money when Mrs Powell was collecting it.'

'That was different,' said Susie.

'How, pray?'

'There she goes again,' said Olly. 'It's getting a *leetle* bit spooky.'

Tiffany watched the Cat Kin leave. Had Mrs Powell felt like this at the end of lessons? Suddenly alone and empty? Many times Tiffany had meant to stay after class, to get to know her pashki teacher better. There was so much they had never talked about. Probably Mrs Powell would have been glad of the company, for she had lived all alone except for Jim, her gorgeous silver cat. The thought that she might be lonely had never occurred to Tiffany. Not until it was too late.

Tiffany blinked and found she was the only person left. And the Sunday School's chairs still needed putting back. Huffing and puffing she got them into crooked rows before the car rolled up outside. Tiffany scrubbed off her face-print with wet wipes, locked the hall and prepared a smile for Dad. He settled her into the back seat and checked her safety belt. Ugh. Would Mum later tuck her in bed with a mug of warm milk?

At home she found Rufus curled upon her pillow, whiskers still damp from his saucer of milk. He gave his greeting-call and she crumpled his ginger ears. Slippers dragged on the landing carpet.

'Hello, stranger.' Stuart leaned on the door jamb. 'Still fooling them, then?'

She stiffened. 'Don't know what you mean.'

Her little brother smirked and walked stiffly into

her room. From his knees to his ankles he wore the outlandish supporting braces that his doctors called KAFOs but which he referred to as his cyberman legs. His chubby face looked pale today, his dark brown hair unbrushed.

'How are you feeling?' Tiffany asked.

Stuart shrugged. The effort seemed to drain him and he flopped onto her mattress, where he lay chuckling weakly. 'Great. Now I can't sit up. Help me.'

'You should be in bed.' Tiffany propped him upright. 'And don't say you are already.'

He gave his withering look. Probably he had been lying down most of the day. Most of his life, come to that. For a kid with muscular dystrophy, visiting his sister's room counted as an outing. She pulled her black velvet beanbag alongside.

'Do you want to play cards for a bit?'

'No.' Stuart looked sly. 'I want to know what's so special about your exercise class.'

'Nothing. It's just that.'

'You hate exercise!'

'I hate school sports,' she corrected. 'This is more like yoga.'

'How much like it?'

Her beanbag rustled. 'It's something I do.'

'It's *all* you do.' Stuart leaned forward. 'Ever since… I mean, you'll give up anything else if Mum and Dad tell you to. Except that. Why? Oww-ow-oo!'

'Someone needs to mind where he puts *this*, I think,' Tiffany said before releasing his nose.

'Only making conversation.' He sniffed, then brightened. 'Hey. I've got some more heavy lifting for you.'

'Of course.' Smiling, she helped him walk back to his room. His bedspread was covered with cut-up scraps of newspaper. 'All these?'

'It's two weeks' worth. This is the best one.' He waved one cutting. It was a headline from a local paper: PARTY-GOERS REPORT ALIENS IN DALSTON.

Tiffany took the scraps from him one by one, pinning them onto his cork notice board. Stuart lacked the strength to push in a drawing pin. The board was already a patchwork of articles on UFOs, mingled with snapshots of blurred saucer-shapes.

'You're really getting into this stuff.'

'The truth is out there,' said Stuart. 'One day planet Earth will accept that we are not alone.'

'Don't I know it.' She took another cutting from him and ironed it between her palms. Then, all at once, she did feel alone, very alone. That pashki class had been awful. No-one was taking it seriously anymore. And why couldn't Ben have come? Then at least they could have said sorry to each other. The thought of him sulking at home made her angry. Angry and sad. She had thought he was bigger than that.

THE GREY CAT

Ben was woken by his triceps cramping. With his arms held behind his back, fixed to something immovable, he could only writhe like half a worm until the sweat was wrung out of him. The pain ebbed, leaving traces of memory. Hours hunched in darkness on a numbing floor. Silent shadows, watching. A headache. Then either passing out or falling asleep. A red glow through his eyelids made him open them.

Anglepoise lamps stood like metal birds, peering light. Among them sat two children, a boy on a plastic chair and a girl on a stool. Both had bloodshot eyes, as if they had stayed awake all night. Apart from a small cupboard and a half-empty crate of cola cans, there was little else in this poky room to tell what kind of place it might be.

Cramp or no cramp, his arms were killing him. He found they were tied to the leg of a wooden desk which dug into his back. The desk itself was attached to a wall tiled like a bathroom. Wriggling into a sitting position he saw a door, also made of wood. It had a steel lever-handle and a roll-blind that might have covered a glass pane.

The girl whispered, 'He's awake.'

Her skin matched the porcelain tiles, milky pale behind curtains of lank dark hair.

'Thomas, he's awake. We should tell.'

'It's four in the morning. Kevin would kill us.'

'But he said to tell. When he…' The girl flapped her hands at Ben.

'Who–' Ben's mouth felt rough. 'Who are you?'

'Perhaps you could give him a gentle shake,' said the boy.

'No! You got to come with me.'

'Someone has to stay on guard duty.'

'I'll stay,' said the girl.

'That would mean leaving you alone with him. He might be dangerous.'

'Hey,' said Ben.

'I'm not waking Kevin up,' whimpered the girl.

'He's quite reasonable sometimes, Hannah.'

'You said he'd kill us.'

Ben took a deep breath. 'Excuse me–'

'He's known you longest,' said the boy.

'But Thomas–'

'*Oi!*' yelled Ben. A stunned silence settled on the pair. 'Talk to me!'

'Quiet.' The boy folded his arms. The movement jogged Ben's memory. He was one of the three bag snatchers. The smaller boy who'd played dead on the rails so his friends could spring a trap.

'I tried to help you,' Ben snapped.

'Sssshhh!' The girl pressed fingers to her lips. With a clunk of lock the door flew open. Ben's guards shrank before a tall, powerfully built boy with a mane of conker-red hair and freckles on his cheeks. His bare feet, T-shirt and frayed tracksuit trousers looked like clothes that someone might wear to bed.

'Are you deaf or just stupid, Thomas?' He seized the boy and girl by their collars as if to crack their heads together, although he didn't. 'I told you to come and get me. What have you said to him?'

'N– nuffink, Kevin.'

'He's literally only just this minute come round,' Thomas pleaded.

Ben sat up straighter. 'Leave them alone.'

Kevin turned. Ben, remembering too late that he was helpless, smiled weakly. Kevin ripped a can from the crate of fizzy drinks. Ben was so thirsty that he actually dared to hope, before Kevin popped the ring and shook the contents all over him. Cola seethed down his neck.

He tried to speak calmly. 'If you let me go now, you won't get into trouble.'

Kevin fetched a second can, shaking it.

'Think!' said Ben. 'I didn't come home last night. My dad's already called the police.'

The drink spurted, soaking his clothes. Something splashed in a foamy puddle. His phone. On the screen, a text message: *Hi Dad. Staying tonight at Yusuf's house. Hope it's OK. Ben.* When had he sent that? Then he twigged: he hadn't. Someone had ransacked the address book, finding his name and a likely friend. With one lucky guess they'd robbed him of a whole night.

Still he rallied. 'My dad won't believe that. I'd never

stay at Yusuf's, he lives in… Scotland.'

'Stoke Newington.' Kevin sniffed. 'Your dad already rang. I can't play you the message as there's no signal down–' He broke off. 'But he's cool about it. What great parents you have.'

Ben strained furiously at his bound wrists. What was this place? What had he stumbled upon? Fizzy liquid stung his eyes.

'Kevin.' The boy called Thomas yawned. 'When's the next guard shift? Only Hannah's really sleepy.'

'Then slap her. You've got three hours till dawn. If you want to eat tomorrow, you'll stay awake.' Kevin trod on Ben. 'Back for you later. Don't get comfortable.'

The door locked behind him. Ben sat in his wet clothes. The damp became a sticky, itchy varnish. He imagined ants on his skin.

'Tell me what is going on,' he sighed.

His young guards blanked him. Ben searched for a less uncomfortable way to slump. His legs went to sleep so often that it became a way of marking time: ten minutes between the pins and needles. Twice he shut his eyes and tried marshalling his catras. If he could summon up Mau claws, those brief ghostly blades might cut his bonds. It was no good. His fingers had no feeling. He flexed his legs for the seventeenth time.

The girl slipped off her stool and began pacing the floor. After a few laps she picked up a packet of tissues, scurried over to Ben and began to wipe his face and neck. The cola had evaporated long ago, but

Ben almost choked with surprise and gratitude.

'I'm really thirsty,' he murmured.

She hesitated, then brought him a can. Oh well, if there was nothing else. Hannah did her best to tip it into his mouth, mopping up the rest with more tissues.

'You know,' said Ben, 'sooner or later my parents *will* wonder where I am.'

That got no reaction. He tried again. 'Do your folks know you're here?'

Hannah said, 'Maybe.'

'Maybe?'

'I don't know.' Hannah shrugged. 'I lost them.'

'We can't talk,' said Thomas.

'Your mum and dad died?' said Ben.

'No. I don't know. Maybe they–'

'It doesn't matter.' Thomas gave her a warning glare.

'Mm.' Hannah nodded. 'I got a new family here. This is our family now. And yours.'

'Not mine.'

'Don't antagonise Kevin, and you might get breakfast,' said Thomas. 'It's smashing at the weekend, there's usually eggs.'

Who *was* this kid? His accent stood out like a salad in a chip shop. Thomas talked like someone from an expensive school, even posher than the one Tiffany went to. What was he doing here? What were any of them doing here? Where was *here*?

'How about your parents, Thomas? Are they lost?'

'No. I see my daddy.'

And who said *daddy* these days?

'Several times a week,' said Thomas, then shut his mouth.

Ben had no patience for riddles. 'Just untie me.'

The silence stretched. They weren't going to answer. He lolled against the desk, cooling his brow on the white tiles. He had seen these white tiles before, he was sure. Only not in a bathroom, not in a house or a shop or a school. Somewhere else, somewhere that had rows and rows of tiles, white and blue and green, curving round corners, soaring in arches, dry winds billowing through them… A kick in the calf jerked him awake.

'I said don't get comfortable.' It was Kevin, dressed now in clothes that resembled combat fatigues, dyed in the shades of concrete and asphalt. A pen-knife glinted in his hand and Ben felt it cut in jerks through his bonds. In one smooth movement Kevin helped him to stand while putting him in a half-nelson. 'Move.'

Grey gloom waited on the other side of the doorway. Ben shuffled towards it, one arm tingling back to life, the other twisted in a new and painful way. He caught a whiff of stale air, fresh enough after the suffocating room. Feeling a wider space around him, he had what his mum would have called a rush of blood to the head. He couldn't let a teenage thug push him around. He did pashki, for heaven's sake.

Pretending to trip, he turned it into a Corkscrew Flick. Clumsy as it was, it broke the arm-lock and he spun clear of his captor and ran. Or tried to. Three strides later came a crippling pain in his neck,

Kevin's fingers, hard as pincers. He fell to his knees and out came all his breath in one whoosh. Kevin knelt on his chest, pointing the knife.

'Let's try again,' Kevin panted.

Now that wasn't meant to happen. For a moment Ben could only lie there in shock. It was as if he had tried to eat a cupcake and broken his teeth. He didn't even struggle as Kevin hauled him upright.

A shove forced him forwards into the twilight ahead. Some sort of broad passage. It looked a bit like a street at night. Lighting came from desk lamps, table lamps or orange workmen's lamps, spaced between shapes like tumbledown houses. They were dens, built from cardboard boxes and bundled with blankets. Some of the bundles snored. Other nests lay empty, littered with sweet wrappers, socks and the occasional comic or children's book. The floor was concrete and, oddly, just half the width of the passageway. A deep ditch ran alongside, cutting them off from the left-hand wall, which curved up to become the roof. At last he understood what he was looking at.

'It's a platform.'

'Platform 2,' said Kevin.

'This is a Tube station.' Wonder distracted him. There was the platform edge; the rails; the doors to staff offices. A blank oblong where he would expect to see a Tube map. And there, upon his left hand side, was the familiar roundel: the red circle with the blue crossbar that bore its station's name in neat white letters.

HERMITAGE

Ben searched his brain. '*Hermitage?* There's no such station as Hermitage!'

'Then you can't be here. Get it?'

His eyes ran across the tiles, patterns of blue and grey punctuated with signs. White words on black told him NO SMOKING. Around the next corner a larger banner pointed back TO THE TRAINS. Every detail was stranger for being so familiar. He was staring at a black arrow and the words PLATFORM 1 when Kevin pushed him through an archway labelled NO WAY OUT.

They entered an even dingier space. Ben recognised it as an escalator hall. He looked for the escalators and saw twin ravines sloping up into darkness, gutted hollows where the metal steps should have been. A tall black girl bounded from the shadows. From her trainers to her baseball cap she wore more brands than a shop window, her jacket still sporting its price tag. The only garment without a logo was her black silk headscarf, which gave her the look of a pirate.

'Hey Kev. Is this him?'

Kevin tightened his hold. 'Stay there, Antonia. He's a live one.'

'Yeah, I heard. Jeep says he hurt Alec. Kicked him or somefin'.'

'That's not all. He followed their team into the tunnel. Jeep managed to take him down but Alec's still walking funny.'

She laughed. 'So what is it? This guy's like us?'

'No. You can tell he's not. But there's something

about him. I have to show him to the Ferret.'

The girl flicked her springy hair. 'Na. He's in one of his Pits. Seeing no-one.'

'Except me, he means. He always sees me.'

'I seriously wouldn't.'

'Oh, get a spine. Come and stand sentry.'

He dragged Ben by the collar to the far side of the escalators and stopped outside a door that was set into the wall beneath the stairs. 'Stand there. Face that wall. Antonia's watching you.'

Kevin twisted the doorknob and went in. Ben dithered. Should he run? As puny as he felt right now, he could surely fight his way past one girl. Then he changed his mind.

He had never heard the scream of someone being murdered, but it probably sounded much like this. His skin gathered itself up in bumps. Out of the corner of his eye he saw Antonia cowering. The shriek tore the darkness, more animal than human, yet the real terror came when the echoes returned from the tunnels and he caught the mangled remains of two words: '*GO AWAY.*'

Kevin stepped from the doorway and shut it. He looked different. Ben realised this was because his freckles had disappeared. Now his face was a single shade of pale.

'Okay.' Kevin's voice was husky. 'He'll see you later.'

He grabbed Ben by the sleeve and dismissed Antonia with a grunt. All the way back to the stationmaster's office that was serving as his jail cell, Ben could feel himself trembling. And he didn't know whether it was comforting, or more frightening still, that most of this quivering seemed to be coming not from him, but from the grip of Kevin's own hands.

SLEEPWALKING

Tiffany had been in airing cupboards less stuffy than this travel agency. Watching her mum browsing a whole quilt of holiday brochures, she was seized by a yawn that made her jaw crack.

'Not boring you, I hope?' said Dad, who looked bored himself.

'Maybe she didn't sleep well last night.' Stuart smirked. 'You look terrible.'

Tiffany sighed, 'S'my impression of you.'

'Oi. Squabbles will cease,' said Mum. 'Give me ideas. Where do you fancy going?'

'Disney World!' said Stuart, as always.

'We did mention Italy,' said Dad.

'Devon,' mumbled someone. Tiffany realised it was her.

'*Devon?*' Mum scoffed.

'Uh… Cornwall?'

'Dearest, I don't work all hours for the Mayor of London just to go on British beach holidays. Pass me the California one.'

'No, *Florida*,' pleaded Stuart.

'There's always pony trekking in Dartmoor.'

'Please ignore my daughter.' Mum managed to

scowl at Tiffany while beaming at the flustered travel agent. 'Her brain has got jammed in one corner of England.'

In the end they packed the brochures in bags and drove them home. All the way, Tiffany yawned.

'Busy night?' murmured Stuart.

She looked at him sharply. 'Rufus kept me awake, if you must know. Miaowing.'

'Ah.'

Probably he was only baiting her. In truth, she had slept much less than her cat. Squirming among wrinkled sheets, she had skidded around on the surface of sleep unable to break through. A nameless dread lay in her stomach. By 1a.m. she could barely close her eyes. In despair she grabbed some tracksuit leggings and a sweatshirt and spent an hour walking rooftops, returning only when she lost sight of her own. It didn't help. By the time dawn seeped through the curtains, she was just about throttling her pillow.

Dad set to marinating salmon for dinner while Mum studied the brochures. All this talk of holidays jogged Tiffany's memory.

'I have to take in my cheque on Monday. For Paris.'

Mum paused. 'Paris?'

'You know. My school trip.'

'I thought that wasn't till Easter?' said Dad.

'Yes, and they need the money now.' The conversation missed another beat. Tiffany smelt a rat. 'You said I could! You promised!'

'Let's discuss this without going berserk, okay?' said Dad.

'We already did discuss it.'

'You know there was a school trip recently,' Mum remarked, 'where a boy got drowned by a freak wave because his teachers were too busy playing beach volleyball.'

Tiffany was going to ask how many freak waves struck Paris when Dad chimed in.

'You've never stayed away from home by yourself before, Truffle. At least, not – Ouch! Blood and *sand*.' He had grated away a sliver of his knuckle on the lemon zester. As he ran the bleeding finger under the tap, the unspoken end of his sentence hung in the air. *Not intentionally*.

'All the French sets are going,' Tiffany pleaded. 'Everyone is.' *Everyone* included Susie, Yusuf and Olly from Cat Kin. Yusuf had been helping her get ready. Being outrageously good at languages (he often answered his home phone in Arabic) he had forced Tiffany to improve by speaking only French when they met at lunchtimes for a chat.

'Well.' Mum thinned her lips. 'We'll look into it some more.'

'They need the cheque on Monday!' She was talking to brick walls. Tiffany flounced out of the kitchen. It made her feel righteous, so she flounced up the stairs too, through her bedroom door, and with one last flounce flopped down on her bed. Oh, to have the one cat talent that eluded her: sleep. She was exhausted. Only this wasn't just tiredness. It was an itching of the mind, a sense that something, somewhere, was terribly wrong.

'Ben... *Doesn't answer. Please leave a message at the tone.*' She must have absent-mindedly picked up her phone and dialled Ben's number. But wait a minute. He still hadn't said he was sorry, had he? Let him be the one who called. Dropping the phone on her bedside table, she happened to glance through the window. She saw a man.

He was standing quite still on the opposite pavement, looking up at her. Well, surely not at *her*, but at this row of houses. He stood with one hand hooked in his jeans pocket, pushing aside the hem of the black leather jacket that hung below his belt. Moppish brown hair, flecked with grey, tumbled to his collar. With his stubbly face he might have been a tramp, but somehow Tiffany knew he wasn't. Their eyes met and she caught a glint of blue, and then he was walking off down the street. She stared after him, feeling cold, then came to her senses. Perhaps he hadn't been staring up here at all. Perhaps he'd stood there only a moment, reading a For Sale sign or something. She had to stop being so jumpy.

'What's the matter with you, Tiffany Maine?' she said to her wardrobe mirror.

Thc wardrobe creaked in reply.

She yanked open the door and pulled Stuart out by the nose. 'You! You had your warning.'

'Leggo! Ow! You mustn't, I'm an invalid –' Stuart's squeals were muffled by the duvet she bundled over his head, really very gently in spite of her temper. When he was trussed at the foot of the bed she glowered over him.

'Spies are being shot.'

Stuart cringed. It unnerved her. He looked genuinely frightened.

'Okay, I'm not going to eat you. You shouldn't earwig, that's all.' She waited for his cheeky retort. It didn't come. 'Sorry. Was I too rough?'

'I saw you.' It was a whisper.

'Eh?'

'Last night. Coming home.' Stuart took a breath and plunged in. 'Across the roof.'

Tiffany stood silent for a long time.

'Ah,' she said.

Stuart struggled out of his duvet chrysalis and slumped on her bed. She sat beside him.

'I have trouble sleeping too.' He coughed, wetly. 'My body gets tired so fast but I'm still wide awake in my head. So I sit near the window and do astronomy. Watch for UFOs and stuff. And, well. You know we can see each other's windows.'

'You saw an Unidentified Feline Object.'

'A what?'

'Never mind. You saw…' Enough. He had seen enough. More than she could ever explain away.

'You… *jumped.*' Stuart spoke breathlessly, as if watching it all over again. 'From the chimney pots, down onto your flat bit of roof. I nearly screamed. I thought you'd fallen. But you landed on your feet and hardly made a sound. And before that you walked along the narrow bit at the top. You never wobbled.' He broke off. 'Is it to do with that exercise class?'

She nodded. Where to begin? To her astonishment, a tear rolled down her cheek.

'Hey. Why are you crying?'

She didn't know. For the life of her she didn't know.

'Tiffany.' Stuart cuddled her. 'I won't tell. Is that what you're upset about?'

No, it didn't seem to be. She felt relief more than anything. The tear had a more mysterious source. Nonetheless, Stuart had a point.

'I really won't tell,' he promised. 'Not anyone. Especially not Mum and Dad. I know how these things work.'

'Er… you do?'

Stuart used one of his favourite new words. 'It's protocol. Secret identities, all that stuff. You're talking to the superhero expert!'

Tiffany had to laugh. 'I'm hardly that. I learn pashki, that's all. Because– because…'

'You're going to have to tell me everything.' Stuart sat up like a boy in the peak of health. 'I can't keep half a secret or a quarter secret.'

'All right. Later. I need to take a nap now or I'll die.'

'Ohhh.... Okay. I could get working on some passwords and so on?'

'That sounds lovely.' Tiffany bolted the door behind him and collapsed onto her mattress.

She managed to snooze and awoke refreshed, ready

for Stuart's barrage of questions. It was surprisingly easy. He devoured every word, including the things she had trouble believing herself. Tales of treetop training sessions, bus surfing and high-rise acrobatics drew Stuart ever closer to the edge of his chair, until he seemed to float in mid-air supported only by his KAFOs. Hearing the truth about why she went missing last summer, he shrank away, pale and distressed. Tiffany assured him she was still the same person, still his big sister.

She held back only when he asked about Mrs Powell. That was a tale Tiffany wasn't ready to tell. She wondered if she ever would be. How she had seen her teacher gunned down, and how she had grieved for her dead friend, only to be left with the bitterest of comforts: Mrs Powell was probably alive, but gone. Tiffany had combed through her old flat but found no note, no letter, nothing to tell her what she ought to do now. So she had done her best to fill her teacher's shoes, hardly knowing if she should or not. Oh, she knew so very little.

And now she lay awake again, her clock burning midnight. The rumpled sheets were as comfy as rubble and the horrible feeling was back: a red knot in her stomach, tugging, pulling. It was painful to lie still.

Oshtis. She'd done pashki long enough to recognise it. The Oshtis catra, the core of instinct, was crimson energy from the belly zone of the Mau body. Why would it flare up without being summoned?

Rolling off the bed she salvaged her pashki kit from

the laundry basket. Secrecy was not needed there – Mum washed it as she washed all sports clothing, with no curiosity, at forty degrees. Tiffany shook out the creases and pulled it on. For good measure, she inked up her tabby face print and pressed the cat markings onto her forehead and cheekbones. The paint hid her pale skin from the glow of the street lamps.

She crept next door to Stuart's room.

'Are you awake?'

'Yes.'

'I have to go out.'

'Now?'

'Sshh. Can't explain. Thought I'd let you know.'

'Okay,' Stuart whispered. 'Want me to cover for you? If they wake up?'

'What would you say?'

'Um…'

'Work on it.' She mussed up his hair in farewell.

Opening her window she shivered. Even a real cat with fur would want to be indoors tonight. She climbed to the crest of the roof, balanced, then ran full-tilt along the ridge until it disappeared under her. Slamming both feet into the slates she launched herself out across the night.

In such split seconds, weightless and alone in air, she barely knew who or what she was. Then moss fragments tumbled off the neighbours' guttering and she was back in the world of hard tiles and chilly night dew. She stood on the Mansfields' loft extension and reached up at the moon, arching her back, exulting. She could caterwaul so well that even cats were fooled.

This was the way to unwind. Feeling calmer, less strung-up, she stalked to the end of the terrace of town houses and thought about returning to bed. No, not yet. First down to the ground via a handy tree, a cut through the playground of her old primary school, then a leg-up from a parked lorry to put her back among the chimneypots. Every stride put her more at ease. But she found it was not movement, exactly, that relaxed her. It was movement in certain directions. She would skip across this garage or that garden wall, only for the ache inside to tug her back the way she'd come. And she noticed how certain landmarks, such as the castle-shaped pumping station that was now a rock-climbing centre, drew closer and closer. Soon there was no ignoring it. Step by seemingly random step she was travelling steadily northwards.

Aglow with neon colours atop a rank of fast-food shops, she peered across the blackness of Finsbury Park. Turning once more – for home this time, she was sure of it – she veered instead around the climbing centre's forked turrets. On she roamed, still farther from home, passing the moon-frosted reservoirs and waterworks, before another mystifying tug sent her looping left again, towards a bridge over a slim black river.

Somewhere along the way she had picked up a splinter of fear. Unnoticed at first, it was sticking in deeper every time she stopped to rest. With it came a ridiculous thought: that for the last quarter hour someone or something had been following her. Whenever she looked over her shoulder there was no-one there. No-one could have been. Only Ben, of all the Cat Kin, had the skill to walk this route, and it definitely wasn't him. As for any normal person, forget it. That could not have been a human silhouette, over there, blotting out a sequence of roof-level stars. It would have been a regular night-creature, a fox or a cat, or some flibbertigibbet from her own dreamy head. Just to make sure, she bolted through the scaffolding of a new housing development, fast enough to lose even an imaginary stalker. There she rested, clinging to a ladder.

Large buildings loomed on the far side of the road. Squat barns of glass and steel, afloat on a sea of ground mist. An industrial estate. Red night-lights twinkled in the vapour, beckoning. Then something happened. One minute she was sliding down the builders' ladder, the next she was hugging a scaffolding pole that froze her lungs as she panted for breath.

She was exhausted. She had to stop. And turn back now, right now. For heaven's sake, where was she? She saw the street below as if for the first time. Blank-eyed windows, faceless houses and that eerily silent business park.

Rung by rung she made her sluggish way down to the pavement. The urge that had been driving her was gone, leaving in its place utter weariness. She could have fallen asleep standing up. At least her shadowy pursuer had faded away too – if he was ever there. In despair she cast about, knowing she was as good as lost. The one visible street sign read Hermitage Road, which rang no bells at all. A wild guess placed it somewhere between Finsbury Park and Tottenham. Achingly far from her warm bed.

'Oh, why didn't you count sheep?' she moaned.

On legs too tired to lift her above the grimy streets, she trudged home. Though it took less than an hour it felt like crossing the Antarctic. Staring up at her open bedroom window, she admitted defeat and used the emergency key Dad had hidden inside an air brick.

Well, she'd succeeded. She was dead beat. Sleep was rushing towards her. Sinking into the bedclothes she closed her eyes. Only one speck of thought floated between her and blissful nothingness. Like an irritating tune that gets stuck in the ear, the name of a street swirled around in her head as her consciousness drained away. Herm. Hermit. Hermitage Road.

THE WHITE CAT

After hearing that terrible cry, Ben was almost relieved to be back in his cell. By bracing himself against the wooden desk while Kevin tied him up, he had managed to steal a little more room to move, though not quite enough to wriggle free. Kevin sent for someone called Jeep. Ben recognised him at once. His bruised neck still ached from when those tattooed arms had choked him unconscious. A second boy, with fair hair matted into dreadlocks, yawned and sat on the stool. Kevin went out. So these were his new wardens. Now what?

Now, apparently, nothing. Ben had stewed in traffic jams, he'd endured a six-hour delay in a Spanish airport, but none of it prepared him for this. Boredom crushed all else, even hunger. His guards spoke little. By the time he could put a name to the rope-haired boy – Gary – it was lunchtime. For them, anyway. Ben could only stare at their stack of peanut butter sandwiches. Later Gary played with a pocket games console while Jeep read to himself, a magazine called *Guns and Ammo*.

'Good magazine?' He had almost given up trying to talk to them. 'You into military stuff, then? Is that why they call you Jeep?'

Gary turned off his game. 'It's not a nickname. It's his name.'

Ben had no idea why he sniggered. Maybe his brain had turned to mush. Jeep closed his magazine. Reaching into a deep jacket pocket he drew out a spindly object. Its hinges unfolded ominously. What was it, a catapult?

'That is funny, isn't it,' he said softly. 'Really funny.'

The object clicked into shape and Jeep produced a slender rod, feathered at one end. Oh no. That was no catapult. It was a miniature crossbow. Jeep nodded to Gary. Gary took a can of coke and placed it on top of Ben's head. Ben freaked out.

'I'm sorry, I didn't mean to–'

'The trouble with laughing…' Jeep placed the feathered bolt on the crossbow's slender stock and slotted three more bolts between his fingers. 'The trouble with laughing is,' he pulled back the string and aimed at the can on Ben's head. 'Laughing makes you shake.'

'Don't,' said Ben.

Thwuck. The bolt missed the can and glanced off the desk behind his head, scarring the wood.

'I had a large family,' said Jeep. 'Do you know what my brothers were called?'

'Please.' Ben tried not to flinch as Jeep took aim.

'Their names were Dodge–'

Thwuck. The bolt hit the white tiles by Ben's ear.

'Chrysler–'

Thwuck. To the right of his eye.

'– and Chevrolet.'

Thwunnk. The last bolt skewered the can on his head and fizzy liquid drenched him yet again. Ben swallowed his pride, and some of the cola. His mouth was that dry.

After that he didn't speak. Jeep read his magazines. Gary played on his console. At long last their guard shift ended. Ben wilted with relief to see Antonia, already in a new cap and jacket. She gave him a cereal bar and a can of lemonade, though her companion Dean drank half of it first. Later, after he begged, they took him to a small toilet tucked between the platforms. A sign on the door said STAFF ONLY.

The tedium blunted his mind. He had almost stopped wondering why he was here. If he didn't think of an escape plan soon, he might lose the power to think. He scanned every inch of the room, then turned his attention beyond the door. His Mau body crept out of hiding, lending him powers of hearing and smell. The rumble of trains mixed with voices and a faint electrical hum. Scents jostled for attention: food both fresh and rotting, mice, dirty bedclothes, unwashed bodies, the toilet, more mice. At least one adult male. And something else. A hot, animal odour. Musty.

'Hello again,' said someone. Ben looked up. Thomas stood there with Hannah.

Dean scowled. 'Cut that out. This isn't Butlins.'

He and Antonia left, locking the door. Ben tried to stretch.

'What time is it?'

'Sorry,' said Thomas. 'You heard him. Talking to you is expressly forbidden.'

'Five past eight,' said Hannah.

'In the evening?'

'I suppose. It's morning for us.'

A draught went down his neck. Dad would have missed him by now. Voicemail messages would be piling up. It was a good thing his parents lived apart, really – Mum wouldn't find out yet. She and Dad didn't talk to each other, they just sent messages through him.

Had it been like this for Tiffany? He wondered if he now had an inkling of what she'd gone through. If only he could tell her.

This train of thought raised his spirits. Tiffany, of course. When she tried to get in touch she might realise he was missing. Then she'd come to the rescue, as he had done for her. He saw where the train of thought was taking him, and derailed it. No. Hopes like that were dangerous. If he sat here waiting for help he might never get out. He had to assume he was on his own.

Hannah saw him shiver. She draped a blanket over him. Thomas took out a slab of fruit'n'nut chocolate and broke it into thirds. The taste brought tears to Ben's eyes and worked a peculiar magic on his guards. They started talking to him. Hannah wanted to become an air stewardess one day, she said. Thomas's favourite crisps were beef and mustard. His great ambition was to learn the bass guitar. Hannah said her socks were full of holes and did

Ben have a nail clipper? Ben didn't.

Night, Ben thought. Somewhere high above this twilight cell, darkness had swallowed the city. His mind tried to reach up through the layers of rock and clay, towards a sky of dim stars through diluted neon haze. Slowly turning. Twice he slipped into a doze; twice he woke up, sweating, the dream of a scream ringing in his ears.

Okay. He had faced dangers before. He didn't scare easily, or so he liked to think. But those had been sudden threats, met in the heat of battle with quick-as-thought reactions. Now, as hours piled on hours, he could feel his courage creaking beneath them. Who was being kept behind that closed door beneath the escalators? What kind of person, what living creature, could utter a scream like that?

His fear overflowed. Straining in a crazed attempt to snap his bonds, he realised he was asleep. In the dream he had no arms. Two severed cat's paws lay at his feet.

'Hey. Wake up.'

A prod in the middle of his forehead. He flinched.

'Steady.' A hand on his shoulder.

The hand wore a fingerless black glove. He saw a man, kneeling, clad in black silk garments that made him think, absurdly, of pyjamas. Meanwhile the bright blue eyes reminded him of…

'Geoff's the name. Geoff White. Sorry I yelled at you the other day.'

'*You?*' Ben whispered.

It was the man from the pub. The unshaven

jawline, the old-rocker hair. The same face, with one electrifying difference. From forehead to cheekbones his skin was bleached white, in a pattern that was eerily familiar. The mask of paint around the sapphire eyes gave him a look somewhere between the Lone Ranger and the Phantom of the Opera.

'Who are you?'

'Geoff or Sir. I don't much mind.'

Geoff passed his hand between Ben's tied arms. Plastic cords fell to the floor with a sound like plucked strings.

Mau claws? Ben's mind reeled. He bent his elbows, flexed his numb fingers.

'Fancy going home?'

'How did you– Why–?'

'I know, too many questions. Sorry about that thing with the paw print and so on. My little test. All to be explained, etcetera. It's lucky you ran into me when you did.'

He twitched. From the corner came a rustling. Two heads popped out of blankets.

'We weren't asleep,' blurted Hannah.

'That's not–' Thomas bounced to his feet, hands raised ready to fight. In an eyeblink Hannah was beside him, crouched and quivering. Everything childish about them was gone.

'Here's an idea.' Geoff's voice was very, very quiet, yet it filled the little room. 'You both fell asleep. You woke and found your prisoner gone. Okay?'

Thomas darted sideways and stood before the door. His on-guard stance trembled. In Geoff's shadow he looked pitifully small. Ben had the feeling that here was a man capable of violence.

'S- sorry, Ben,' stammered Thomas. 'We can't let you leave. Nor you.' He looked at the intruder and gulped.

Ben held out his hand. 'Come with me.'

Hannah froze in mid-creep. 'Where would you take us?'

'I don't know. Back to your families. Wherever you like.'

A tremendous battle seemed to be raging behind their frightened eyes. Geoff shuffled his feet.

'No,' said Hannah. 'We can't.'

'Our family is here,' said Thomas. 'Why would we leave? It's ridiculous.'

'Listen–'

'No,' said Geoff in his ear. 'Not now. A time may come when you can help these kids. But we have to move. At once.'

'I'll– I'll come back,' said Ben. 'I promise. Now do as he says. You'll be all right.'

Thomas and Hannah traded glances and edged aside.

'Thank you,' said Geoff. 'Remember. You saw nothing. Asleep.'

They crawled back among their blankets.

'Kevin will kill us,' Hannah moaned.

Ben looked away. These children had been his jailers, yet he felt he was not escaping so much as abandoning them.

'Bye,' he murmured. They did not answer him.

Geoff opened the door and stole out onto the slumbering platform. Ben kept close. Along the cardboard dormitory the shaded lamps burned.

'Where did you find the key to the office?'

'Didn't. Got a way with locks. Simple ones.' Geoff wiggled a finger mysteriously.

'You're a – I mean, you know –'

'Sssh. This lot aren't exactly hard of hearing either. Down here.'

Geoff dropped off the platform into the railway trench. Ben, bursting with questions, followed him at an Eth-walk into the tunnel. The dimly glowing opening behind them had shrunk smaller than a fingernail before Geoff made another sound.

'Through darkness I walk in day,' he murmured.

Ben steadied himself on the blackened brick wall.

'You're a pashki master.'

'That certainly would explain a lot,' said Geoff.

'And now you run a pub?'

'Nah.' Geoff chuckled. 'Earning pennies behind the bar. A nice thought, mind you. Landlord of the White Lion. It'd suit me, do you reckon?'

'I suppose.'

'One day, then. If I ever settle down. Now–' He froze in mid-step. 'Did I catch your name back there?'

'Ben.'

'Yes, I did. Great. Answer me this, Ben. How well can you see?' He pointed. 'Can you make out those chalk marks on the track where it curves?'

Ben widened his eyes. 'One. Seven. And the letter J.'

'Ha! Twenty-twenty night vision. Only three people

in the country could have taught you that. I'm pretty sure it wasn't me. I'm going to guess.' He looked hard at Ben. 'Felicity. You've been around Felicity Powell.'

Ben had to nod.

'I knew it!' Geoff's cry echoed alarmingly. 'Didn't I know it right away. Never say I'm losing my touch.'

'You know Mrs Powell?'

'As well as anyone ever has.' Geoff's voice sank again. He tightrope-walked along one steel rail. 'We wore away footpaths together. Over rooftops, through jungles. Yes, I know her. Or I did.'

He blinked his blue eyes.

'It's been so long. Tell me, Ben. How is Felicity? How's she doing?'

Ben felt the night dump all its weariness on him at once.

'This could take a while,' he said.

THE COMPASS

The knees of Tiffany's jeans had gone grey. Her dustpan rattled with grit, fluff, crayon bits, biscuit crumbs and two plasters. Welded to the hardwood floor she found a wad of chewing gum, which she picked off with her thumbnail, grimacing. The shiny patch underneath showed up the grime everywhere else. Should she get a mop? There wasn't time.

She put away the dustpan and cast a critical eye round the church hall. The Sunday School's drawings looked more out of place than ever. Maybe she could take them down for this evening. First she had to change her dusty clothes. It also seemed important to get her face-print just right, with no smudges. She was checking the tabby markings in her hand mirror when she heard the door crash. Ben walked in.

'Hello.'

His expression was mysterious – as mysterious as his phone call yesterday morning. It had gone something like this:

'Ben, Hi! Ouch, it's only seven a.m. I meant to say, I'm sorry about what I said the other day.'

'What?' said Ben. 'No, no, forget that.'

'O...kay. That means you're sorry too, does it?'

'Yeah, of course. Listen. We need a Cat Kin meeting tomorrow. You have to book the hall for Monday evening.'

'*I* have to?'

'Yes. Can't explain on the phone. Too tired. But there'll be a special guest.'

'Guest? Did you say guest? We can't let other people –'

'Trust me. This is someone you really want to see.'

It was this tantalising hint that had persuaded her and made her come here far too early to start a frenzy of cleaning. Now she did her best to decode his face. Despite the twinkle in his eye he looked frayed around the edges, as if he'd had a hard day at school.

'So,' said Tiffany. 'What's the big surprise?'

'Wait for the others.'

Olly, amazingly, was one of the first to appear, and even the usual stragglers showed up on the dot of seven. Yusuf put his face round the door. 'Someone having a birthday?'

'Did Ben say we've got a visitor tonight?' Cecile asked, and Tiffany could only shrug.

Susie cried, 'Tickle him till he tells!'

'Cut it out!' Ben pushed her off. 'He'll be here in a minute.'

'He?' said Tiffany. A hope inside her, so frail she had barely noticed it, fell like a tree's last leaf.

The group sat in awkward silence. Perhaps they had wondered the same as her. Feeling more and more foolish, Tiffany rubbed her wrists across her mouth, the way Rufus did when he fell off the sofa while napping. How could she have been so silly as to imagine, even for a second, that…?

There was a knock. Instantly Ben was on his feet to open the door. In stepped a man in a black leather jacket. Tiffany caught her breath. She had seen him before. But where?

'Here we are, Geoff,' said Ben. 'Our little team. Everyone, this is Geoff White.'

The newcomer stood still, taking in the room, the stacked chairs, the high windows, the Cat Kin sitting in a loose semi-circle. Then he wandered over with a tentative wave.

'Interesting place.' He looked round some more. 'Nice finger-paintings.'

Tiffany saw puzzled faces. Yusuf mouthed a question. She helplessly shook her head.

'Floor's uneven.' The man scratched a scar on his cheek, a pale path through the stubble that was almost a beard. 'Narrow. Bit grubby. And those pictures…' He turned to face the group at last. 'You realise you can't possibly learn pashki in here.'

'Ben, who is this man?' Tiffany demanded.

'I beg your pardon.' The interloper squatted among them, his feet flat to the floor. 'Felicity Powell called me Geoffrey, mostly. But Geoff will do.'

'Mrs Powell?' Daniel exclaimed.

'They're old friends,' said Ben.

'Less of the old in my case, please,' said Geoff. 'But yeah. Friends, associates, comrades-in-arms…

and teacher and pupil, both ways round. I could tell you some tales… and I will. Only not tonight. More important is the story Ben has for you.'

'Wait,' said Tiffany. Things were running away from her. 'You can't just walk in here. We don't even know you. And I saw you–' now she remembered, 'lurking outside my house!'

'You must be Tiffany. Sorry. You got me bang to rights.' Geoff held out his wrists, as if for handcuffs.

'Why were you watching me?'

'Because they don't list the Cat Kin in the Yellow Pages.'

She returned his blue gaze, determined not to blink.

'You're cautious.' Geoff blinked first. 'Good. And you want proof that I am who I claim to be.' He chuckled. 'Well. I could tell you lots of facts about Felicity. She hates dust and clutter. She subscribes to the National Geographic. She has a beat-up old radio that she keeps repairing. Etcetera. I know all that. Does it prove I'm her friend?'

Foreheads wrinkled as they tried to follow his meaning.

'Of course not,' said Geoff. 'No more than Tiffany can prove that her cat belongs to her. Friendship is hard stuff to get hold of. So it's no good me just telling you who I am. That's for you to decide.'

Tiffany felt a twinge of recognition. She'd known someone else who said things like that. With his scarecrow hair, taxi-driver's accent and sturdy, powerful build, this man seemed almost a different species from the sleek Mrs Powell. But it was the difference of pepper and salt – in that she could, so easily, picture them together.

Geoff pulled up a chair and sat on it back to front.

'This is sudden for me too,' he said. 'I will make time for us to get to know each other. Now there are more important things. Ben, go ahead.'

Ben stood up.

'I, er...' He laughed nervously. 'I had a bit of an interesting weekend.'

Ben's tale upset Tiffany in two ways. The first shock was how much it got to her. She saw Susie's incredulous face, Daniel craning forward. Yes, they looked alarmed, but no more than if Ben had been telling a ghost story round a camp fire.

'How long was you tied up?'

'Ugh, you've still got the marks...'

'Didn't they give you any proper food?

'You went to fight this kid and he *beat* you...?'

'But who was it in that room under the stairs?'

'If I'd heard that scream I'd've been outta there...'

They were lapping it up. For Tiffany it was different. It came too close. The more Ben talked of his ordeal, of loneliness and helplessness, darkness and captivity, the more her own nerves rang, like a glass, in the note that would shatter them. This made the second shock even harder to bear. When Ben revealed that his prison was a derelict station called Hermitage,

Tiffany fled the church hall in tears.

'I knew where you were,' she said the next day, when an anxious Ben phoned her from his school during morning break. 'Something in me knew.'

In the dead of Saturday night she had stood in Hermitage Road, drawn by a gut feeling. Turning to the internet she proved her guess correct. In the 1960s, when the Victoria Line was dug, a station had been planned between Finsbury Park and Seven Sisters, before construction was abandoned for reasons unknown. It would have been on that very spot.

'I was right there,' said Tiffany. 'Directly above you. And I left you down there to rot.'

'You didn't know I was missing, remember?' said Ben. 'It's okay. Geoff got me out.'

Yes, exactly, Tiffany cried inside. *It should have been me. Not some stranger.* Her cruel words to Ben had turned out to be true. 'I said you'd never get any help from me. And you didn't.'

But she was wrong about that.

On Friday she dragged herself to the pashki class, arriving last of all. Geoff White was there again. His leather jacket and jeans had been replaced by a rumpled black outfit he called a pashkigi, its sleeveless tunic showing off arms that looked hard as iron. He asked her if she minded him taking the lesson. She sat in silence while the others pelted Geoff with questions: who were the sinister kids who had abducted Ben? What was that Hermitage place? He quelled them with a stare.

'No,' he said. 'First you've got to give me something. I don't like wasting my time, and I don't like putting minors in danger. So I need to know. How well did Felicity teach you?'

Better than you ever could, thought Tiffany. Geoff lined them up in the Sitting Cat pose and put them through their paces. He watched Daniel's Chasing the Bird, Olly's ungainly Felasticon, Susie's Tailspin and Yusuf's Ratbane Lunge. Most of the time his face was unreadable, although when Ben ran up the wall to place a glass of water on the high window ledge, he clapped.

'Nah,' he said, when Ben offered to fetch it down. 'Let the Sunday School figure it out.'

Tiffany felt as if she were watching her snowman melt. It wasn't fair. She was the one who'd kept this club going. Who'd booked the stupid hall and collected – *tried* to collect the money. Who'd vainly trawled the net in search of new things to teach the class. *Her* class.

As for her, nothing went right. Her balance wavered and she couldn't feel her whiskers. It was like being back in Miss Fuller's P.E. class. When Geoff brought round a plank of scratched chipboard to test their Mau claws, her heart sank. Summoning that invisible cutting energy at one's fingertips required total concentration, and hers was miles away. She bodged her way through the remaining exercises, sat down and sulked.

Geoff held the chipboard aloft and, with a flick of his wrist, scored his right hand across the four deep marks made by Ben. The top half fell off with a splintering sound as Geoff's Mau claws cut clean through. The class gasped. Their teacher gave a slow blink.

'You've got some promising talent here,' he said. 'Felicity must've been thrilled to find you, Ben. Yusuf, nice footwork, tight circling. Cecile, good sharp senses. The rest of you… ah, you'll soon be up to scratch.'

Tiffany sat with her chin in her hands, wondered what TV she was missing tonight. She felt a touch on the head.

'Hey now.' Geoff winked at her. 'An off-day, was it?'

'Dunno.'

'I think so,' said Geoff. 'You're better than this. When did you learn to use the Oshtian Compass?'

'The what?'

Geoff looked perplexed. 'Ah. Felicity may have called it something different. The Lodestone of Pasht?'

His words meant nothing to her.

'Interesting,' Geoff purred. 'You've no idea what it is. Yet you used it anyway. Like a great jazz pianist I knew. Never had a lesson, couldn't even read music. But a wizard on the keys.'

He orbited them on tiptoe and they craned their necks to follow him.

'You know what cats are famous for, Tiffany? I mean apart from the falling thing and the indestructible thing and the mice thing… all those things. Look, what should you do with a cat if you move house? Shut them indoors for a week. Or they go looking for their old home.' He paused. '*And they will find it.* Cats have this homing instinct, as strong as a pigeon's. Ten miles, a hundred miles, it doesn't matter. If the cat loved his old territory, he's likely to find his way back.' Geoff made a sudden bound, springing over their heads to land crouched before them. 'It's another skill we've copied from them. The Oshtian Compass. And it was helping us to get around long before they thought of Sat-Nav.'

Olly chuckled. Daniel elbowed him into silence.

'But Tiffany, you look puzzled. As you should. For what I've told you is only part of it. The easiest part.' Geoff held all of their gazes with his own. 'More remarkable yet is when a cat's owner goes away. Leaving it behind.'

Her heart kicked. She'd read about this.

'As bizarre as it sounds,' said Geoff, 'some cats can actually follow them. I met a Nottingham lad when I was in the army. He was three weeks into basic training when his cat Garibaldi showed up at the barracks, in Surrey. A hundred and fifty miles away. And he knew it wasn't a lookalike because Gari was missing two vertebrae in his tail. These stories aren't rare. I heard of one cat crossing the width of the USA, coast to coast, two thousand miles, just to find the sick lady who'd had to give him away when she moved.'

Geoff looked up at the lead-crossed window. Speaking in a murmur, he seemed to be addressing the night outside.

'That the cat has such a power is astonishing,

I suppose. I'll tell you what's more incredible. The wish. The *will*. What kind of force could drive a creature from warmth and safety, make it trek day and night across hostile wilderness, through illness and starvation, in search of one special person? That is what gives me chills.'

He closed his eyes.

'That night,' said Tiffany, beginning to grasp it. 'Something *was* guiding me.'

'The Oshtian Compass,' said Geoff. 'Drawing you to Ben.'

'And someone...' she groped for the memory, 'was following me.'

'Yeah, that was me.'

Geoff made a guilty face. He'd been watching them both, he confessed. He'd moved to this area after noticing signs that there were pashki students about. It was nothing much – distinctive footprint patterns in the park, a spent Christmas cracker on the church roof – but it got him searching. He set a simple test in the yard behind his pub, which soon netted a catch. After that he kept a watchful eye on Ben, and a good thing too. When Ben didn't come home one Friday night, Geoff feared the worst ('More than my dad did,' said Ben, wryly). Geoff started shadowing Tiffany in case she too was in danger. He couldn't believe his luck when she helped him by setting out across the rooftops.

'Why didn't you come and tell me?' asked Tiffany.

'Too risky,' said Geoff. 'You were following the merest thread. You meet me, you're distracted, it snaps. My best bet was to track you unseen. Turns out you did see me. What can I say. You're good.'

A smile caught Tiffany unawares.

'And it worked,' said Geoff. 'You led me right to him. To use the Compass without training is remarkable. The fact that Ben was in trouble might have helped.'

'Can't you do the Oshtian Compass, though?' asked Cecile.

'Course he can!' chided Susie.

'Actually,' said Geoff, 'the answer is yes and no. For Ben, I couldn't. I'd only met him once, you see. And you couldn't really say we bonded. In fact, I think you told me to get a haircut.' He paused for the class giggle. 'That's why I talk about the will. It's the driving force, the magnetism in the needle. To put it simply, your Compass can only point to a person if you already have a very strong bond.'

Tiffany saw Ben turn away. Were his ears normally that red?

'Okay then,' said Yusuf. 'How did we score? Sixes? Sevens?'

Geoff frowned. 'Come again?'

'He's talking about your side of the bargain,' said Susie.

'Are you going to tell us who those creepy kids are, why they kidnapped Ben, and why they're living like moles in a hole,' said Olly, 'or have I just knackered myself out for nothing?'

'Moles? No. They're not moles.' Geoff laughed darkly. 'Okay. You've proved yourselves. And it is safer if you know. Though not much.'

His eyes darted around.

'Not here. I can't talk about this next to a drawing of Winnie the Pooh.'

'Sorry.' Tiffany felt frosty again. 'This hall was the best place I could find. Or afford.'

'I'll find us somewhere better,' said Geoff.

FERAL CHILD

Ben had always liked Abney Park Cemetery. There was no better place to chill out. Here in a walled-off corner of Hackney the evergreens grew thick as a witch's wood. Trees and shrubs sieved out the street noise, letting birdsong bubble through the stillness. Sleepy, creaking boughs watched over the graves and the wind whispered with the rustlings of squirrels, foxes and field mice. This cemetery was a place of life, not death. Only once had it made Ben afraid.

He'd been eight years old, walking with Mum and Dad, back in the days when they were still together. Then he lost them in the labyrinth of graves. Sighting a church spire above the leaf-line he headed towards it, for he knew his own way home from Stoke Newington church. To his shock and bewilderment, the path took him not out of the graveyard but to a clearing, where stood a hollow-eyed chapel he had never known was there. Its doors were planks, its rose window broken. It seemed to howl with loneliness. *Lost.* He had turned in terror, running through a nightmare of ivy-bound headstones until Mum and Dad's distant shouts finally brought him back.

'He's right!' Daniel, clinging to the rose

window, peered out through the stone petals into the thicket. 'This place rules.'

'Well. It's still a church.' Tiffany's voice rang flatly.

'A shell of one,' said Geoff. 'No-one's used it for years. Most classes we can hold outside, so long as you hide from passers-by. Then if it rains we can exercise in here. We are allowed to be wimpy about the rain.'

Ben wandered up the twilit nave, long since stripped of pews. He had to admit (with a twinge of disloyalty) that Geoff had found the perfect headquarters: secret, vaguely sinister, walled in by woodland. They didn't even have to bring three pounds. The old chapel was tiny really, far smaller than the horror-film abbey in his memory. Funny to think he had once been scared of it. Then the gloom brought to mind a similar place, a lost and forgotten Tube station, and the laughter stayed inside him.

'Duh-duh daaaaah!' Arms raised, Olly mimed playing a huge church organ.

'It *is* a bit creepy,' Susie frowned.

'Hey, if there were ghosts around, I'd see 'em,' said Geoff. 'Everyone find a space to stretch.'

During the rigorous warm-up, Ben noticed something interesting. Geoff had his own way of performing certain pashki movements. For instance, he did not kneel for the Sitting Cat pose, preferring to squat flat-footed instead. In his Hunter crouch he curled one hand flamboyantly behind his head. He showed them a new Freeze stance which he called Siamese Stone. Other moves he performed exactly like Mrs Powell. He had learned a lot from her, Ben guessed – but not only from her.

They poised for a long minute upon their left toes while Geoff studied them, pacing up and down. 'And… sprawl at ease.'

Down they sank upon their sky-blue yoga mats. A blackbird twittered from the rafters and whirred off through the pointed window.

'Hey! No dozing,' said Geoff. 'That was meant to help you concentrate. You know all those questions you've been bugging me with?'

Everyone sat up.

'I'll be straight with you.' His uneasy glance flicked towards Tiffany. 'Not everyone is thrilled to have me here. I know that. But I won't throw a strop if you don't like me at first. All I ask is that you hear me out. Because this is to do with what happened to Ben. And it's one story I really don't like repeating.'

Fourteen autumns ago, in the village of Kings Langley, it was a grey and misty morning. It was too grey, too misty, around an old farmhouse. Fire had left only a shell of charred beams. The house's registered occupant was Charlie Gladwell, an elderly recluse with no family or friends. Firemen found his blackened skeleton in the bathtub.

Nearby was a large shed untouched by the blaze. The first man inside was a paramedic and the stench made him throw up. The building was stacked with what looked like rabbit hutches, though nearly all contained ferrets. Later the RSPCA also counted four mink, twelve polecats, eight stoats, a pine marten, a blind weasel in a box and one dead bitch otter. The hutches looked as if they'd never been cleaned. However, the paramedic found somebody cleaning one.

It was a boy. He looked under ten, though later guesses put his age nearer fifteen. Pictures of him taken at the time were considered too upsetting for the newspapers. Police also photographed chains and shackles bolted to the shed wall. It seemed that Charlie Gladwell had kept this boy imprisoned here. For how long? There was one clue. The boy wailed and struggled when they tried to take him outside, only calming down when he'd fetched a scrap of rag, which he cuddled tight. Later, when hospital staff got a look at this comfort blanket, they saw it was a tiny frayed shirt. The label inside said *2–3 years*. A nurse was taking the stinking thing to the incinerator when a doctor stopped her and put the rag, filthy as it was, back in the sedated boy's arms.

Who was he? No relative of Gladwell's, that much was clear. The police re-opened every case of missing boys as far back as a decade and a half. Blood tests were carried out on three families. All were negative and the boy went unclaimed.

Emma Leech, the psychologist on his case, held little hope. Living in chains, in the dark, alone except for caged animals... what would that do to a child?

This boy, instead of crying, wailed like a polecat. He gibbered, he hissed, he curled up to sleep. With a mind as starved as his body, he would be a feral child, lacking human speech, probably insane.

After a week he startled Dr Leech by throwing his uneaten sandwich at her and demanding, 'Mouse.' He could speak. She found, to her astonishment, that he had a reading age of six. Apparently Gladwell had read him newspapers, not so much to entertain the boy as to lord it over him. While the old man basked in the sound of his own voice, his sharp-eyed prisoner was learning to read, literally behind his back.

Charlie Gladwell thought his captive docile. He was wrong. After months of patient work, the boy filed through his chains with a stone. That night he stole into the house and torched it with white spirit. True escape proved more difficult. Terrified by the vast outside he fled back to his shed, to the warmth and cosy stench of the ferrets.

With proper food and medical care he grew quickly, filling out into a tall teenage boy. His carers had called him Adam but he hated this, so Dr Leech encouraged him to choose his own name. By now he had a favourite book, all about the mustelids – animals such as ferrets, pine martens, fishers and minks – and soon his choice was made. But carers quit their jobs in tears rather than look after young Martin Fisher, who seemed more beast than human. The slightest upset could spark off his temper, and in one savage tantrum he bit through Dr Leech's index finger (it was successfully reattached). On other days he would curl into a ball at the mere sight of human beings. Emma Leech was desperate for someone who could help. Unfortunately, she got Geoff White.

Geoff took a swig from a water bottle. The blackbird was back on the window ledge, its beak full of fluff.

'I've tried many day jobs over the years,' said Geoff. 'At that time I'd found a niche in mental health. St. Hubert's in Middlesex had a top psychiatric unit, so that was where Martin Fisher ended up. Given his background, they wondered if animal therapy mightn't be a way to reach him. You know, traumatised kids can express their feelings with pets –'

A phone made a noise like an air-raid siren. Tiffany blushed and answered it.

'Yes… No… Yes Dad. I'm at Susie's house, like I said. What? That's because we're in the garden. Yes. Yes I will. No I won't. Okay. Bye.' She shut the phone with a loud snap. 'Sorry.'

'Pets,' said Geoff, petulantly. 'Animals have a calming effect. That was my thing, my specialist area. I found a good-natured calico kitten to see if Martin would enjoy handling it. You live and learn. I had to put the poor thing out of its suffering.'

Cecile winced.

'I probably cared too much,' said Geoff. 'About

helping Martin. See, I had no kids of my own. Still don't, come to that. Never met the right girl. But… where was I?' He stared at the window, where budding blossoms were peeping in. 'Yeah. I was ready to try anything. I thought I'd teach him some pashki exercises, to relax him. Simple ones like the Omu meditation. No good. Cats made him freak out. The only time his face lit up was when I gave him a ferret. Which is how I hit upon my genius idea. My ingeniously stupid idea.'

Geoff had wondered for some time. Was pashki unique? Ancient Egyptians revered the cat, so they had made an exercise system to awaken the feline inside them. But suppose they'd worshipped a different creature? Might other animal selves lie hidden within us, waiting to be discovered? Geoff saw a chance to answer this question and help Martin at the same time.

He bought two more ferrets and an illegally-trapped Welsh polecat at no small expense. For many weeks he watched Martin interact with them, and stayed up whole nights to study their movements. Geoff read every book he could find on the mustelid family. Step by step he adapted pashki routines to reflect these animals' whip-like movements. As he gained confidence he began sketching plans for a whole new system. At the time it did not seem crazy. He was younger, keen to prove himself, anxious to help this poor boy.

When Geoff explained his plan, Martin laughed for the very first time. Perhaps it was the one occasion when he knew happiness. Throughout his childhood he had watched the ferrets in their hutches, the only beautiful things in his world. He had loved them but he envied them too, because – abused as they were – they had Charlie's love and Martin did not. No wonder he longed to be like them.

Geoff held secret one-to-one classes. They practised in the hospital's basement rooms, or amid the expansive gardens, and no-one ever found them out. Martin attacked his training in the manner of a boxer with a grudge. He proved fiercely intelligent. In another life, with proper parents, he could have been anything – a Grade A student, an athlete, anything. Soon he was inventing moves of his own, forcing Geoff to work more nights writing up his notes. As the new system grew it became as much his creation as Geoff's, though it was Geoff who named it *mustel-id*. He said this meant 'Soul of the Polecat', and Martin, who knew no better, devoured it.

Compared to pashki, refined by Egyptian priests and Eastern gurus over a hundred or more generations, mustel-id was brutishly simple. Against that, it was easier to learn. In less than ten months Martin had grown quick, strong and acrobatic. He could fit through spaces that looked narrower than his waist and could sniff out a coin in a pitch dark boiler-room, even though his vision would never reach cat levels. Mustel-id offered no equivalent of Mau claws, but still Martin's fingers grew strong enough to tear the seams of a straitjacket. Trying to soak up this furious energy, Geoff adapted Ten Hooks to create a mustel-id fighting system, and they sparred for hours at a time. And Geoff, who would cheerfully face in combat any pashki master you cared to name, found Martin becoming quite a handful.

Then came the breakthrough. As Martin honed his polecat skills, he became at other times more like a normal teenager. It was as if his human and animal selves were drawing apart, so that they no longer waged war inside him. Martin let carers into his room. He would talk and read storybooks aloud to Dr Leech, even though he never seemed to follow the stories. He learned not to smash televisions, stopped asking for mice and grew fond of cookery programmes. Given a sketchpad he revealed a gift for drawing. The staff even introduced him to a visiting princess. Geoff patted himself on the back. He'd done it. Martin was calmer, healthier, and at least half sane. And Geoff had achieved something extraordinary: a brand new form of pashki based on one of nature's deadliest predators. What could possibly go wrong?

'To throw away a young life,' said Geoff, 'is an unforgivable thing.'

Ben had the nastiest feeling that he knew what was coming. Susie gnawed a corner of her yoga mat.

'What happened?' Yusuf murmured.

'I betrayed him,' said Geoff.

His words fell into silence.

'Martin was transferred to a care home,' said Geoff. 'And how smug was I? I'd found his cure. He had a new room, his own TV, posters on the walls. He tolerated those around him. There was even this boy named Carl who knew how to cook real pizzas and who might have become his friend.

'So I left. I didn't say goodbye, I just stopped visiting. Because that's what pashki masters do, right? We're footloose. Free spirits. You look for us and one day we're not there.'

Ben stole a glance at Tiffany.

'I was three weeks and fifty miles away by the time I heard the news. The care home had been destroyed in a fire. One girl was dead and a boy was missing. Martin Fisher.'

Ben shaded his eyes. The chapel's rose window was flowering, the intricate stonework catching sunbeams through the firs, so that it sprinkled green-gold light. The effect lasted seconds before the angle was lost, but its magic lingered in a sweet breeze that wafted down the aisle. Ben heard the bark of a dog outside, the giggle of young children, a pair of parents strolling a nearby path. He had a sudden longing to be elsewhere.

It was Tiffany who said it. 'You know where he is now.'

'I tried to track him,' said Geoff. 'He gave me the slip. For years he's been off my radar.'

'Then he found that empty station,' said Yusuf.

'He was bound to go somewhere like that,' said Geoff. 'All over the Underground there are stations that are no longer used – Aldwych, Down Street, City Road. Martin would have liked the name Hermitage. A home for a loner.'

'Did you see him, Ben?' asked Daniel. Ben shook his head. Somewhere deep inside him that scream was echoing still. *GO AWAY*…

'All these years,' Geoff mused. 'He must be thirty by now.'

Susie looked doubtful. 'If this loony is such a hermit, what about the other people Ben saw down there? Those weird kids?'

'Martin can't bear human company,' said Geoff. 'But he must have found that loneliness is worse. So he recruited children and he trained them, just as I trained him. Maybe he thought he could tolerate humans if they too lived the way of the polecat.'

'Good job it was Mrs Powell's advert that we saw!' said Olly.

Geoff glared, not amused.

'Olly's got a point, though,' ventured Ben. 'Martin didn't put adverts in the Hackney Gazette. Where did his pupils come from?'

'And how could anyone want to live like that?' Susie demanded.

'Think about it,' said Geoff. 'Not all are as lucky as you. Everywhere you see broken families, latch-key kids, waifs and strays. Kids whose lives came apart. I used to be one myself. There's boys and girls out there who feel lost, with no-one to care. Until they meet Martin.'

Ben fidgeted. For a moment Geoff's words had felt uncomfortably close to home. But then, who was he to feel sorry for himself? Mum and Dad might be cut off from each other, but they weren't cut off from him. His was a happy life compared to some. What had that girl said about her family? *I lost them. I got a new family here.* Hannah and Thomas, his oddball guards. Both so distant, so afraid, so *lonely*. The way they stood trying to block his escape, pitifully defiant, threatening and beseeching him not to leave. Their faces of dread as he slunk out of the door.

'We should do something.' His own voice startled him. 'We have to try and help them.'

Geoff looked at Ben as if he'd lost his mind.

'But of course we do,' he said. 'Why else do you think I came to find you?'

HUNTING HUMANS

'Tiffany. Tiffany?'

It was like hearing a dripping tap beneath a waterfall. Tiffany pictured a green cat's eye and drew more deeply on Mandira, the face catra that governed the senses. It took a moment to tune in.

'–we can walk to Covent Garden–' '–amazing film that was–' '–grab a coffee in the Square–'

The clamour of the ticket hall broke into its component parts, each one twinkling and clear. Her ears panned through the muddy mass of chatter, flick-flacking barriers and thrumming escalators, straining to find the voice saying her name.

'Tiffany, any luck?'

'No,' she sighed. 'If I had more idea who I'm looking for...'

'You know them when you see them. They wear black bandanas. And there's this feeling they give you.'

'Speak up!' Susie's voice floated on the din. 'I didn't catch a word of that.'

'Nothing,' said Tiffany, glad for once that Susie's listening skills needed practice. The seven of them were spread across the donut-shaped concourse of Leicester Square tube station. Daniel and Yusuf loitered near the exits while Susie, Tiffany, Olly and Cecile leaned at intervals around the circular office in the centre. A tense and twitchy Ben prowled everywhere else. Thanks to cat hearing they could talk across the noisy space, with only a little confusion from Chinese Whispers.

People poured in from the streets above. Escalators pumped crowds from below. Daytrippers surged in search of films, shows, fast food and Sunday shopping, ebbing and flowing in a ceaseless tide. Tiffany stifled a yawn. She could feel her weekend trickling away while thousands around her had fun. But Geoff insisted this was their best chance to watch Fisher's children outside their lair.

'He needs cash to keep everyone fed,' Geoff had explained. 'So he sends them out on thieving raids. The Tube is like a rabbit warren, which happens to be a polecat's favourite hunting ground. They'll target the busiest stations, the tourist traps. I want to know where they go, how far they range, how many there are – as much as you can tell me. And look for the misfits, the unhappy ones. They may come in useful.'

Tiffany was puzzled. It should have been exciting to work with the Cat Kin in such a good cause, a slightly dangerous cause at that. Why, then, did she feel so reluctant? Of course she wanted to help those poor kids, as much as anyone did. What she didn't much like, she decided, was Geoff White telling her to do it.

Was she being a brat? It wasn't as if Geoff was

a bad pashki teacher. She no longer minded that he had taken over her class. He had awesome skills, a real sense of fun and a bucketload of patience to match. In fact there was nothing about him to dislike, except for the fact that he wasn't Mrs Powell.

Daniel piped up: 'Anyone else hungry?'

'Yes,' said Olly.

'*Your* hearing's improved,' said Ben. 'Okay. Let's make it short.'

They climbed the steps into Leicester Square and felt the pull of an ice cream parlour. Tiffany got the last tub of Chocolate Midnight Cookies flavour and shared it with Cecile, who had brought no money. Perched on a window seat she let her eyes loose on the house-sized posters that crowned the cinemas, wondering which film she was missing most. An odd conversation made her turn round.

'Mustelids form one of the broadest families in the order Carnivora,' said Yusuf. 'While some eat fruit, most have strong jaws that can slice or crush bone.'

'What's that? Cecile looked at the book Yusuf had opened on the table. '"*We are the Weasels: A guide from badger to zorilla.*" What's a zorilla?'

'Sounds like an ape with a sword,' said Olly. 'You know, like Zorro?'

No-one laughed.

'Got it from the library,' said Yusuf. 'It can't hurt to know a bit about these creatures, can it?'

'Creatures?' Ben poked the book with his plastic fork. He had a tub of vanilla that was still untouched. 'We can't think like that. Those kids aren't polecats any more than we're really cats.'

'I know.' Yusuf looked at him oddly. 'I'm talking about the animals. We read up on the polecat family to try and understand Fisher's gang. That's all I meant.' He turned a page. '"The ferret and the polecat are close cousins, ferrets being the domesticated form. Some experts joke that ferrets are just polecats with addresses."'

Ben picked at his ice cream. Tiffany could tell his mind was elsewhere. His gaze kept wandering through the window.

'"Ferrets are commonly used as hunting pets-"'

'There!' Ben pointed, sending Susie's sorbet flying. 'Over by the Odeon.'

A squad of four figures was breaking through the crowds of cinema-goers, moving with one wilful stride. They circled round a busker with a banjo and on past the Vue cinema towards Charing Cross Road.

'That's them.' Ben pulled Olly and Daniel from their chairs. 'Come on!'

'I was still eating that,' protested Susie.

Tiffany slurped one last chocolate chunk and flicked her tub sadly and accurately across the room towards the bin. They piled out after Ben into the Square.

'That guy with the messy hair is Gary. The girl's called Antonia. I don't recognise the other two.'

The gang crossed the road. Ben and Yusuf broke into a run, following them across the road and into the Tube station. Tiffany, lagging behind the others, made her way down the congested steps and got sour looks from all the people Ben had barged aside.

She was surprised to see that the four youths – the polecat kids, as she now thought of them – were still in the ticket hall, loitering outside a tacky souvenir shop. Ben had gone into full shifty mode, lurking near a ticket machine and casting suspicious glances. Yusuf did better by burying his head in his book.

'"Like cats, ferrets are insatiably curious, a trait which gets them into no end of trouble,"' he read. '"Sadly, unlike cats, ferrets have very little homing instinct, so a lost pet rarely survives as a stray unless some kind person takes them in."'

Tiffany pretended to study her nails so she could stare at the group through her fingers. The three boys wore wolfish grins and had an aura of danger that cleared space around them. The willowy black girl watched the crowds. She wore her bandana as a head scarf, while her companions had tied theirs round their necks. These were masks, Tiffany reminded herself. Bandit masks.

'Are they waiting for someone?' Susie hovered at her side.

'Look,' Cecile murmured. 'They're splitting up.'

Two of the boys ambled towards the gateway to the Piccadilly line.

'"The American fisher, *martes pennanti*,"' read Yusuf, '"resembles a very large mink. An adult male can weigh as much as a terrier dog. They don't actually fish; their name comes from fitch, an old word for polecat."'

A logjam of tourists was forming at the top of the escalators. They appeared to be foreign students. Some fiddled in purses or wallets for unfamiliar Travelcards, while the more confident filtered through the barriers into the ticket hall. Tiffany's keen ears plucked a thread of their conversation.

'*Il est pour ma mère. Maman aime des ours.*'

A girl with a brown fringe and glasses was holding a teddy that wore an I Love London T-shirt. A gift for her bear-loving mother – Tiffany understood that much. She'd been working hard at her French, supposedly for her school Paris trip which Mum and Dad were still umming and ahhing about. The happy faces of the French students made her wince. They were having fun in her city, while she would probably never visit theirs.

'"Fishers are exceptionally fierce and agile predators,"' Yusuf read. '"They can outclimb a squirrel and are one of the only animals able to kill porcupines." Hey, this is good. "The fisher's cry is notorious, often mistaken for a human scream. Shaken Boston residents have even imagined it to be the sound of a child being murdered–"'

'Shut it, Yusuf,' said Ben. 'I think something's happening.'

The two boys had lapped the hall and were now strolling back towards Gary and Antonia, quickening their pace. The barriers were now clogged with bemused Europeans, forcing an inspector to unlock a side gate.

'"As well as preying on everything from mice to

small deer, fishers have been blamed for slaughtering domestic cats–'

'I said that's enough!' Ben tried to snatch the book and so missed the moment. Tiffany felt a spark jump between the polecat pairs. The four pulled their masks over their eyes. Then they moved like the wind. They really did, for they themselves were harder to see than the path they blew through the crowd. Tiffany's cat vision slowed other moving figures to a crawl as her eyes tracked the attackers. The leading pair shoved people hard, knocking them off balance long enough to let the others breeze past and harvest purses, phones, money-belts and iPods. What most witnesses might later describe as a random smash-and-grab was in actual fact an elegant and orderly dance. Someone screamed. The girl with the teddy bear groped on the floor for her glasses.

Dreadlocks flying, the boy named Gary vaulted the ticket barriers, two handbags and a plastic carrier hooked in his right arm. He had hardly hit the ground before his friends leaped over. The whole strike, from first nod to breakaway, had taken all of five seconds. Tiffany stood dazed for the sixth. Then:

'After them!' Ben cried.

'We can't go down there,' Tiffany blurted, 'we haven't bought tickets–'

Ben cleared the barrier in one bound. Susie was right on his tail, flinging herself aloft with the help of both hands. Tiffany heaved a sigh, called on her inner cat and leaped. She landed on the other side in the path of a cross mother's pushchair, skipped aside with a quick apology and grabbed the nearest shoulder, Olly's.

'What's he playing at? Geoff said to watch, not chase them.'

'Uu-uh.' Olly gulped. 'This looks hairy–'

The packed escalators hadn't slowed the thieves' escape. The polecat kids had jumped onto the partition between the staircases, making its sloping surface into a slide. As for Ben, his splayed shape was already halfway down it and dwindling fast, with Daniel and Susie close behind. Olly shut his eyes, whooped and hurled himself after them. *Hey ho*, thought Tiffany, *why not?* As soon as she was plummeting she remembered why not.

'Yow!' Olly yelped, slithering down below her. 'Mind the– Yerk! Mind the No Smoking signs. They're lethal!'

Just in time Tiffany tilted herself, bobsleigh style, to slip round the side of the first jutting sign. Olly continued to hit every single one until he reached the bottom and plopped off the end in a groaning heap. Tiffany skimmed over his head for a prim toe-pointed landing.

'Ben?' The escalator hall was bedlam, hoards of taller people hurrying, blocking her view. 'Olly, did you see where they went?'

'I'm fine, thanks for asking,' Olly whimpered.

Perspex-faced posters for the latest shows and films lined the corridors leading to the two Tube lines. The Piccadilly line was closest. Taking the passage straight ahead she zig-zagged against the tide of alighting passengers, took the steps in one jump and caught up with Susie on the westbound platform. A train was leaving, whining up to speed.

'Where are they?' Tiffany demanded.

'Here.' Ben stood in the thinning crowd, arms folded, staring after the train. Before its lights dimmed into the tunnel, Tiffany spied two small figures hitching a ride on the rear carriage's back bumper.

'We lost them,' Susie panted.

'The doors closed!' Ben thumped his palm. 'And then they went and jumped on anyway. We could have done that! They use the doors between the carriages to get inside the train.'

'An idea that I give zero out of ten,' said Yusuf. 'Those guys have had a load of practice, Ben. If you'd tried it we'd be scraping you off the tracks.'

'Lucky for you I chickened out, then.'

'There were four of them,' said Susie. '*I* wasn't going to get on their train. We'd have been ambushed and beaten up and dragged off to that nasty place.'

'Well, I've been there before,' snapped Ben. He glowered at the tunnel until the train winked into darkness, and Tiffany could not guess his thoughts.

Had she said she didn't mind Geoff taking charge? No, she minded, she minded lots. The Cat Kin was meant to be her group, yet now, for much of the week, she was the outsider. On most weekdays she had to languish safe at home while the others met without her. Her contact with Ben was reduced to snatched phone calls, and even then he seemed cagey, as if there were things he wasn't telling her. She was forced to scavenge scraps of news from Susie, Yusuf or Olly during school lunch breaks. Apparently Ben (and anyone free to join him) was spending every spare minute on the Underground, tracking the polecats' movements.

'We think they target four stations, mostly,' Yusuf told her on Wednesday, speaking English instead of French after she threatened to throw water at him. 'Tottenham Court Road, Oxford Circus, Piccadilly, and Leicester Square.'

'Those stations link together on four different lines.' Olly showed her on his tattered Tube map. 'This helps them avoid being caught, Ben reckons. If someone raises the alarm, then pow! they switch lines at the next stop. We're calling this rectangle the polecat patch.'

'Nice of you to let me know.'

'We tell you as soon as we can,' protested Yusuf. 'You're just not around as often as the rest of us.'

'When I was the teacher, it was you lot who weren't around. How come Geoff can get you to come four times a week when I was lucky to see you once?'

'There's just...' Olly smiled weakly, 'more stuff going on now.'

Tiffany gritted her teeth. So much was happening without her. It wasn't jealousy, well, all right, it was a bit. But more than feeling jealous she felt afraid – afraid they were getting in over their heads. Most of the Cat Kin were treating this as a game. Then there was Ben, who seemed to be taking it far too personally, and Geoff, who was simply doing his job, she supposed. None of them saw things the way she did. Yes, a man like Martin Fisher ought to be stopped. She just didn't remember volunteering. Her homework timetable said nothing about fighting a maniac per week. She had been there, done that, nearly died.

Here was a horrid thought. Maybe her parents really had turned her into a wet blanket. Was this common sense or cowardice? If only someone would help her tell the difference.

That evening she lay on her bed, stubbornly learning French verbs in the hope that Mum or Dad might *entre* and find her. Instead it was Stuart who interrupted, calling from his room. 'I need you to push in some pins.'

Beside his board of newspaper cuttings, a map of the British Isles had been tacked to the wall. It was speckled with many coloured pins, which Mum had presumably swiped from her office and then helped Stuart to push in.

'What's this for?'

'I'm keeping track of mysterious sightings around the country,' Stuart explained. 'Yellow pins are UFOs. Blue ones are ghosts, and so on.'

'You're branching out.'

'There's so much to keep track of. Scotland's

full of ghosts, look.'

'What are these ones?' Tiffany fingered the black pushpins that were clustered in England's south-western foot.

'Black pins are... mysterious big cat sightings. Green pins are the Loch Ness Monster –'

'Did you say *big cats*?'

A headline on Stuart's notice board leapt out at her. *Dartmoor's Sheep Slayer.* He had printed it off a news website. *Mutilated carcass resembles 'jaguar kill' say experts.*

'How long have you been collecting these stories?'

'Not long. I only started on the cats last week. You gave me the idea. I've been finding old reports...'

She was no longer listening. Her mind was in a spin. Where was this wild thrill of hope coming from? She couldn't help noticing that all the black pins were stuck in one corner of England. Devon, to be precise.

Tiffany came early to Friday's pashki class, hoping to speak to Geoff alone. As the shadowy chapel loomed through the leaves she heard low voices. Ben had got there before her. He and Geoff were talking about the polecat gang, as usual, though they stopped when she walked in. She waited until the class was over, then went to help Geoff roll up the mats.

'You've certainly found your form,' he said.

'Thanks.'

'A shaky start's nothing to worry about. New teacher and all. You're a Powell pupil through and through, that's your only problem. My style's a bit different.'

'You're still great, though.'

'Purrr-r-r-r.' Geoff rolled the word with his tongue. 'Now then. No-one's ever nice to me unless they want something.'

'Um.' Tiffany flushed. 'You know the other week. You said I'd used this pashki skill. The Oshtian Compass.'

'Oh... yeah.'

'That was an accident. I don't know how I did it. When are you going to teach it to us?'

'One day.' Geoff paused in his mat-rolling. 'It's not top of the list.'

'Why not?'

'Too hard. If pashki had belts this'd be the black one.'

'You could show me, though.'

'Eventually,' said Geoff. 'I can't see the Compass being much use to you now. We're in London, right? You've got the *A to Z* if you get lost.'

His tone irked her.

'Not much use? I found Ben for you!'

'I would have found him anyway, given another day.'

'What if I need it again?'

'Give me strength–'

Tiffany stepped backwards. He had never raised his voice before. The place felt very quiet and dark. Isolated. Geoff scratched his nose.

'Let's leave it, yeah?'

She was trembling slightly. 'I don't understand. I want to learn. Won't you teach me?'

Geoff slapped a mat as if to brush away dust. 'You know the catras, don't you? You know how they work. If this… *parlour trick* is so important to you, figure it out for yourself.'

For a ridiculous moment Tiffany feared she might cry. At last Geoff's blue eyes met hers. They had softened.

'Oh. Hey.' He held up his hands. 'Can I say sorry? That was mean.'

Tiffany went to gather her things.

'I'm not stupid, Tiffany.' Geoff half-smiled. 'Not all the time. I see what's on your mind. All you are doing is tormenting yourself.'

She tried for a poker face.

'You want to be taught,' Geoff said. 'But not by this teacher. Right?'

Tiffany looked away.

'It's Felicity you want,' said Geoff. 'Mrs Powell.'

'She,' Tiffany swallowed, 'she never even said goodbye.'

'It's hard.' Geoff wiped his hands on his jeans. 'I've been there myself. But she's gone, Tiffany. And she means to be gone. If she'd wanted the pair of you to meet again, it would have happened by now.'

'She wasn't any old teacher, though. She was my…'

'Yes,' said Geoff. 'For what it's worth, Tiffany, I'm sure she counted you as a friend.'

'Tell me about her.'

Geoff looked surprised.

'I mean,' Tiffany stammered, 'you call her Felicity. I call her Mrs Powell. So it feels, I don't know, like we're talking about different people.'

'You want to meet the person I knew?' Geoff pondered the chapel roof. 'To me Felicity was lots of things. First she saved me from a wasted life. I was a young thug who robbed people on the streets, till I chose the wrong lady's bag to snatch.'

'You didn't!'

'Go on, laugh.' Geoff played with a coin, rolling it to and fro across his knuckles. 'Anyway, she took pity. Said I had potential. Etcetera. She paid for my air ticket so I could travel to see her mentor, Mr Singh. For years I lived at a hill station in Kashmir, the most beautiful place in the world. I learned my pashki rudiments in the snow.'

A vision of mountains swept Tiffany away.

'Then I stayed in Cairo. I was in my twenties when I met Felicity again. She looked young as ever. We became… colleagues. Her life was this great mission, of course, and she roped me into it. Hunting big cat poachers in places like Thailand, smashing the trade in bogus medicines. It was fun. I got to see the world, meet interesting people, and ram their illegal tiger bones down their throats. And gradually I became more than just her henchman.' The coin fell from his fingers. He let it twirl on the floor to a stop. 'Friends can be scarce in a life like ours, but without a doubt she was the closest friend I ever had.'

Tiffany felt suddenly foolish. How could she compare her troubles to his? She'd hardly lived. Her deepest feelings were mere paddling pools.

'Let me tell you something,' said Geoff. 'Felicity and I were once so close that, even hundreds of miles apart, we could look up at the same new Moon, at the same moment, and we would *know*. But now…' His voice went over a bump. He stared out at the dark sky, sniffed the breeze through the window, turned his head as if to listen with each ear, seeming to reach out with every volt of his senses before sinking back into himself. 'Nothing. I can't feel her. We've drifted too far. That's what happens, Tiffany. The closest ties you have, they decay, they wither away if you let them. And the people you loved become strangers.'

'I'm sorry,' said Tiffany.

Geoff touched her forehead, where the M of her face paint faintly tingled.

'Don't be. All I want is for you to understand. What you think will make you happier may end up doing the opposite. It can be better to let go.'

She bit her lip.

'Forget the Oshtian Compass,' said Geoff. 'Focus on the friends you still have.'

'But – I can't just forget –' Her reply fell apart as she heard her phone wailing. 'Ohmygod! What's the time? My dad'll be waiting outside the church hall!'

'That way.' Geoff pointed. 'Go dead straight and skip over the wall. Remember to scrub your face.'

Tiffany caught the pack of tissues that he tossed to her, grabbed her bag and hightailed it out of the door.

Top speed and some reckless grave-hurdling meant she was only ten minutes late, so all she got was a lecture. By Sunday, Dad had calmed down enough to let her go out again. Cecile and Susie would meet her at the cinema to see *Croftville*, the hilarious new Scottish rom-com. After twice losing her nerve, Tiffany rang Ben to invite him too. He couldn't, he said. He had plans. She tried not to sound disappointed.

Today, she had decided, she would be *normal.* Her inner voices, however, were having none of it. All the way to Leicester Square they pestered her. *You know the catras, don't you? You know how they work.* Geoff wouldn't teach her the Oshtian Compass and had even warned her not to try. Yet she had done it before, unaided.

Her Tube train rattled its rhythm on the rails, awakening a rhyme in her mind.

Ptep is my head, the balancing blue sky
Mandira is my green all-sensing eye
Kelotaukhon, copper maw, my mystery
Golden chest of Parda strongly glows
Lower crimson Oshtis feels and knows
Nimble tail is Ailur, indigo.

So. How did you make the Oshtian Compass? Start with Oshtis, she supposed – no prizes for guessing that. She remembered roving the rooftops in her unknowing search for Ben, feeling the blood-red pulse of Oshtis in her stomach. Yet there had to be more to it.

Kelotaukhon? That was the most enigmatic catra and the one she used least. She tried it now, picturing a copper eye to blend with the red one. Ugh, that just felt weird. She ran over the rhyme again. *Mandira is my green all-sensing eye.* Sensing. Surely the Compass was a kind of sense?

Waiting on a sunny bench near the Odeon, she gave in to temptation. On her mind's dark screen she projected the red eye of Oshtis, then steadily turned up her Mandira. A flutter in her solar plexus suggested she was on to something. Okay. She would try to predict where Susie and Cecile were coming from. Imagining their faces, she concentrated. From the right, she decided. They would come from the right.

'Boo!' cried Susie, in her left ear. 'Dozing off?'

Tiffany snapped her eyes open, embarrassed. So much for that idea.

'Hi,' she said. 'Want to get a burger before the film?'

'Dunno if we should see it now.' Cecile seemed excited or anxious. 'Daniel called.'

'To say what?'

'Ben's been caught by the polecats.'

'*What?*'

'It's okay.' Susie nodded vigorously. 'It was planned.'

'Planned?' Tiffany stared from one to the other. 'I don't understand. Who planned it?'

'They did,' said Susie. 'Geoff and Ben.'

For a moment Tiffany couldn't think. Then her hand shot out and grabbed Susie's jacket with such lightning speed that a flock of pigeons took flight.

'Start telling me stuff *now*,' Tiffany hissed.

GOING UNDERGROUND

Ben had been riding the same route all morning and had seen neither hide nor hair of a polecat. Knowing his luck they had probably taken the day off. In an effort to keep alert he had flicked through every newspaper littering his train, then read rows of advertisements for everything from vitamin pills to religious cults. Now he was left with just the door sign at the end of his tube carriage: *Risk of death if used while train is moving*. He was still reading it when the door opened.

Red-haired Kevin came first. Then the gangly Alec, no longer limping from that lucky kick in the dark. Behind him, a boy Ben had never seen – he would have remembered such a big nose. At the rear, sporting sweatbands on his tattooed arms, was Jeep. Their eyes browsed the busy carriage as if it were a rack of DVDs. Ben took deep breaths. So far they hadn't seen him. There was time to change his mind.

'I couldn't plan a steak lunch in a slaughterhouse,' Geoff had confessed to him on Friday evening, before Tiffany arrived at the chapel. 'I don't do strategy. So tell me if I'm daft in the head.'

Geoff said this had kept him awake day and night. In a single week the polecats had made over thirty thieving raids. That was far more than they needed, for riches meant nothing to Martin Fisher. Geoff suspected the polecats were hoarding, stockpiling supplies of money, food, clothes and valuable items. It all pointed to some sort of plot.

'Fisher's a natural planner,' said Geoff, with a hint of envy. 'For years he had nothing else to do. If he has a scheme on the boil we need to know what it is. I can think of only one way to do that. Ben, you're not going to like it.'

Kevin, Jeep, Alec and Big Nose were sidling along the carriage. Passengers pulled feet and bags out of their path. The boys clearly enjoyed the ripple of fear they pushed before them, daring people with their eyes. Ben waited till it was fractionally too late. Then he rose from his seat and hurried away from them down the aisle.

'Kev, look, it's him!'

Ben fumbled with the carriage door until he felt hot breath on his neck. The four boys crowded him into the corner. He tried to look afraid and succeeded.

'Small world, isn't it?' said Kevin.

'What do you want with me?'

'It was very rude, running off like that,' said Kevin. 'You wanna guess how much hell you caused me? Totally blew my morning schedule. Now you're coming back with us.'

He seized Ben's right arm and Jeep took the left, painfully bending his fingers. Ben pretended to struggle. It was an Oscar-winning performance.

'You lads! What are you doing to him?' A balding man with a shopping bag got to his feet. Ben's heart didn't know whether to leap or sink.

Without slackening his grip, Jeep half-turned and slashed with the knife that appeared in his hand. The carrier bag split and a plush grey elephant tumbled out, spilling the stuffing from its trunk.

'Shut,' Jeep snarled, 'up.'

The man sat as if the knife had cut his backbone. The train's windows blurred with reds and blues as they rushed into Oxford Circus, slowing sharply.

'Here's our stop,' said Kevin. 'Come on, Ben… you got a last name?'

Ben said nothing.

'You don't. Good. Let's go home.'

Kevin led them off the train, his three henchmen hustling Ben between them so they looked like one friendly group. Through the station's airless passages they shuffled, flowing with the crowds that followed the blue signs towards the Victoria line.

'I see your point, Geoff.' Ben had picked his words with care. He hadn't wanted Geoff to think him a coward. 'But think about it. There's no way I can join Fisher's gang.'

'I understand.' Geoff paced the chapel's nave. 'It's not that you're afraid. You're thinking of your family. I forget how it is. I never really had one myself.'

'You know what would happen if I went missing,' said Ben. 'My parents would–' He couldn't imagine it. And there was no reason to imagine it, because it was not going to happen. 'It's all right for people like you and Mrs Powell. You sort of... don't exist. But I'm in Year Nine!'

'Easter holidays coming up,' Geoff remarked. 'Ah, forget it. I can't ask this of you. I'm just saying what needs to be done. After all, Fisher stole those children from *their* families.'

'Can't you do anything?'

'I haven't been sat eating pies,' Geoff snorted. 'I've gone back to the Hermitage five or six times. It's not easy spying on folks who have sharpened senses. I wouldn't fancy my chances if I got nabbed. Even in the old days Martin fought almost as well as me.' He cracked his knuckles and winced. 'I haven't found out much, but I've caught a scent. And something's rotten. This may be about more than saving a few missing kids.'

That was when Tiffany had stepped through the chapel doorway, and they stopped talking.

Later, tired and aching, he flung down his kitbag in the hallway of Dad's flat – home, he reminded himself – and pondered dinner. Dad let him choose his own meals, so now he lived off crispy pancakes, seafood pizzas, spicy chicken drumsticks and ice cream. This was ideal – wasn't it? Without Mum around there was no-one to tell him courgettes were full of vitamins, or claim that bananas were desserts. He never had to chop at little trees of broccoli or shovel pebbly soya beans. All the same, it was puzzling. Although he would never choose such foods for himself, dinner without them didn't taste like *his* dinner any more.

He laid a wedge of frozen fish among chips on a baking tray. On an impulse he added a second fish and upped the chip count. Dad was out on an emergency call, a localised power-cut, and had probably forgotten to eat. Ben set an extra place at the table and lined up two cans, one of Coke and one of beer. By the time Dad's key scraped in the lock the whole flat was simmering with a golden smell.

'Mm! You'll make me hungry now.' Ray Gallagher put down his toolbox with a clank. He saw the two sets of cutlery. 'What's this? Special occasion?'

'Not partic'ly.'

'Nice one, son. You'll make someone a lovely wife one day.'

Ben served up. No peas, he noticed, then pushed the thought away. He put on the CD they both liked and set the volume to stun. When all was gobbled up except for three burnt chips, Dad finished his beer and went on a dessert hunt. There was a long-uneaten Christmas pudding gathering dust, so they had that.

Lying stuffed on the sofa, Ben remembered he had a letter from school. Dad read it while surfing TV channels.

'Parents' evening,' exclaimed Dad. 'What a drag, eh. I remember hating that as a kid. The oldies poking their noses in.'

Actually Ben had never minded it much. He enjoyed showing Mum and Dad round his classrooms, as if welcoming them into his den. School was like another secret life, one he could, occasionally, share with them.

'Mum says to tell you she can't make it this year,' said Ben. 'She has to work the evening shift.'

'That must be a relief, eh?'

Ben wasn't relieved so much as disappointed. He had hoped Mum would get to see his art project, a modrock sculpture of a pinball machine that had real flashing lights. He was particularly pleased with this idea.

'Well, I know you do well at school,' said Dad. 'I don't need your teachers to tell me that. Why don't we say I'm busy as well?'

'Er...'

'Your friends'll be so jealous!'

Ben sighed. 'Suppose so.'

'Let's play safe, though. You'd better tell your mum that I am going. We don't want you getting into trouble with her, do we?'

'Suppose not.' Ben picked up a blackened chip and chewed it. Bitterness filled his mouth. A memory came back to him: arriving home at daybreak after his escape from the Hermitage, having been missing two nights and a day. He'd expected to see police cars outside. All he'd found was Dad having a lie-in, and instead of a telling-off he got a jokey reminder to phone the next time he planned a sleepover. At the time he'd felt glad: Dad was so cool. Now he wondered how long it would have taken Ray Gallagher to remember he had a son, and what might have become of him, were it not for Geoff White.

That stung him into saying what he said.

'Dad, I've decided. I want to go and stay at Mum's this weekend. And, uh, stay there until after the Easter holidays. I can travel to school from there in the meantime. See how it works out.'

As he spoke he realised it was a test. Everything depended on how Dad reacted.

'Oh.' Dad frowned a moment. He rubbed his upper lip. 'Okay, Ben. If she agrees, I guess that's fine with me too.'

Ben watched him. Dad was supposed to argue, to ask questions, or be upset. Instead he just picked up a TV guide and began reading it with intense concentration. And there was silence. Nothing more to be said.

Ben cleared the dinner plates. Fine, if that was how things were. If Dad wasn't bothered, he would find someone who was. He went to his room and dialled the newest number on his phone.

'Okay,' he said, when Geoff picked up. 'I'll do it.'

The test had become the first step. To carry out

Geoff's mission he'd have to disappear, for at least a week, without his parents wondering. Impossible – unless you had a family like his. Dad would think he was staying with Mum. Mum could be told he was at Dad's. Only from each other could they find out the truth, and (here was the beauty of it) they no longer spoke except through Ben. The final spanner in the works – school – was easy. A phone call from Geoff, posing as Ray Gallagher, explained to Ben's form teacher that he had tonsillitis. That covered the week until the holidays.

But planning it and doing it were very different things. On the Victoria line train he sat sandwiched between Kevin and Big Nose, facing Jeep's and Alec's mocking sneers. Trying to stare past them he locked eyes with his reflection in the opposite window, a ghost that blurred when the jolting train rattled the panes of glass.

They braked into Euston. He must have tensed, for Kevin pinned his left wrist to the arm rest. Passengers disembarked and boarded. A young man in a rugby shirt took the seat next to Kevin, settling down with his earphones yammering. Doors clunked and they moved off.

In two minutes they'd be at King's Cross. Then onwards to Islington, on through Finsbury Park, then the long, long tunnel in the depths of which hid the station that appeared on no map. Already his home – wherever *that* was – felt far away.

I don't understand. This morning's phone call to Mum still hurt. *Ben, what's the matter? We agreed you'd spend the holidays with me.*

I want to stay in London this Easter. Where my friends are.

It was done now. He had to forget their conversation. Those lies he had told were to spare her from worry.

Are you cross with me, Ben? Because I moved out of London?

No.

I hoped you could come with me. I still do.

He shook his arm free of Kevin's, ignoring the warning glares. It did nothing to silence the voices in his head.

I'll come in the summer holidays.

Will you though? You say you'll come at weekends and you don't. You don't even call much. I'm scared, Ben.

Scared? Why… why should you be?

I get this feeling. You're drifting. Out of my reach. Like I'm never going to see you again.

Ben met the stare of his spectre in the window, hurtling through emptiness. This was wrong, this was *mad*. Guilt rose in him and kept on rising, pounding him into submission. He couldn't let Mum think those things. Geoff was asking too much. He hadn't thought this through at all.

Highbury and Islington. The doors chirruped and clunked.

He had to escape. As the train gathered speed his mind raced with it, getting flashes of a crazy plan. He rode on this route at least once a week, knew every bump and swerve. There was something about this stretch of the line…

Rat-tat-tat-ah-ratta. The man with the earphones must have been deafened, his music louder than the clash of steel wheels. Ben stole a glance past Kevin. The iPod lay upon the guy's knee, the wire snagged on the collar of his rugby shirt. The pieces of Ben's plan fell into place. But Finsbury Park was only minutes away. It was now or never.

He shut his eyes and invoked his catras, one after the other, his Mau body bristling awake. He lingered on the last, Ailur for agility. He was going to need it.

'Kevin,' he said. 'That last name you asked about? It's Gallagher.'

As Kevin turned his way, Ben reached past him, his left hand darting as fast as a cat's paw. He grabbed the young man's earphones and jerked his iPod up like a fish on a line. It landed in Kevin's lap, blaring into thin air.

'What the – ?' Too slow to have seen Ben move, the man rounded on Kevin. 'Give that back you – !'

Kevin knocked the grabbing hands away, and right on cue all hell broke loose. Jeep and Big Nose sprang to help their leader as he struggled with the burly man. The carriage's other passengers cringed in alarm and it was left for Alec to yell, 'He's getting away!', which Ben heard from the far end of the carriage. Hoping Alec was right, he ran to the connecting door (*Risk of death if used while train is moving*) and yanked it open to the smell of metallic winds.

A horrified shout came from behind him. He looked back and saw the man in the rugby shirt clutching his blood-soaked right hand. Jeep's knife flashed a second time and Kevin caught his arm.

'Leave it! He's the one we want.'

White-faced the bleeding man slumped into a seat. Ben felt sick. That had been his fault. Tearing his eyes away he slipped through the door and edged his body into the gap between the train cars. With every bend the cars flexed around their couplings, squeezing him when they turned left. He had a moment's terror. If the bend got any sharper, the bunching carriages might crush him.

But the track straightened. The carriages parted on his side, freeing him enough to climb. Scraping paintwork with his Mau claws he dragged himself, gasping, to the train's curved roof. The noise stunned him. He had thought tube trains were loud inside, but out here, hemmed in by echoing walls, it was like being in the throat of a roaring Tyrannosaurus rex.

The tunnel's brick roof would shear off his scalp if he rose out of a crouch. He crawled along the top of the carriage, into the wind. Wheels rasped on rails and it was hard to hear himself think. Why had he come up here? Because… because he hoped to do something so stupidly dangerous that even the polecats would think twice about it.

All his life Finsbury Park had been his local station. Nobody knew their back garden better. It served two lines, the Piccadilly (great for getting to the cinemas at Leicester Square) and this one, the Victoria. To switch from one to the other you had to walk across the platforms, for the two lines ran through separate tunnels. There was only one point where those tunnels joined.

Knowing he shouldn't, Ben looked back. A spark from the electric track whitened the walls, and he saw Kevin's red hair, the flash of Jeep's bared teeth. They were clambering onto the carriage roof behind him. Kevin shouted something, lost in the roar. Ben ducked his head and kept crawling. Thirty seconds more was all he needed. Thirty seconds and luck.

Something zinged off the bodywork near his hand. Flying gravel? He looked round again. His pursuers were closer. Jeep held something in his outstretched hand. A T-shaped thing. With a lurch of dread Ben recognised the mini-crossbow. Kevin was still bawling as if someone had pressed his mute button. *Stop. Stay there.* Ben clung on as the train rattled and bounced. This was it – this was the place. But the thing he had banked on was not happening. His plan collapsed. What a mad gamble it had been. He'd trusted his life to London Transport.

And then it appeared.

For a magical moment it seemed as if the tunnel was walled with mirrors. A second tube train, all lit up, was cruising alongside. In this short stretch of tunnel, where the two lines briefly merged, he'd often stared out of the window to see this synchronised train, bound on a slightly different course. A different course that he now had the power to take.

Jeep rose to one knee. He levelled the crossbow, squinting along the shaft. Kevin yelled inaudibly.

Ben caught the gleam of amazement in his eyes. Maybe he couldn't quite believe it, but Kevin had guessed.

On rushed the trains to the fork where the track began to pull apart like a giant zip. Ben leaped. Parda, the strength catra, burst golden in his mind, catapulting him across the widening gap. He crashed onto the roof of the parallel carriage and pinned himself to it with his claws. In the same instant the trains dived into their separate tunnels, carrying Ben to one side of Finsbury Park and the polecats to the other.

His train pulled into the platform, just one of dozens every day. Passengers spilled out. Ben peered down on the tops of their heads. The doors stayed open an agonisingly long time. He knew that his last-second leap had only bought him breathing space. Should he make a dash for it through the station, or stay put? Running seemed too risky. Staying on this tube line would take him farther away from the Hermitage, and right now that was all he cared about.

The train moved off. Ben crawled to a gap between the cars and let himself in through the door he wasn't supposed to use. He found a seat and let a station go by, getting off at the next, Turnpike Lane. There weren't many people around. Ben headed for the escalators. Any of the buses that went down Green Lanes might get him home in time for lunch with Dad. He could say he'd changed his mind –

'One more step,' hissed a voice behind him, 'and it's

a bolt in your back. I'll do it.'

Ben stood as still as he knew how.

'Turn around.'

He obeyed. Jeep stood half-hidden in an archway, the arrow of his crossbow pointing at Ben's heart.

'Yeah,' said Ben. 'I know you would.'

Slow handclaps rang off the tiles. Kevin stepped from another arch.

'Nice one. That was class.' He closed until he and Ben were face to face. 'Really, you're one slippery guy. A shame you can't outwit me. Especially not on the Tube.'

Ben took deep breaths, trying to calm his Mau body down. There was a real danger that the wildcat inside him would make him do some dumb cat thing, like trying to fight his way out.

'Kev, you're in my firing line,' said Jeep.

'And you're in my slapping line. Gimme that stupid bow before you poke someone's eye out.' Kevin peered at Ben. 'Okay, jumping Jack Flash. Who taught you that stuff?'

Ben counted his remaining options. Just the one, it seemed. Fortunately it was the one Geoff had prepared him for. Time to go back to the script.

'I learned it from a guy I used to know,' said Ben. 'But he went off and left me.'

'He left you? What was his name?'

This was it. The magic words. 'He called himself the White Cat.'

Kevin and Jeep blinked.

'No way,' said Jeep. 'That's the guy who taught–'

'Not *Geoff* White?' said Kevin.

'Might have been.' Ben shrugged. 'I ain't seen him for months and I don't want to.'

Kevin took him by the elbow with a firm but not unfriendly grip.

'There's someone you really have to meet,' he said.

THE WEASEL DANCE

'Your mum and I have been having a talk,' said Peter Maine. Tiffany paused with her sardines on toast half-chewed. That phrase could mean a divorce or simply that her room needed hoovering.

Mum started laying two places for dinner. 'We've discussed that Paris trip, and we think it'll be good for you to go.'

'You what?' Tiffany spat crumbs. 'Duh! It's no use saying yes *now*. They did the bookings ages ago.'

'I phoned Mr Devereux on Friday,' said Mum. 'There's a spare place. One of your classmates had to cancel.'

Of course. Jason Wilks had busted his ankle playing rugby.

'So, I can go to Paris now?'

Dad took a lamb joint out of the fridge. '*Mais oui!*'

Tiffany felt peculiar. Happy, of course, yet in a distant way. School trips, Easter holidays, these seemed alien things at the moment. She remembered to smile back and look *tres heureux*, but inside she was stewing.

For starters, she was furious with Ben. She was furious with everyone, herself included. All the

Cat Kin had known about the plan except her.

'How could you?' she yelled at Geoff, as soon as she arrived at the chapel that evening. Geoff didn't even take Sundays off, and now held Cat Kin meetings whenever anyone could make it. Tiffany had told her parents she was round at Cecile's to watch a DVD – well and truly scraping her barrel of excuses. 'How dare you send him back there?'

'Send him? You can't send Ben out for a pint of milk.' Geoff looked tired, his stubble scraggier. 'This is something he wants to do. For him the Hermitage is unfinished business. He has to go back. And I have to find out what Fisher is up to.'

'Mrs Powell never sent us into danger on our own,' Tiffany retorted. 'She'd have handled it herself.'

'No doubt.' Geoff stretched towards the chapel ceiling. 'But then, Mrs Powell wouldn't have this problem in the first place. Mrs Powell would never mess up the way I did. Mrs Powell is perfect, isn't she, Tiffany?' He dropped his arms with a hiss of spent air. 'But I'm not. So cut me some slack.'

Tiffany smarted from his words until Cecile caught her at the end of the class.

'Sometimes,' said Cecile, 'you can be a clot.'

''Scuse me?'

'Around Geoff. He misses her too. Maybe more than you do. Don't you see?'

Yes, she did. Geoff slouched in the corner, trying to unknot a lank of his hair, scratching inside one ear. Had she passed such a man on the street, Tiffany might have given him her loose change.

'He's sore talking about her. It's obvious,' said Cecile. 'And you keep picking at it.'

'Tell him I'm sorry, then. It doesn't change the facts. Think, Cecile, where is Ben? What's happening to him right now?'

Kevin led him along the platform, through the Hermitage's cardboard dormitory. Wind ruffled Ben's hair and he heard a roar.

'Train passing Platform 1,' said Kevin. 'They still go through that bit of tunnel. We sleep here on Platform 2, where it's quieter. This'll be your bed. It's just become free.'

Ben looked down at a nest of split grocery boxes.

'Why has it just become free?'

'Because no-one else needs it anymore.' Kevin scratched a spot on his chin. 'No blanket. Get one before bedtime. We dim the lights at eleven-thirty. After that, no talking. Routine is important.'

Where would he find a blanket? It gave him an excuse to explore. Wandering the Hermitage, Ben found himself thinking of a crab he'd seen on a beach in Spain. Instead of a shell it had a Fanta can. Funny – of course, that would have been a hermit crab. Yet it wasn't the name that struck a chord. It was the way these kids had managed to make a home out of something so wrong for it.

He climbed the stairs between the unfinished

escalators and found what would have been the ticket hall. It reminded him of the one at Seven Sisters. The floor space formed a wonky crescent with the stairways at one end and a tunnel at the other, blocked with concrete. There were two other exits, similarly sealed. Ivy-wreathes of electric wires wove along the skirts of the walls, feeding the forest of brightly burning household lamps. Probably they drew power from the train tracks below. Here was a kind of leisure area, with a TV, stereo system, pool table, even a pinball machine (for a moment he was tempted, then moved away with a shudder). He found a ticket office that was serving as a sort of kitchen, piled high with grocery boxes, a microwave and a fridge.

Another office had been turned into a wardrobe, or rather a mineshaft through a mountain of clothes, exposing seasons of fashions stacked in geological layers. A small blonde girl was working to sort mounds of shopping bags into piles. Ben learned her name was Lisa. She unearthed some Calvin Klein pyjamas, still in their wrapper.

'We're out of bedding,' she said, after more digging. 'Use this.'

The angora shawls, silk shirts and fake fur coat that she gave him would have paid Mum's housekeeping for months. Ben said an awkward thank-you over the bundle and took it down to line his cardboard cot. The shirts would pass for sheets and the bundled up shawls could be a pillow. He had almost finished making his bed (another first for him) when he sensed a presence behind him.

'You're wanted,' said Kevin. 'On the training ground.'

The training ground proved to be the escalator hall. Most of the polecats were already assembled, among them Dean, Gary, Alec and the lad with the big nose whose name turned out to be Ritchie. They had lined up in loose ranks, looking very much like the Cat Kin preparing for a pashki session. Except that these kids didn't do pashki, did they? They learned mustel-id. Unsure of where to go, Ben hovered at the end of the back row, next to Antonia. Kevin, up at the front where Geoff or Mrs Powell would have stood, put him straight.

'Not you. You watch. Over there.'

He went to sit at the hall's edge, his back to a wall of locked wooden doors, utility cupboards perhaps. Something troubled him about the group. He realised he was looking in vain for two familiar faces. Thomas and Hannah weren't here. He hadn't seen them since he arrived, nor had anyone mentioned their names. Maybe there was an innocent explanation.

Kevin got the session going and Ben almost relaxed – it was so familiar. Those bends and balances, the stretches that made his calves ache in sympathy. Ritchie and Lisa were the wobbliest ones but Dean was gifted, he could tell, and so was the spindly Alec. Jeep was one of the best.

As the lesson progressed he noticed subtle differences. A stretch like pashki's Scratching Tree became even more extravagant, so that the wave of reaching bodies swelled even higher. Coiled feline poises were replaced by looser, shiftier stances, and Eth walking had transformed into a frantic bounce. Most strikingly, no-one ever stood still, so that instead of pashki's weightless grace the polecats gave off a feverish giddiness. Mustel-id was like pashki, yet unlike. One was the flow of a gliding stream, the other, a water-tap turned full on.

Ben's interest became fascination. He knew he had a nagging worry, something about two children who weren't here, but couldn't quite place it now. He saw Kevin make a gesture like the AOK sign, but with the thumb to the middle finger, palm out. The straight fingers formed a W.

The crowd began to move as a single body. They swayed first one way, then another, resembling dancing cobras, though the only music was the shuffle of their feet on the concrete. Keeping track of any individual was too hard. Now he would see them on the hall's far side, then he would feel their draught as they passed close. He couldn't tell if the swaying forms were near or far, or both at the same time. The surrounding walls melted into darkness to leave only the figures writhing before him.

And a shadow.

That thought came from nowhere. He did not see it but he sensed it: another presence, bigger and bulkier than the rest, yet even harder to pinpoint... an extra figure gliding in and out of the crowd. It wasn't Kevin. At the same time there came a stir in the patterns of the dance, like the flurry through the pigeons of Trafalgar Square when a pest-controlling falcon crossed the sky. In sudden fear he tried to stand and found himself glued to the floor. There was something else here in the hall, something *frightful*, and he couldn't move.

Even as the dread ate him up, one corner of his mind held firm. It understood. This was no mere exercise. This was for him. He had read about how weasels danced to mesmerise their prey, muddle their wits and break their will to escape. This must be how the polecats subdued their new recruits. Now it was hard to blink, hard to think. He saw the dance, the dance, only the dance. He stared, helpless as a rabbit.

No. His inner cat seethed indignantly. *I am no rabbit.*

His eyes finally got a grip on the tangle of bodies. They picked the vision apart with catty disdain, until the hypnotic patterns unravelled to become just a lot of clowns prancing about.

'*Stop*.'

The polecats froze at a shout. He saw the new figure among them. It was tall, taller than Kevin, and oddly drained of light, so that at first he mistook it for someone's elongated shadow. Then he knew what it reminded him of. Mum's best friend Lorelei had once kept a statuette in her living room, a man-shape twisted out of bronze wire. It had frightened him so much when he was little that he wouldn't be left alone with it. Now here it was, life-sized and alive.

The man's arms were cables of muscle. Cropped hair, light brown, revealed the roundness of his skull.

He turned into the light, but the shadow clung to his features. Was this some kind of ghost? No. The face was tattooed with spectacled markings, so that it appeared to be wearing a hangman's mask or weeping huge dark tears. The figure's clothes, a sleeveless tunic and trousers, were rags of fur stitched together.

Ben thought of a dark stinking shed, a starving child chained in the corner. He was looking at Martin Fisher.

The polecats shrank back as if from a fire. Fisher turned, his eyes sweeping over them, coming to rest on Ben. Fisher walked towards him. With every step he appeared to grow until the lofty roof seemed too low to hold him. Leaning over Ben he cocked his head to one side.

'Hello. How are you?'

'Er,' said Ben. 'Okay.'

'My name is Martin Fisher. What's yours?'

'Ben,' said Ben.

'I am very well, thank you,' said Fisher. He frowned suddenly, as if someone had corrected him. 'I am very pleased to meet you.'

Ben's skin wanted to crawl away and hide. He had the feeling that a puppet was speaking, not a person at all.

'Make yourself at home,' said Fisher. 'The Hermitage has everything you want. Kevin has looked after you well.'

Was that a question? 'Yes… he has.'

'Kevin has looked after you well?' Fisher repeated. 'Yes, he has.' He nodded thoughtfully. Then, in a single movement, he stooped and lifted Ben to his feet. He was as strong as a machine.

'Kevin is my friend,' said Fisher. 'He told me about you. You are the cat child.'

Ben was too afraid to nod.

'You are the White Cat's child,' said Fisher.

Ben steeled himself. Geoff had rigorously coached him on how to play this. He hoped Geoff was right.

'He used to teach me pashki,' said Ben. 'Then one day he disappeared. That was last Christmas. I haven't seen him since.'

'Haven't seen him since,' said Fisher.

He circled away. Ben stared at the fur of his tunic, fearing to see tabby, calico, tortoiseshell. No, it was the warm, brown beige of mink. Mad Ferret wore the skins of his cousins. He reappeared suddenly on Ben's blind side.

'I am very well, thank you.' Again that frown, a facial tick. Then: 'I am very unhappy.'

The air was as still as an exam hall. Ben could no longer hear the polecats breathing. The silence ruptured as a train passed Platform 1. Martin Fisher's face twisted.

'I am sorry about the noise. People are noisy. They go by in their trains. They trample everywhere. The streets. The tunnels. Their breath gets in my mouth. There is no hiding from them. Not even here. Not even here.' His voice rasped like a wheel on a rail. 'Not even here.'

They were back in exam silence. Kevin coughed and Fisher snapped out of his trance.

'Welcome, Ben.' His mouth stretched in a smile. 'Welcome to the Hermitage. The Hermitage has everything you want. Kevin has looked after you–' The tilt of the head, the frown. He dropped to one knee and took Ben's hand in a painful grip. When he spoke next, the puppet-like manner was gone. It seemed for the first time that Fisher's words came from a living person inside.

'The White Cat abandoned you, didn't he?' he whispered. 'He abandoned me too, Ben. It is what those cat-people do. They always do.' His eyes glimmered. 'But I will never leave you. Only turn around and I will be behind you. When you sleep I will watch over you. And wherever you are, I will–' his voice rose to hiss, 'I will *always find you*.'

The rest of the day passed in a blur. At one point he imagined he was coming down with flu. He remembered eating a hamburger and fries, which Lisa reheated for him in the makeshift kitchen upstairs. Then an evening that seemed never to end, sitting stiffly on a chair watching the others play pool and table football in the games area, while music hammered and consoles flashbanged around him. He couldn't have joined in even if he'd wanted to. He was too strung-up looking around for Fisher, and the fact that Ben never saw him didn't mean that Fisher wasn't there.

Down on Platform 2 he queued for the toilet. Glad as he was of the flannel, towel and toothbrush that Kevin had pressed on him, telling him hygiene was important, he didn't see anyone else washing. He scrubbed his hands and face over and over, stopping only when someone thumped on the door.

He bedded down among his silk shirts and fur blanket, propping his boxes into a flimsy fortress of solitude. It was like camping, he persuaded himself, closing his eyes. He heard Antonia yell that she'd lost a shoe. Next-door to him Dean and Gary were guffawing at a brain-dead joke. Alec and Ritchie played cards with someone else. Lisa sat rocking back and forth to tinny pop songs from her phone. Other music blared from other players. And every few minutes Kevin yelled at them to go to sleep. Ben covered his ears. Camping? More like the sleepover party from hell.

It was pashki that saved him from going mad. Curled in a despairing ball, he slipped by accident into the Omu meditation. If cats had one great talent, it was sleep: any time, any place. He lay in the O shape and a shell of calm coiled around him. The noise that continued to fill his ears no longer stirred his mind, so that he had the odd sensation of sinking into sleep while hearing everything that went on. The thunder-gusts of night trains came farther and farther apart, the children's voices grew wearier, falling away one by one, and the jumble of music petered out, until nothing remained except a faint stain of sound upon the blackness.

He awoke.

The platform was swaddled in gloom. Filaments glowed in the low-burning bulbs. Ben blinked at his watch. It was half-past-three on a Monday morning, and felt like it. He lay still, a railway sleeper in the long line of slumbering forms. What had woken him?

Gary shifted in the bed next to his, muttering without sense – it sounded like *water and water and water and water*. Dean's hands knotted at his blankets as he huffed and sighed. Ben became aware of a background murmur. The hairs rose on his neck when he realised what it was. All the kids were talking in their sleep. Someone was whining – it was Antonia – *please, pleeeaaase*. A deep voice, surely Kevin's, cracked high as it yelped *No! No!* before gurgling to silence. Others mumbled fragments too obscure to make out. It all flowed together into a hum, a meaningless conversation in which every voice was alone.

He couldn't close his eyes to that lullaby. He crawled from his box nest and stumbled along the platform, groggy with sleep. Even in the escalator hall the murmur followed him, borne along the passages. Maybe he could sleep in the wardrobe. He was setting foot on the stairs when he stopped short.

Now he remembered. One sound in particular had awoken him. A squeal, a shriek. Lines from Yusuf's library book came back to him. *The fisher's cry is notorious… like a human scream.* He revolved upon the ball of one foot until he faced the platform again, his Mau whiskers probing the air. He felt a ripple, the stealthy passing of a body. He Eth-walked to the lip of an archway and pressed his goosebumped back to the wall. Had a shadow moved in the corner of his eye? He stiffened, his heart pounding, the Mau claws springing unbidden from his fingertips. He peered round the pillar.

Something touched his arm.

'Gaah!' Ben lashed out and hit it.

'Ow! Pack it in.' The shadow shrank away and took shape.

'Tiffany!'

His amazement turned to dismay.

'Tiffany, oh no – are you hurt?' He grabbed at his right hand with his left. 'I didn't know it was you. I had my Mau claws out. Let me see.'

Tiffany stepped into a puddle of light. She examined her forearm, squinting through her tabby face-print.

'Don't think I'm cut. Maybe you snagged my sleeve.' She brushed at the sleek black of her pashki kit. 'No. Not a mark. Lucky me. Lucky you, pal.'

Ben's relief was huge but it didn't last long.

'You idiot!' he whispered. 'Why'd you come here?'

'I'm making up for last time,' said Tiffany. 'Now let's go.'

'Go? I don't need rescuing. Didn't Geoff explain? He sent me here on purpose. To find things out.'

'Oh. So you're a spy.'

'Yes.'

Tiffany considered him.

'Nice pyjamas.'

'What?' Ben looked down at his Calvin Kleins. 'Oh. Er. They gave me these. They've got tonnes of stuff. It's all nicked.'

'Ben, you shouldn't be doing this. I'm afraid.'

'Yeah, well. Live with it.'

'Come on, get out of here. This is wrong.'

Ben bit at a thumbnail that had almost nothing left. The sleepers' burblings were louder. He had a sudden urge to check his blind spots.

'Escaping isn't the problem,' he whispered. 'I could walk out now. Martin Fisher is the problem. He'll come looking. He'd hunt me down.'

'Thanks to Geoff.'

'Geoff's trying to sort it,' Ben snapped. 'But he needs our help. You could have wrecked everything by barging in.'

That earned him a catty glare.

'Sorry,' he sighed. 'And thanks. I am glad to see you. Really.'

A new and awful sound pulled him up short. Someone on Platform 2 had started to cry. And this wasn't snivelling. It was sobbing, wailing, moans and howls. Ben's first fear, that the noise would wake everyone, was swamped by deeper terrors that had no name. The boy was clearly not awake, he was weeping in his sleep, blubbing out prayers of despair to the darkness. Tiffany stood still beside Ben as if the same icy spear had pierced them both. At length the cries dissolved into the general whimpering. She let out her breath.

'Are you sure you want to stay here?'

'When I was here before,' said Ben, 'there was this boy and girl. They were sort of... nice to me. They said they'd get in trouble if I escaped. I told them to come with me but they wouldn't. And now they aren't here.'

'What do you think's happened?'

'You see? I have to stay. If only so I know what I did to them.'

He found Tiffany holding his wrists, as if arresting him.

'Whatever happened isn't your fault. You didn't do anything.'

'Exactly.' He took his hands back. 'I did nothing. And if I walk away now, I'll be doing nothing.'

Instead of replying she prowled an ever-shrinking circle in a way Ben knew well. It meant she was thinking.

'Ben. I could do something else.'

He guessed what she'd say. She would offer to join the polecats herself to keep him company. A sweet thought, but a ridiculous one.

'I think...' She hesitated. 'I know that, somewhere out there, Mrs Powell is still alive.'

'Thanks, but I'm– *What* did you say?'

'I even have a rough idea where. Sort of a hunch.'

Ben was getting a hunch too, an ominous one.

'If I can persuade Geoff to help me–' Tiffany spoke faster, 'I could track her down. Geoff can teach me the Oshtian Compass and I'll find her. I'm sure I could, I, I...' her Adam's apple bobbed, 'I think about her every day. So it ought to work.'

This was too much to take at four in the morning.

'Tiffany, I know you miss her. But what's that got to do with the mess I'm in?'

'Because when you leave this place, Fisher's going to come after you. Do you think Geoff can stop him alone? Because Geoff doesn't, I can tell you that now. I say we need Mrs Powell as well.'

'Why stop at her? Go and fetch James Bond too. If you can find him.'

Tiffany's face twitched and he realised he'd hurt her without meaning to. He looked away, fumbling for the right words to say sorry. He heard her shuffling feet.

'Ben.'

'I know. You have to go.'

'School in five hours. Haven't been to bed yet.' Tiffany rubbed her temples. 'I had to wait in that stinky tunnel until you lot fell as– aslee...' She gave a cavernous yawn.

Ben had to smile.

'Go then. Don't worry.'

'I'll worry all I like.'

'I'll be okay.'

He crept with her to the mouth of the tunnel. She took two steps into the gloom and returned.

'Here. I brought your stuff.'

She threw him a drawstring bag. Inside was his bundled pashki kit, along with his face-print and a vial of paints.

'I can't keep this here.'

'Hide it,' said Tiffany. 'Even if you never use it.

It'll remind you.'

She gave him a hard look and stalked off between the rails.

'Tiffany!' Ben hissed after her. 'Remind me of what?'

Only her gleaming eyes were visible.

'Who you are.'

If it hadn't been a sunny day she might have fainted during history. Luckily the weather had let her cat-nap on the gymnasium roof at lunchtime, so that now she only felt a little bit rubbish.

Mum and Dad were downstairs tutting at a programme about London youth crime. Stuart had fallen asleep after visits from both his physiotherapist and his maths tutor. Tiffany sat on her bed, holding the letter and the cheque she had forgotten to take in today. Mr Devereux had assured her that tomorrow would be fine, if she still desired to come.

The letter paper was Mum's personal stationery. *We would be delighted for Tiffany to join her classmates on their visit to Paris next week… Please find enclosed cheque for the full amount of…* Her mind thrilled with place-names she knew only from textbooks, *Louvre, la Tour Eiffel, les Champs-Elysees, Versailles*, stirring to life like delicate winged creatures. She thought of Stuart's map with its cluster of black pins in the corner. The choice wavered in the balance.

Tiffany dragged her right hand across the letter. Her fingertips tingled, and the letter and the cheque fell in ribbons to the floor. Then she had a good cry.

SECRET AGENTS

Kevin woke Ben with a cup of tea. Fortunately it was cold.

'Yurgh!' Ben sat up, mopping his face. 'What was that for?'

'You overslept.' Kevin dropped the crushed paper cup in Ben's lap. 'We get up at six. Routine is important.'

Six? *Six?* Ben peeled off his soggy bedclothes. Dean, already dressed and lacing his trainers, chuckled.

'Got to catch the rush hour commuters. Here, set the alarm.' He tossed Ben a battered mobile phone.

It was like waking up in an army barracks, or perhaps a submarine: the long, tubular hall, the uniforms, the pale faces pickled in cold electric light. He laid out his tea-stained pyjamas to dry and made a show of tidying his cardboard bed, checking that his pashki kit was well hidden among the shawls. It was his only evidence of Tiffany's visit, which already had the texture of a dream.

He washed and brushed his teeth in the old staff toilet cubicle, found a cereal bar and a carton of juice in the kitchen, then went to scrounge some clean clothes from Lisa in the storeroom. He got socks and boxer shorts wrapped up in a T-shirt, along with a pair of grey combat trousers. She also gave him a black silk scarf with eye slits cut in it, and showed him how to fold it into a bandit mask.

'You'll get used to Martin,' Lisa assured him. 'Everyone thinks he's a bit funny at first.'

'How long have you been here?' Ben asked.

Lisa held up his bandana. 'There. Now you can wear it round your neck.'

Ben sat for hours among the bits of his bed, feeding his head with an iPod. Not even his favourite songs tasted right, so in the end he listened to passing trains. The place felt emptier. Most of the gang had caught southbound tubes for what Dean called 'rabbiting raids'. As for the rest, he could only guess. Already his skin itched to feel sunlight. Tonnes of London clay were piled above his head, and he seemed to be breathing yesterday's air. New recruits had to stay in the Hermitage for the first week, Kevin had explained, 'to give you time to adjust.'

Taking a stroll upstairs he felt sick and dizzy. He fought an insane urge to try and burrow through the walls with his bare hands. He shut his eyes, lost his balance and had to sit down, gasping, on the floor. There was no way out. No escape. And no-one knew. Dad thought he was at Mum's. Mum thought he was at Dad's. He could be buried here and they'd never know. Panic rose in him before he remembered. Tiffany knew. And Geoff. Geoff would not abandon him.

He grew calmer. It was as if his teacher stood just

behind him, a hand on his shoulder. He ran a hand through his hair, the way Geoff did with his long, stringy locks. Ben pictured him there, almost within reach, a comforting phantom smelling of roof tiles and beer.

Something's rotten, Geoff had said. *If Fisher has a scheme on the boil we need to find out what it is.* He was here for a reason. That thought too was comforting. He returned to the escalator hall and pondered the wooden doors he had supposed were utility cupboards. Two of them were marked *Danger, High Voltage*, a third warned *Private* and the fourth was blank.

First making sure the hall was empty, Ben tried each door in turn. They were locked. He looked to see if there were any more doors and found the one beneath the staircase. His fingers were closing on its handle when he remembered in the nick of time. This was the door to Fisher's room. He let go as if he'd been burnt and fled upstairs.

Up in the games area he collapsed onto a beanbag and watched cartoons on TV.

The morning crawled by so slowly that he had to call 11 o'clock lunchtime. In the kitchen he found microwaveable hotdogs and ate them alone on a plastic chair. With a full stomach he felt brave enough to get back to spying. He investigated an office stuffed with books of all kinds. In one dogeared pile he found a hardback he'd read years ago, an omnibus of Redwall tales, full of talking ferrets and stoats. Before he knew it he had retreated to the stool in the corner and blotted out the whole afternoon. Coming to his senses he closed the book and stiffly got up. Smells drew him towards the kitchen. A couple of other kids were there now, preparing a single tub of Pot Noodles. Ben stopped dead.

'You!'

'Ben! You see, I told you he'd come back,' said Thomas.

'Did you?' said Hannah.

'I thought you were–' Ben broke off. It didn't matter what he'd thought. A monstrous weight had lifted off him.

'You remember,' Thomas was telling Hannah, 'last week in the tunnel, when I was helping you hold the drill, and you said you couldn't do this anymore, and I said they're only punishing us until Ben comes home, and you cried, and I said he'd be back soon–'

'No you never.'

'You were sleepy. I have a distinctly clear memory–'

'Er. Hello,' Ben tried.

'Hiya,' said Hannah. She and Thomas grabbed plastic forks and attacked the tub of noodles between them. Hannah looked as if she couldn't shovel them in fast enough. Ben was puzzled. The kitchen was bursting at the seams with snack foods. Why did she seem so ravenous, and why was she having to share?

'I, er, decided to join you after all,' he said. 'Hope I didn't get you in trouble.'

Thomas paused in his chewing.

'We got Night Shift. It was okay. Actually it was quite interesting. Peculiar seeing the Northern Line so quiet, with no trains.'

'Scary, though,' said Hannah.

'What did you have to do?'

'Well, when we got past Embankment we had to–'

'The Ferret made us work especially hard,' Thomas broke in. 'But that was interesting too. He's never spoken much to us before. Have you had your Welcome yet, Ben?'

'Yesterday.'

'You're really staying?' Thomas gripped his sleeve. Ben saw his fingernails were filthy, clogged with grey-black dust. 'You won't leave again, will you?'

'No. This is my family now.'

Hannah beamed. Ben hid his queasiness by smiling back.

'By the way. You know that guy who fetched me last time? You never told anyone, did you?'

'Who was he?' asked Hannah.

'Doesn't matter. You never saw him, okay?'

This idea was having trouble sinking in.

'Okay?' Ben repeated. 'It's important.'

They looked dubious. He should never have brought this up. He was groping for a way to change the subject when Thomas winced, as if from a sting. Ben heard a familiar soap opera theme tune meandering from the recreation zone.

'Hey, Thomas!' Alec called across the hall. '*Eastenders* is starting.'

Thomas turned away.

'It's okay,' said Alec, coming over. 'Kevin says you can watch TV now that Ben's come back.'

'Really?'

'Does that mean I'm allowed dinner tonight?' asked Hannah excitedly.

'I suppose.' Alec returned to the television corner, where Thomas had already nabbed the best seat.

'Kevin stopped you eating?' said Ben.

'Only lunch and dinner,' said Hannah. 'I was allowed breakfast and afternoon snack.'

'But Thomas only got a TV ban?'

'Yeah, well, y'know. His dad's Tony Sherwood.'

'Who?'

'Keith Grogan. You know him, right?'

'You mean the character off *Eastenders*?' said Ben. 'The school teacher?'

Hannah nodded. 'The actor who plays him is Tony Sherwood, innit?'

'And he's Thomas's dad…'

'Right. So Thomas always watches it if he can. In case there's a Keith Grogan bit.'

What had Thomas said to him, back in his prison cell? A maddening riddle that had gnawed at his mind. *I see my daddy… several times a week.*

'It's really great that you came back.' Hannah made a beeline for the fridge.

Tiffany's class milled upon the platform in the mighty glass cavern of St Pancras International, humming with pent-up energy like the waiting

Eurostar trains, all except for Olly who sat alone, nervously sipping his Diet Coke. At least, Tiffany imagined that he did. She was not there. Yusuf, Susie and she were far across town at Waterloo station, sitting aboard the 9:20 for Exeter St. David's. The platform clock read 9:18 and had done, it seemed, for the past three minutes.

'Come *on*,' Tiffany muttered.

Last-minute passengers scurried past their window. Yusuf leaned back in his seat, trying to peer out without being seen himself. No-one was likely to recognise them, but if anyone did… Susie fiddled with the tag on her backpack.

'There's still time.'

Time to change their minds, she meant. Time to leave this train, hop on the Tube and rejoin their Paris-bound classmates.

'Don't be dense,' breathed Yusuf. 'We're not on their list anymore, remember? We gave them those letters to explain why we can't go.'

'Oh yeah.' Susie bit her nails.

Tiffany was surprised that these two were here at all. Surprised and grateful. When she'd told Yusuf of her crazy plan, it was only so that someone else would know where she'd really gone. She hadn't dreamed he would offer to help. That he would forfeit his own place on the Paris trip, fake a letter from his parents to tell the school he was unwell, and come with her. And then of course Susie had found out, and Yusuf was going nowhere without her.

The clock clattered to 9:20. Tiffany shut her eyes.

The moment balanced on a knife edge. At last she felt the brakes release and she sighed with them. The train eased clear of the platform.

Susie giggled. '*Au revoir.*'

'The scary thing,' said Yusuf, 'is that this *isn't* the stupidest thing we've ever done.'

'What if a teacher saw us on our way here?' Susie wondered. 'Or, or – no, this is the best one! – what if someone we know is actually on this train? Going on holiday to Exeter? And we run into them at the other end, and they go, "Fancy meeting you here!" and we're all like uuuhhh–'

'I'm sure you'll think of something to say,' said Tiffany, sourly.

Yusuf made settle-down gestures. 'We'll be fine. This plan is watertight. Ten out of ten.'

The train threaded through Clapham Junction and Tiffany dared to hope he was right. The trundling wheels spun out their soothing rhythm. Yes – for Olly's idea had been the cherry on the cake. He'd found a London gift shop that sold postcards of the Eiffel Tower for tourists too lazy to travel any farther. Tiffany, Yusuf and Susie had written in them, saying how much fun they were having. Olly would post the cards from Paris when he'd been there a couple of days.

Susie passed round a bottle of fruit-flavoured water.

'You do know where we're going, right?'

'Of course.' Tiffany secretly crossed her fingers. Five months ago Mrs Powell had vanished with a pantheon of big cats in tow, and now there were reports of beasts on the moors of south-west England. That was all she had.

'I still say we should have told Geoff,' said Yusuf.

'No. He'd have talked us out of it.'

She very nearly had told him. About to ask him one last time to teach her the Oshtian Compass, she had finally understood that he would never agree. Geoff knew what she wanted the Compass for and made no secret of his disapproval.

She had to believe she could succeed without him. If she'd done it once by accident, she could make the accident happen again. She had tried for hours at home, convinced she was close to cracking it. Picturing Mrs Powell's face in her mind, she summoned Oshtis and joined it with Mandira, then tried it with every other catra. She even attempted tricky groups of three. Mostly nothing happened, or she merely felt strange. Once, she could have sworn that a ghost wandered through her bedroom, in the shape of a young boy, making her yelp. Stuart lurched in on his cyberman legs.

'Did you see a mouse?'

'Hardly.' She shook herself to clear her head.

'You're up to something weird again.'

'If you must know, I'm trying to make a sort of compass. It's difficult to explain.'

'Oh, I know how to make a compass,' said Stuart. 'You float a needle on a slice of cork in a saucer. I wanted to try it but I can't cut the cork.' He stopped to think. 'No, wait, you have to magnetise the needle first. You get a magnet and you stroke the needle with it, over and over, until it has its own north and south pole.'

'Sounds fun,' mumbled Tiffany. He wanted to help so much, but what did her brother know?

The train rushed onwards. The great city began to dissolve at the edges, tightly-packed office blocks and terraces giving way to houses with big gardens. Flooding into the widening spaces came green seas of parks, woods and farmers' fields. The morning sun flashed gold on water and Tiffany identified the river Thames, miles and miles upstream, looking unbelievably young and slim.

Yusuf unfolded a computer printout.

'I found these youth hostels. We can stay there without an adult so long as we're fourteen or over.'

'But I'm still–'

'*Fourteen.*' Yusuf looked her hard in the eye until she nodded.

'Then what?' asked Susie. 'Hope we bump into Mrs Powell out walking her tiger?'

'Devon's quite a thin bit,' said Yusuf, studying his pocket map. 'How hard can it be?'

It was time to think positive, Tiffany decided.

'We'll know where to go. The Oshtian Compass will guide me.'

Susie looked doubtful. 'I still don't see why Geoff couldn't track her down for us.'

Tiffany had reflected long and hard upon this.

'I don't think he can,' she said. 'Not anymore. He and Mrs Powell have spent too long apart. They don't have that link anymore. If they did,

I think he'd have traced her years ago.'

'But now he doesn't want you searching either,' said Yusuf. 'What's that about?'

'Search me. Maybe he's afraid I'll be disappointed too. Or maybe…'

'Yeah?'

'I wonder if it's pride.'

'Pride?' said Susie.

'You know. If your parents fight ever. No-one wants to say sorry first. Mine can go silent for hours. Geoff's like that sometimes. When he talks about Mrs Powell. Sort of prickly.'

'So they argued about something?' said Yusuf.

Tiffany shrugged.

'Smashing,' said Susie. 'We could be walking into the middle of the world's longest sulk. That's if we don't starve to death on the moors first. I knew we should have gone to France.'

On they pressed from station to station, through level crossings, racing traffic on the roads, scattering rabbits up steep grassy cuttings, walloping past farmers on tractors. Tiffany leant her head against the window.

ANIMAL MAGNETISM

The longer they waited, the more Tiffany wished to be on her bunk bed at the hostel with a mug of hot tea. The wooden post beside them was looking less and less like a bus stop and more like a practical joke.

'Why doesn't one come? Susie lamented.

'I expect there aren't so many buses in the countryside.'

'Huh.' Susie kicked the dubious bus stop, which wobbled. 'There aren't *any*. And they're not even the right colour. Buses are red.'

Yusuf squinted at a faded timetable nailed to a stump. Tiffany zipped up her waterproof. Stern grey clouds were peering above a stand of fir trees, in a sky so much bigger than she was used to.

Any minute now, her friends would be fed up with her. After going to such trouble and coming all this way they'd done… what? Arriving after lunch on Friday, they had made their base at the Exeter Youth Hostel and hired some bikes. That was when Tiffany realised. She had no idea what to do next.

But she could hardly tell them that. So she'd jingled her bicycle bell and set off in front, leading them along the west road towards Moretonhampstead. If it was true that there were big cats loose on

Dartmoor, and if she was right to think that this was connected with Mrs Powell (two *ifs* so big it was hard to hold them in one head) then it made sense to look in the villages close to the moors. Didn't it?

So from Friday afternoon until sunset on Sunday they rode until their hands blistered, whizzing down lanes, puffing up hills, dodging tractors, stopping for snack breaks in tastily named villages like Drewsteignton, Hennock and Bovey Tracey. Susie complained that the air stank of farm animals, but the wind washed over Tiffany's face and through her hair. There was a quiet so deep that it pressed on her eardrums. She found darkness here too, true darkness, so that waking in the dormitory at 2 a.m. she had needed her cat eyesight to find the loo. Tiffany peered up at the night sky, rinsed of city lights to an absolute black and dusted with inexplicable glitter... she boggled when she realised what this was. It was stars, hundreds. Back home she had seen a few dozen at best, and assumed that was all you got. This was like being flung out into space.

Each morning they would get up, raid the hostel kitchen for someone else's cornflakes, choose a village from Yusuf's map and climb back on the bikes. Tiffany led, and with every push at the pedals she silently wished. She wished for the feeling to kick in.

She remembered how it had taken hold of her, that night on the rooftops. A feeling somewhere between butterfly nerves and the ache from a punch to the stomach. Sending her out in search of Ben when she didn't even know he was missing, homing in on him with an urge as strong as pain. Now she willed it to come again. She pedalled, she willed, she pedalled harder. But through mile after mile of chocolate-box countryside her heart's radar screen stayed obstinately blank. Was anyone really here to be found? Or was she only chasing her tail?

On Sunday afternoon, on their way to a new hostel closer to the moors, it bucketed down. Come Monday they were damp, weary, saddle-sore and poor. Their Paris spending money hadn't stretched as far as expected. Unable to face the bikes this morning, they plodded to the bus stop and waited. And waited.

'No buses, no tube trains,' Susie grumbled. 'Not even any black cabs. You'd think they'd have black cabs.'

'We could hitch hike,' said Yusuf.

'I'm not getting in some yokel's Land Rover,' Susie snapped. 'I've seen films. They'd lock us in a barn and pitchfork us and turn us into cattle feed.'

'We're only in Devon,' said Tiffany.

Susie shuddered.

'Uh-oh, my friends, here comes the rain.' Yusuf ducked under a tree.

Surrendering, they trudged back through Dunsford. Halfway to the hostel the rain became a power-shower, forcing them to shelter in the local tea shop. By now Tiffany was thoroughly miserable and could only sniff at Yusuf's gift of a cream tea. When she filled her cup, her flattened hair dribbled rainwater into the milk jug.

The lady who ran the shop brought their scones.

'Spread the clotted cream on first, then top it with the strawberry jam,' she instructed. 'In Cornwall they do it the other way round, but we don't talk about that.'

Tiffany ate three scones and tried to feel better.

'It's no good.' She wiped cream off her nose. 'I'm sorry I dragged you out here. This is ridiculous. It's like looking for a needle in a haystack when you don't even know if there *is* a needle.'

'Finding a needle in a haystack's easy,' Yusuf remarked. 'All you need is a magnet.'

'Yes,' said Tiffany. 'And I don't have one. I've tried to make the Oshtian Compass every way I can think of. I know it must be the Oshtis catra plus Mandira. It has to be. But it doesn't work. I don't get any…' She had to stop and swallow a mouthful of tea. 'She's not here, is she?'

'It was a good guess,' said Yusuf softly.

'Wishful thinking. She's gone. I'm never going to see her again.'

Her tea spilled in the saucer. It reminded her. Mrs Powell used to pour tea into a saucer for her silver cat Jim to lap. She'd been funny that way. All ice and steel on the outside, melting with warmth underneath. You could never tell when she was joking, never knew if it was safe to laugh. Tiffany remembered the night she'd opened up, confessing the story of what had happened to her son, her green eyes bright with unshed tears.

And how she'd tried to say goodbye, taking back her harsh words from before: *I do care. I care very much indeed.* How Mrs Powell had nurtured talents in her that no-one else could see. The smiles that said *well done*, as rare and reviving as January sunshine.

Memories came like cramps, welling inside her until she wanted to burst. Mrs Powell saving Olly from falling in the woods. Mrs Powell fearlessly facing a gun. Mrs Powell being shot down… They truly did hurt, pulling at her insides, pulling –

Tugging.

She sat up with a gasp, startling the others.

'Tiffany?'

As these memories scoured through her, it was as if they left something behind. Trails of force, gently tingling. What had Stuart said about making a compass? She should have listened. *You have to magnetise the needle… You get a magnet and you stroke the needle with it, over and over.* Could it be as simple as that?

She shut her eyes. In the darkness Oshtis glowed ember-bright, Mandira flared emerald, and the pair fused at once into a bar of red and green. Even in the heartache of remembering, she exulted.

'Where is it? Where'd you put it?'

Yusuf recoiled in alarm as she scrabbled at his coat.

'Your pocket map!' Tiffany cried. 'Give it, give it now!'

'Take it easy!' Yusuf fended her off with it. The tea-shop lady had paused in mid-cake arrangement to stare. Tiffany's fingers tore through page after page.

'Hey,' Yusuf protested.

'We have to go.' Tiffany struggled to get the words out. 'Mrs Powell's not here.'

Yusuf and Susie shared a glance.

'I'm sorry,' said Susie. 'We didn't want to be the ones to say it.'

'No.' Tiffany slapped the map on the table and planted her finger in the heart of Dartmoor National Park. 'She's *there*.'

They couldn't check out of the hostel fast enough for Tiffany. There were bills to pay, bikes to return and bed sheets to hand in to the laundry, and the other two wanted lunch, though she couldn't swallow any. Despite their dwindling funds she phoned for a taxi. By the time it had carried them along the moorland roads and up the lonely track to their new hostel, a grey stone building that Susie said looked like an orphanage, it was mid-afternoon.

'We'll start a search tomorrow,' said Yusuf, and Tiffany nearly bit off his head. She was terrified her new-found sense would fizzle out. Packing essentials such as waterproofs, drinks, cereal bars and an ordinary walker's compass, they struck out on foot along a track cut by walking boots and horses' hooves. Very soon Tiffany strayed off the path, across the face of the hill on their left.

'West-north-west,' said Yusuf.

The view from the hill's crest was like the surface of the Moon, if the Moon had grown lichens and moss. It plunged and rose and rumpled every way until it fused with the sky, three hundred square miles if you believed the guide book – it looked like more. Tiffany felt a fleeting despair, then her feet moved again, carrying her down towards a shallow valley that sank under a veil of trees.

They walked for an hour. Often she changed course wildly, once nearly doubling back, deaf to all protests. By the time they reached the valley floor, their shadows were stretched long and the light had the quality of weathered copper.

'I'm done in.' Susie gulped water. 'Let's head back. Or we'll be walking in the dark.'

'Which bothers us how?' Tiffany peered hard at the woods on their right. The spring foliage gleamed in the lowering sun.

'It bothers me,' said Yusuf. 'Haven't you seen The Hound of the Baskervilles?'

'Where?' Susie glanced all around.

Tiffany made for the trees. They could follow if they liked. Her Oshtian Compass was thrumming, its needle quivering. She was close. As Yusuf and Susie caught her up, grumbling and stumbling, all three were nearly driven off their feet by a gust of wind that rolled along the edge of the wood, making the newly minted leaves roar.

Susie said, 'We're not supposed to be here.'

Tiffany hesitated, pricked by the same thought.

But the pull of the wood was stronger. She walked among the trees, under a leafy canopy which seemed to be held up by a scaffolding of sunbeams. There were no real paths, only breaks in the thicket. The leaf mulch underfoot cushioned her step and her feet sank beneath a sea of bluebells. Wading more and more as if through a dream, she almost blundered into the chain-link fence that stretched between the tree trunks.

'What's this doing here?' asked Susie.

'Must be private property,' said Yusuf. 'Someone wants to keep us out.'

The fence was more than twice Tiffany's height and woven of stout wire that wouldn't bend. It curled away from them at the top to create an overhang. Something about this struck Tiffany as odd. She slipped off her rucksack and threw it over the barrier.

'You're kidding,' groaned Yusuf, sounding very American. Tiffany climbed the chain-link and swung her legs over. A Pounce Drop and the soft soil landed her light as an acorn. The others followed reluctantly, awkward in their walking clothes. They pressed on deeper into the wood.

Squeezing through a corridor of shaggy leaves they came to a glade where the air tasted moist. Yusuf sank to one knee. His fingers traced an impression in the mud: a triangle with rounded corners, crowned by four dimples. Susie crouched beside him.

'Is that what I think it is?'

'Uh-huh. A footprint.'

Tiffany's mind flicked to rewind. That fence they

had scaled. Now she realised what was odd about it. To deter trespassers, the overhang should have been on the outside. Instead it bent inwards. So it wasn't designed for keeping people out. It was there to keep something in. In here.

'It's not the Hound, I hope,' said Susie, trying to giggle.

'I think it might be worse,' said Yusuf.

'A big cat!' cried Tiffany. 'I knew it! She's here somewhere, Mrs Powell, I've really found –'

Yusuf dragged her to the ground and covered her mouth.

'Could you please not shout.'

The penny dropped. She sat bolt upright, her eyes scurrying back and forth, scanning for movement in the leaves. The shrub layer seemed to bulge with menace.

'We're in a big cat enclosure!' Susie whimpered.

'There!' Yusuf pointed.

'What is it?'

'Not sure. Something. There it is again. Behind those bushes.'

'What –' Tiffany wetted her lips. 'What did it look like?'

'Spots. Black spots.'

'It's a leopard?'

'I think worse.'

Susie gaped. 'Worse than a leopard?'

Movement flashed across the clearing downwind of them, a tangle of shadows solidifying and then melting into wispy grasses.

Yusuf's eyes glazed over. It was as if he had one of his cherished natural history books in front of him.

'Its name comes from the native South American, *yaguara*,' he murmured. 'It means *The beast that kills in one bound*. Although most cats bite prey in the neck, these kill by crushing the skull. Pound for pound it's the strongest mammal in the world.'

Susie's voice was a squeak. 'What *is* it?'

'It's a jaguar,' said Yusuf. 'Very slowly. Move.'

Staying in a crouch, Tiffany shifted her weight to the tips of her toes. The beast had to know they were here. Was it choosing its moment? Was it bunching its hindquarters and shimmying, like Rufus before he rushed at a bird?

'Can we climb a tree?'

'No better than it can,' said Yusuf. 'Maybe those brambles. Over there. Might slow it down.'

Lifting their feet with agonising stealth they Eth-walked towards the thicket. Tiffany sensed a change in the texture of the air, her Mau whiskers stirring.

'It's following. We have to split up.'

'Bad idea,' said Yusuf. 'Prey animals stay in herds. Better protection from predators.'

'Listen to him, Tiffs,' said Susie. 'He knows his stuff.'

'No, listen to me,' Tiffany snapped. 'I know why animals herd together. It's so the hunter will pick off the weakest one. All in favour?'

They digested this.

'I want to go to France,' Susie whimpered.

'We have to outwit it. Force it to chase the hardest

target.' Tiffany swallowed. 'Which is me. As soon as it comes, go opposite ways. Get up trees. It'll see me on the ground.'

Yusuf said, 'I am never–'

'If you want any of us to live,' snarled Tiffany, 'you'll do as I say.' Her gaze caught on a knot of trees, their trunks choked with rhododendrons. The waxy weeds convulsed and vomited a shape into the glade. 'Go!'

They didn't need telling twice. Yusuf and Susie sprang apart, vanishing into the wood. The thing running at them faltered, before locking on to its new target.

When Tiffany thought of something beautiful, she thought of a cat – any cat. But if she had to name a hideous one, this jaguar was it. That head, like something made for ramming down doors. That shovel jaw, more bulldozer than animal. Where a leopard would have dapper spots, this beast had blotches. It covered the distance to her in a blink.

She slung her rucksack at it and leaped, as high and far as she could, launching herself over the jaguar's head. Even so surprised, it reacted. Like a kitten after a moth it sprang straight up in the air, all paws and jaws, and she had to tuck in her feet to snatch her shoelaces from its grasp. A stunning roar hit her. Falling headfirst she landed on her palms, somersaulted to her feet and ran for her life.

Her only thought was to lead it away from her friends. As for herself, she had to hope that it would tire or lose interest. That it wasn't hungry, only curious. Because this much was immediately clear: she wasn't going to outrun it. In and out of the trees she wove, over a hollow log, smashing a shell of blue-green fungus as she dodged behind a stump. Slithering down a steep ditch that might have been a brook, though it held mostly mud, she flung herself up the opposite bank with the jaguar's hot breath sawing in her ear.

Cat skills learned in an after-school club were no match for the real thing. Her one advantage was a human brain, only hers was too terrified to work. She ran for the nearest tall tree. No – if it climbed after her, she'd be trapped. There was one option left. She whirled around.

The jaguar gripped the earth in its paws while its wasp-coloured eyes sized her up. Tiffany prepared to leap over it again. Then her courage died. The beast was ready. It knew what she would do. Steadily, one step at a time, it closed the distance between them, its body bunching, ready to spring.

'P- please,' she whispered. 'I helped you.'

She had no time to scream as the jaguar lunged.

It jerked back as if caught on a leash. A queer sound, sharp as a pistol shot, rang off the tree trunks. A human shape dropped from a tree, dim behind bars of sunset and shade. The jaguar fanned its whiskers and growled. The sound spat out again, oddly metallic, the noise of someone flicking an empty can. The cat flinched.

'Frieda. Tsss!'

The figure waved an arm. The jaguar u-turned,

as if remembering an appointment elsewhere, and vanished into bushes. On a high branch a bird whistled.

Tiffany peeled herself off the tree that had become stuck to her back. She squinted through the twilight. The figure was slender, dressed in paint-smeared jeans and a red top that looked like a Liverpool football shirt. Its hair was in a ponytail. The woman turned towards her and the words broke from Tiffany like a sob.

'Mrs Powell!'

She was the same. Always smaller than Tiffany remembered, lithe and straight as a sapling, betraying her age only in her lined face and grey hair. And alive. Tiffany's last lingering doubts disappeared.

'Mrs Powell!'

She ran to her teacher, arms wide to hug her. Mrs Powell stepped backwards.

'Ah. Sorry.' Tiffany let her hands fall. 'I suppose you don't do hugs, do you.'

'What do you want?'

'Well, I –' Tiffany composed herself. 'I'm *here*. I came to find you. And I did it!'

'I can see that.'

Undergrowth crashed. Susie and Yusuf burst through.

'Tiffs! You're safe. You should have a medal for –' Susie broke off. 'Oh wow – it's her! I mean, it's you! Yusuf, she's really here!'

'Hi,' said Yusuf, shyly.

'Is that the lot?' Mrs Powell cut in. 'You haven't invited your whole school, I trust?'

'No,' said Tiffany. 'Just us.' What was wrong here?

Mrs Powell blinked her cold green eyes.

'I don't know what you think you're doing,' she said. 'But this is private property. I'll thank you to leave.'

She walked away.

'Wait!' Tiffany cried. 'Mrs Powell! I– I don't understand. We've come so far and… and I missed you. And –'

'You made a mistake.' Mrs Powell's voice faded as she withdrew into the trees. 'Now go. Go away.'

The last drop of sunlight drained from the wood. Branches crowded black against an opal sky and a crow cawed upon a nodding spray of twigs. The air felt dank.

Yusuf breathed an Arabic curse.

'Tiffany? Are you going to stand for that?'

She stared into the darkness.

WAIFS AND STRAYS

'No, Dad. Nothing's wrong. Just thought I should call.'

'Your mum's okay, is she?'

'Seems to be.'

Ben had just got off the phone to her. She hadn't seemed okay.

'You coming back home at the end of the week?'

'Mm. 'Spect so.'

'Bet you're bored out there with none of your friends around.'

'Sort of. But Mum likes having me here.'

'Ben, *I* like having you here. You know that, don't you?'

'Yes,' said Ben. 'I didn't mean–'

'Maybe I should have a word with her. Can you pass her the phone?'

'Er... no.' Ben thought fast. 'No, she's having a nap. One of her migraine heads.'

'Better not then.' Dad sniffed. 'Well. Ring again tomorrow, won't you?'

'If I can.'

Ben shut the phone. Thomas climbed off the H of HMV and onto the window ledge beside him.

'That was Kevin,' said Ben. 'Checking up on us.'

Thomas gave him a funny look and carried on climbing towards the roof of the music store. Ben followed, eaten up by worry. What if Dad phoned Mum himself? No, he wouldn't. They never phoned each other direct. But what if they *did* speak? After thirty seconds of confusion they would know that he was missing. For the first time in his life he willed them to stay cross with each other.

His first week among the polecats was at last behind him. For most of it he'd been stuck inside the Hermitage, eating there, sleeping there, going quietly spare. Each day he tried to sand away the hours in the library or the games area, and each night he awoke to the sleep-moans of his bunkmates. When he wasn't scared he was bored. The only things to look forward to (apart from takeaway Big Macs) were the daily mustel-id classes. These broke the monotony and wore off his pent-up energy, but left him feeling more infected than invigorated. Also they made him stand out. The exercises, which had names like Mesmerise and Whip Strike, felt awkward, like writing with his left hand, and he kept lapsing into pashki. Sometimes he caught Jeep watching him.

Martin Fisher rarely showed his face, but the station creaked with his presence. When he did speak it was mostly to Kevin, but sometimes, when the Hermitage was emptier, in the pit of silence between passing trains, a muttering would seep from the walls. In his den below the stairs Fisher was ranting to himself. Ben would creep as close as he dared and every time his nerve failed him before he was halfway to Fisher's door. Even with cat hearing, the only clear word he had picked up so far was *river*.

At least he was allowed out now. When they weren't robbing trains in rabbiting raids, off-duty polecats were allowed to roam the streets in small groups. It was here that Ben remembered the phone Dean had given him to use as an alarm clock. A stolen pay-as-you-go, it had some credit left. Slinking out of earshot he had dialled his parents in turn. It was to double-check that they still believed his cover stories, not, he told himself, not because he ached to hear their voices.

Like abseilers without ropes, the gang swarmed down the side of a pub into an alley off Oxford Street. Ben was impressed at how the polecats could climb. Although mustel-id could boast nothing like Mau claws, it had a technique called the martengrip, which locked the finger joints until bare hands hardened into grappling hooks. Most of these kids could scale a shop-front with ease.

They clustered outside a newsagent's. Anyone daring to go in for a paper ran a gauntlet of taunts, chewing-gum missiles and the occasional banger. Ben, trying to blend in, was dumping ice-cream down some poor girl's neck when he saw Thomas, staring through the window of a television shop on the corner of Tottenham Court Road. Of course, it was Sunday afternoon, when they showed the *Eastenders* omnibus.

Thomas wouldn't talk about his actor father. It

was hard enough getting him to admit that he'd ever had a father. However, by working on him night after night, Ben had learned a few things. Thomas was an only child. Taught at home by someone called Phoebe, he'd never gone to school. He wasn't allowed television, except for *Eastenders* and other things Daddy was in, and his friends were three cousins two or more years younger. Then one day Phoebe took him to McDonald's for the first time. Thomas had insisted on it as his birthday treat. There he met a boy named Alec. Alec was exciting. When Phoebe got up to buy apple pies for pudding, Thomas left the restaurant with Alec's gang.

Now television light washed over his face. Ben watched him watching a dozen identical screens. Did he follow the story, or merely hunt for scenes that featured Keith Grogan, played by Tony Sherwood? Did Thomas see the character or his dad?

Shrieks of laughter nearly took Ben's ears off. Hanging out with this gang was murder. Earlier this afternoon Gary had started a contest to see who could grab the most live pigeons. Although Alec won, two of his seven birds had died, so Gary said he was disqualified. Alec went for him, ramming him into the window of Selfridges, which cracked, at which point security guards rushed out of the department store and everyone fled. Jeep outdid them all. This morning he had stolen boxes of bangers from a firework shop. All along Oxford Street he'd moved sniper-like from roof to roof, igniting the squibs with a plastic cigarette lighter and lobbing them down onto streets thick with shoppers. Screams of shock only goaded him on, until he was making machine-gun noises and spreading his arms like a bomber's wings.

They were all mental. Ritchie marched into shops to eat Easter eggs off the shelves. No-one tried to stop him. At last he'd been sick in a slimy brown splash on the pavement, which explained the laughter. Ritchie laughed too, wiping his chin, and carried on necking his chocolate milkshake –

'Ben!' Hannah's nails raked his forearm. 'Stop him!'

Bewildered he turned. Thomas was running off down the street.

'I tried to– He just –' Hannah babbled. 'He saw his dad on the telly and then… Ben, we got to stop him!'

For a full second Ben stood there. So Thomas was escaping. Good. He would go back home, home to his father, home to Phoebe, whoever she was. Ben felt a surge of triumph, of pure happiness.

And then he was running. He was running after Thomas along the busy pavement, guided by his Mau whiskers through gaps in the crowds, weaving without slowing as only a cat can. Thomas saw him and veered into the road. From the right and the left a white van and motorbike were closing. Ben could hardly bear to watch, and so it was with blind instinct that he plunged through the stream of traffic, neatly hurdled the motorcyclist and knocked Thomas out of the van's path with something that was half pounce, half rugby tackle. They fell against a bus shelter.

'Wait,' Ben gasped. Thomas was scrambling to his

feet. In desperation Ben hit him. It was a gentle enough stomach-jab that Dad had once taught him, but it winded Thomas nicely.

'No,' Ben hissed in his ear, as he doubled over. 'Not yet.'

'Let me go. Or I'll tell. You were talking. To your dad.'

Fear gave Ben heartburn.

'If you want to go home,' he growled, 'trust me. Please. Now play along. It's all right–' he called to the gang, who were catching them up, 'he thought the shop guy was calling the police. Just freaked out.'

'Police!' Gary scoffed. 'Grow up.'

Maybe they guessed what Thomas had really been trying to do, for the gang's mood darkened after that. There were no more fights or jokes. After an hour's slapdash shoplifting it was time to go back. They piled aboard a bus heading out of the city centre. Ben sat so he didn't have to look at Thomas. They were rumbling through Islington Green by the time he noticed who had sat beside him. It was Hannah.

'Thank you,' she murmured.

Ben said nothing.

'You had to,' said Hannah. 'If he'd gone, we'd of got it so bad. Like when you left, only worse.'

'At least he'd be home.'

Hannah gave him an I'm-with-stupid look.

'Ben, no-one makes it home. Mad Ferret finds them.'

'So he says.'

'It's true. I've seen proof. We all thought Hayden

had got away until–'

'Hayden? Who's he?'

Hannah didn't answer. The bus sailed along the shore of Clissold Park. Out of habit Ben glanced across the street into the road where he used to live. It looked as distant as a picture on television.

'Why?' said Ben.

'Why what?'

'Why are you with Fisher? What are any of you doing here?'

'Same as you, I suppose.' Hannah shrugged. ''Cos no-one else wants us.'

'Did you *mean* to join?'

'Martin took me in when I was lost,' said Hannah.

'Lost?'

'Couldn't find my way home, could I? I was only like, six or seven.'

'What happened?'

'Can't remember. We was visiting. My mum came to London for the shops, I think. We lived a long way away. A place called Cambridge. I don't know where that is. She let go of my hand in the Disney toy shop and…' Hannah's pale face crinkled. 'I went outside to look for her. That's where I met Kevin. He said he'd take me to someone who'd look after me. That's it really.'

No. That absolutely could not be it.

'Parents don't just lose their kids,' said Ben. 'They look for them. They call the police. They don't give up and go home.'

'Kevin said people do. After a while.' Hannah got

up. The bus had stopped and the gang was shoving its way off. 'I asked if we could put an advert on the telly, but Kevin said that was expensive. And we couldn't use the internet because... I can't remember why not. For a while I thought Mum would ring Martin up to say she was coming to fetch me. But she never did.'

Ben almost walked into a litter bin. The bus drove off.

'Too late now,' said Hannah. 'It must have been four or five years. And anyway–' she recollected herself, 'I've got a new family here.'

She used those words like a full stop. Ben tried to think of a reply as the gang strolled across the park, over the duck pond bridge, past the tiny enclosures of rare birds and butterflies. No-one seemed in a hurry to get back. Passing the playing fields he remembered Geoff's urgent words: *This may be about more than saving a few missing kids.* He decided to seize his chance while Hannah was talkative.

'What was that punishment you had to do? Night Duty or something.'

'Night Shift,' said Hannah. She had tensed.

'What were you doing? Was Martin with you?'

'Just some work. He wanted it done.'

'In a Tube tunnel?' Ben tried to recall their conversation. 'You said you were near Embankment. On the Northern Line.' He thought he knew Embankment. Wasn't it at the end of a bridge across the Thames?

'Dunno where we were.' It was as if shutters

had closed behind Hannah's grey eyes. 'It was nuffin' much.'

'Thomas talked about a drill.' Ben was sure of this. As sure as he was that Thomas's fingers had been grimy with dust. 'Drilling. You drilled in something?'

'Oi, who are you?' Hannah glared at him. 'The Ferret's put you up to this, has he?'

'No, listen, I–'

'You're not gonna catch me out. I'm saying nothing.'

She trotted to the front of the pack to walk with Alec. Ben tried to catch up just as Thomas looked round, nailing him with a stare. He stooped by a park bench and pretended to tie his shoelace. Fantastic. He'd lost his only two friends in the space of an hour. That was impressive even for him.

A WALK IN THE GARDEN

The slope pulled their feet down through the wood until a mossy rooftop peeped through the leaves. Above the chimney floated a gibbous Moon, shimmering as ghosts of smoke lazily uncurled.

'That must be her house,' said Yusuf. 'Bang on the door.'

Tiffany shook her head. Susie elbowed her.

'Go on! What's the worst that can happen? I mean,' – she wilted in Tiffany's glare – 'apart from what just did happen.'

The house seemed to crouch, its stout walls bulging. Upstairs windows glowed dimly, sunk in stone under drooping eaves. A ring of trees whispered around it.

'Let's go home,' said Tiffany. 'She doesn't want us.'

Yusuf strode to the porch. 'Hey. A cat door knocker. How original.'

His knocks echoed loudly. Silence refilled the clearing. They waited.

'It's not as if–' Tiffany spoke huskily, 'as if I knew her very long. Why should I mean that much to her?'

Yusuf left the doorstep.

'She's gone deaf, my friends. Or else…' He spotted a flint wall skirting behind the house as far as the trees on either side. With a short run he boosted himself to the top of it. He whistled. 'Look at this.'

Susie hurried over. Tiffany trudged. She could barely summon the effort to climb the wall. But what she saw on the other side took her breath away.

The wall enclosed an oval back garden, delving a hundred feet or more into the wood. It looked like a lake of milk. She needed no pashki tricks to see quite clearly, for it seemed as if the glow of the Moon had spilt upon the ground. It wasn't milk. Nor, on this warm spring night, could it be snow, and it wasn't smooth as snow would have been. She saw swirls and eddies of white, woven with darker patches in oddly familiar patterns.

'Wow,' said Susie. 'A Zen garden.'

'What?' Yusuf frowned.

'A sort of rock garden. They're Japanese. I think that's what this is. All that white gravel. You hang around in them and you get enlightenment.'

A spark of enlightenment hit Tiffany. The gravel's snowy patterns resembled a tabby cat's brow.

'It's not a Zen garden,' she said. 'It might be… a *Mau* garden.'

'Or a giant litter tray,' mused Yusuf.

'What are those things?' Susie pointed at a row of tall posts winding towards the end of the garden and back again. Tiffany had zeroed in on them too. Upon one post stood a statue. Her stomach flip-flopped as the statue moved, stepping off its post onto the next.

In awe Susie whispered, 'No way.'

It was Mrs Powell. Mrs Powell was Eth-walking. But this was Eth-walking in its ultimate form. Tiffany had seen those posts in her mind countless times, imagining she was stepping from one to another. Never had she dreamed that they might, somewhere, be real.

'I'm going in.'

Susie chewed a thumbnail. 'Do you think you should?'

Tiffany hesitated. Mrs Powell's words still smarted in her ears. Here was a high flint wall to keep her out. But the garden below twinkled in the darkness like day.

She dropped to the white stones, light on her feet once more. Her footsteps crunched across the garden till she stood below Mrs Powell on her pole.

'You can't get rid of me,' said Tiffany.

Mrs Powell appeared not to see her. She moved a pace farther off, leaving one stick-thin perch for another. The empty post shuddered. In her jeans and football shirt she cut a bizarre figure. Tiffany coughed into her fist.

'I lost a cat once. Before I had Rufus. Her name was Cleopatra. She was a tortoiseshell. She disappeared one day.' She strode to catch up with Mrs Powell, the gravel sucking at her feet. 'I didn't know what was worse. Thinking she was dead, or wondering if she was alive somewhere. If she was alive but had decided to leave me. I worried what I'd done to upset her. I was eight.'

Mrs Powell said nothing, though she had stopped moving away. Her eyes gazed over Tiffany's head.

'Never mind,' said Tiffany. 'I didn't come this far to tell you silly stories. I came because we need you. Ben needs you. He's in terrible danger. And I thought, I had this crazy idea, y'know, that you might be interested.'

Mrs Powell glanced down in a puzzled way. Abruptly she pivoted and carried on walking along the poles. Tiffany lifted her foot to stamp it in fury, then stopped.

Of course.

She retraced the row of poles to the cottage's back door, where there stood a tall stone plinth. She climbed the steps leading up to it and stood on top. The first of the wooden posts was a stride away. As narrow as her ankle, as tall as herself. This was the scene she pictured every time she Eth-walked. There was only one difference: here the stakes were real.

A deep breath in, a long breath out. A twitching left calf muscle; she rotated her foot clockwise and anti-clockwise to soothe it into stillness. From up here she could see that each post had a painted cat's paw-print on top. She mingled two catras, blue Ptep for balance and green Mandira. Her Mau whiskers tingled to life, countering the feeling that she was standing on nothing. She stepped into the void.

Her right foot took her weight and she wobbled. The stick beneath her wobbled too. The trembling fed on itself, shaking her harder and harder until she had two options: fall, or take another step. She stepped.

Again she swayed, wheeling her arms while her perch shivered uncontrollably. She nearly despaired – she was dressed for hiking, not acrobatics. Then she realised she was trying to balance like a human. With the next step she forced herself to be still. Nothing existed outside the ball of her foot. Another step. If she closed her eyes she could see the poles more clearly. Another. Just a blink between strides to check where she was.

Then she found the next post occupied. Mrs Powell looked her full in the face.

'Nobody knows I'm here.' Mrs Powell's soft voice was the night's only sound. 'Not a soul. I'm very curious to know how you found me.'

It was Tiffany's turn to be speechless.

'You had your hair done,' Mrs Powell observed.

'Uh.' Tiffany flushed. 'Yes. Cost my mum a fortune. The rain's ruined it.'

'It's nice.'

A solitary bat lapped the garden. They blinked at one another.

'I thought I'd never see you again.'

Tiffany lost her balance. It was Mrs Powell who had said it. Windmilling her arms she fell to the gravel. Mrs Powell dropped beside her.

'Never mind. Everyone falls.' She helped Tiffany up. Her eyes were full of wonder. 'You can't be here, young lady. At least, I know of only one way that you could be.'

Tiffany nodded, shakily.

'But that is…' Mrs Powell shook her head.

'Terrifying. The Oshtian Compass can only work if... Dear oh dear, Tiffany. What have I done to deserve such love?'

'I was beginning to ask that myself.'

Mrs Powell smiled. All of Tiffany's pent-up tears blew away in a flurry of laughter. Mrs Powell touched her forehead with her own, then withdrew. The gesture seemed more intimate than a kiss.

'From the day I met you,' said Mrs Powell, 'I dreaded this happening. Friendships can appear at the most awkward times. And friends will do such silly things, like risking their lives for you. That's why I had to leave, Tiffany, why I had to disappear. And why I've been doing my best to make you go away. And why I never taught you the Oshtian Compass.' She steepled her fingertips. 'Is there something you've forgotten to tell me?'

Tiffany felt the keenness of her gaze. 'I mostly worked the Compass out for myself.'

'*Mostly* is the word I heard, girl.'

'Er.' She felt oddly reluctant to mention him. 'We met an old friend of yours. Geoff White?'

'Geoff.' Mrs Powell looked suddenly up at the Moon. Pearls glinted in her tilted eyes. 'Geoffrey,' she whispered. 'My cat Geoffrey. White Cat Geoffrey. You old rogue. Where have you been wandering?'

'She knows him, then.'

Tiffany found Susie at her side. Yusuf hung back, trying to peer in through the cottage's windows. Mrs Powell rubbed her wrist across her mouth and, fleetingly, over her eyes, before turning to face them.

'You three have a lot of talking to do. I'll make the coffee.'

They sat at a freshly sanded wooden table that wobbled under their elbows. One glance round the kitchen told Tiffany that this was a million miles from Mrs Powell's old Hackney flat. The floor was a field of flagstones. The low ceiling sagged towards a lumpy black beam. Three quarters of the walls were buttercup yellow, the rest dirty white beyond a ragged tidemark. A paint tin and brush rested on the sideboard, overhung by syrupy wood cupboards with cast iron hinges and handles.

There was so much she wanted to ask. How had Mrs Powell survived being shot? How she had made herself and all those jungle cats disappear? But Ben was in danger and that was more pressing. Hearing about Martin Fisher, Mrs Powell made a face. She knew of Geoff's ex-pupil, she said, but had never had the pleasure of meeting him. Her brow creased in alarm when she learned of Ben's undercover work ('Geoff asked him to do that? Are you sure?').

Fisher seemed to interest her far less than Geoff did. She asked questions that Tiffany found hard (how was Geoffrey? Did he talk about her?) or irrelevant (was he managing not to smoke?). By the time the clock on the plate cabinet chimed the last quarter of ten, Tiffany was still trying to steer the conversation back towards the polecat problem.

Then she opened her mouth and only a yawn came out. Mrs Powell's finger combed the milk froth from the inside of her coffee cup. Tiffany found her voice.

'I think Geoff could use your help,' she managed, lamely.

Mrs Powell licked the froth off her finger.

'It may be too late.'

'Huh?' Yusuf looked up.

'That is –' Mrs Powell blinked, as if she too were half asleep. 'That is, too late to do anything more tonight. We'll sort things out in the morning.'

She left the room to switch off all the downstairs lights. Her last stop was the kitchen.

'Oh,' said Mrs Powell, discovering them still at the table. 'Where are you staying?'

'Er,' said Susie.

Mrs Powell huffed. 'There is space upstairs, I suppose. I warn you though, I don't cater for visitors. You'll have to make your own beds.' She breezed out, remarking over her shoulder, 'You'll find the hammer and nails in the cellar.' Then, from halfway up the stairs, 'That was a joke.'

Yusuf gallantly took the cramped attic with its camp bed, and Susie won the toss of a coin for the single mattress in the guest room. Tiffany, tired out, found a pile of coats comfy enough and slept like a fossil. She stirred once in the small hours to see through a window the Moon setting behind the trees, and felt the tickly rumblings of a curled cat by her head.

'Jim,' she murmured. A whiskered snout caught the moonlight. So Mrs Powell's silver friend had followed her out here. Tiffany slipped into comforting dreams.

Jim was gone when the sun prodded her awake. The house seemed afloat on a sea of birdsong. Without disturbing Susie she rose, performed a few cat stretches and crept downstairs. From the kitchen came the burble of a radio show, the clink of spoons and crockery. Entering she saw Mrs Powell, wrapped in a lilac dressing gown. On the sideboard sat Jim, scrubbing his whiskers. Mrs Powell swirled hot water in a teapot.

'Morning!' chirped Tiffany. 'Can I help with anything?'

'Ssh.' Mrs Powell fiddled with the radio on the table. A gentle pop song grew louder. Tiffany eased the door shut behind her. Mrs Powell stood very still as a fluting, celestial voice sang of finding its way home. Tiffany, though she never listened to old stuff like this, felt a lump in her throat, and even the cat's ears were pricked. The tune swelled, lonely yet triumphant, only to vanish in a cloud of static.

'Oh blast, wretched thing.' Mrs Powell pounced on the radio, prised off the back and stuck a dinner fork into its innards. She waggled the fork and the static cleared, but the song was over and a DJ was prattling about the cost of late-night taxis.

'Nuisance,' sighed Mrs Powell. 'I rather like that one.'

Tiffany considered the radio. It had certainly been made later than the 1960s, though perhaps not very much later. Its aerial was a bit of coat hanger, its casing was as scuffed as a builder's boot, and three of four knobs had fallen off.

'New radios are quite cheap,' she ventured.

'Oh, I know I could replace it.' Mrs Powell shrugged. A bell rang in Tiffany's mind. Something Geoff had said to prove he was a friend of Mrs Powell's. It had meant nothing to her at the time.

'Why the smirk?' Mrs Powell set down teacups and saucers.

'Geoff told us about it,' said Tiffany. 'He said you had this battered old radio that you kept repairing.'

'Really?' Mrs Powell looked shocked. 'But I haven't seen him for at least fifteen years. It can't have been so old then. Oh dear, perhaps it was. A new wireless it may have to be. Pity. I've rebuilt every bit of this one. It's my baby.'

Felicity Powell with a soldering iron. It was hard to picture.

'You're smirking again,' said Mrs Powell. 'I'm allowed to have a hobby, aren't I? Besides, I class cats as electrical animals. For one thing, they can feel electric fields. And I have a devil of a time stopping Jim from chewing the television cable.'

'And there's Ben,' said Tiffany. 'Cats give him electric shocks. Funny – his dad's an electrician.'

'There you go. Must run in families too.'

Tiffany finished her tea and toast. Yusuf and Susie still weren't up, so Mrs Powell offered her a guided tour of her domain. Stepping out of the front door, their feet struck mists from the dewy turf and clouds of vapour rolled before their mouths. A steep trail climbed away from the cottage and into the wood's grey light.

A gravel track ran across their path, an aged Land Rover parked on the verge. Mrs Powell took an umbrella from its back seat and walked on into the trees.

'And then there's Geoffrey,' she said. 'It was he who showed me how to change my first fuse. In the days when we shared a basement flat in Dalston…'

'Mrs Powell. You just laughed.'

'I was remembering something else he did. You see, we were penniless. I'd spent all my inheritance and had to work at a supermarket checkout. Geoffrey didn't fancy getting a job, so he dreamed up a plan for saving money. Right outside our window was a street light. He rigged a wire from it to our mains electricity. Abracadabra, free heat and light! It worked perfectly. That is, until we got the bill.'

'What bill?'

'The bill for the entire road of street lamps. We'd made a mistake in the wiring. We got free power during the day all right, when the street lights were off. But when it got dark, and the lamps came on, the whole lot of them ran off our electricity meter. Geoffrey's language when he opened that envelope…' Mrs Powell watched blackbirds purl and knit through the highest twigs. 'We moved out of there pretty quick. But that's Geoff White. Infuriating, yet somehow –'

In silence they followed the twists of a new and narrow path.

'One misses him,' she concluded.

Tiffany hid a pang of jealousy. Time to change the subject.

'The jaguar that chased us. Is he yours?'

'She. No. She's a cat. Frieda belongs to Frieda.'

'But is she–?'

'Yes. One of those we saved from Dr Cobb's factory.'

Tiffany loved the way she said *we*.

'I care for a few of them still,' said Mrs Powell. 'Most, thankfully, are off my hands.'

'In the wild?'

'Afraid not. They'll never be up to that, after the life they had. But they're comfortable. And the tiger, Shiva, is in India. Home at last.'

'I've been longing to ask.'

'Oh yes?'

'How did you do it? Round them all up and disappear like that?'

'With great difficulty. Ah, now here's a view for you.'

They stepped out of the trees and Tiffany felt herself shrink to a speck. From this ridge the moor flung itself below her, almost frightening in its wild size. Distant lumpy rocks bit through the shadowed land, the low sun turning them to crooked yellow teeth. In the cold wind she shivered. Yet gazing farther she felt a homely warmth, for the hills on the horizon seemed to sit within her grasp, their flanks creased as though kneaded from dough, baking in the glow of the dawn's oven.

Mrs Powell smiled. 'Ra is rising.'

Tiffany looked at her. Ra was the Egyptian sun god, she knew that. The rays of the golden disc bathed Mrs Powell's face, so that fleetingly she looked like a much younger woman with blonde hair.

'Pasht the cat goddess serves the sun,' she said. 'For I am called the Eye of Ra. Watcher and protector.'

It was hard to know what to say to that.

'Mrs Powell. Are you…?'

'Do I follow those lost religions? Pray to Isis? Shun the evil Set? Bury my friends in pyramids?' Mrs Powell turned her back on the sun and in the turn she aged again. Her face was lined and tired. 'There are the things we hold onto. And the things it is best to let go of. The great test is to tell them apart. Come on.' She took Tiffany's hand. 'Busy-busy. Chores to do. Cats to feed.'

A new path led them back among the trees. Tiffany drank in the pure peace of the wood. For the first time in a long while she felt herself safe. Ben's plight back in London seemed far away, now that she no longer feared for him. She had found her teacher. Mrs Powell would sort their problems out. Everything was going to be all right.

THE SKELETON TOWER

It's only a nightmare. The head of Martin Fisher bent over his bed. The plughole eyes glinted in their tattooed mask and Ben got ready to scream himself awake. Then he found he already was.

It was over. His cover was blown, the polecats had sniffed out the spy in their midst and Lucy and Ray Gallagher would spend the rest of their sad lives wondering what had become of their son. Screwing his eyes shut he called on his Mau body to save him. If he could only strike out before Fisher tore him apart…

'Hello,' said Martin Fisher. 'Get up.'

It was no use. Fear was jamming his pashki skills. He clutched his motley bedclothes tight around him. Then he saw Kevin, Jeep and Antonia lingering nearby. Although they looked impatient, they weren't exactly baying for his blood.

'Good morning. It is night time. Nice and quiet. Goodnight.' Fisher cocked his head and frowned. 'A good night for work. You come with me.'

Kevin signalled urgently. *Get up. Get dressed.* Heavy with sleep and a horrible case of the shakes, Ben forced his limbs into their grey combat gear.

He pulled on a pair of trainers that his parents could never have afforded and fumbled his bandana-mask around his neck. Why had they come for him? Not to unmask him, that much had sunk in by now. What, then? It had to be the Night Shift. The thing that Thomas and Hannah had been so cagey about. His fright gave way to a glint of hope. This was the chance he'd been waiting for.

Kevin followed Fisher down the platform at a respectful distance, with Jeep bringing up the rear behind Ben and Antonia. The long line of bodies slept, for a change, in silence, as if they dared not whimper while Fisher passed over them. Ben was sure he would be led down the tunnel, and got a shock when instead they headed into the escalator hall and up the steps.

'Aren't we going to–?'

'What?' hissed Kevin.

'Nothing.'

Now he was afraid again. Was this the Night Shift or wasn't it? But Hannah had said they'd gone down the Northern Line, the Embankment, which was miles from here. What reason could there be for marching him upstairs, unless it was to do something ghastly to him? They trooped through the dining and games areas. Then, in a concealed corner, he saw a ladder. Martin Fisher scaled it and unbolted a trapdoor. The team climbed after him, up into darkness, and wind chilled the sweat on Ben's face. Shapes crowded round him, barns made of brick, glass and steel. The five of them emerged from what appeared to be a manhole and Ben got his bearings at last. This was the industrial estate on Hermitage Road. That secret glint of hope became a ray. The Hermitage had another way out.

'Off we go,' said Fisher.

He broke into a loping run and Kevin sprang after him, leading the team in his wake. Clearing the shadows of the business park they crossed the deserted street, where Fisher scrambled up builders' scaffolding. Then he was off across the terraced roofs and his followers were struggling to keep up. That is, the polecats struggled. Ben found that up here, on the tiles, he was faster and more sure-footed than any of them, perhaps even Fisher himself. Not that he wanted them to know that. Not yet.

Fisher's erratic path lurched from terrace to terrace, his footsteps on the eaves no doubt waking many a light sleeper and filling deeper slumbers with grisly dreams. Ben tried in vain to work out where Fisher was heading, until he wondered if this was a mere training routine, a midnight assault course. Only when he kept noticing bus stops on routes towards Tottenham did it dawn on him that Fisher did have a goal, and that his twisty rooftop trajectory was being guided by these very signs. But where was he leading them?

Apartment blocks propped up the sky. A gasworks glowed in the distance. At last, running after Fisher across a bare square of paving stones, they almost tripped over him, crouched there motionless. Ben noticed his team mates were panting hard.

He pretended to have a stitch.

The night winds blew through a blustery space. Where were they? He scanned the darkness for buildings, before realising that the darkness *was* a building. They stood at the foot of a giant tower block. He hadn't noticed it at first because every other tower in the sky was pinpricked with lights, while this one was black as a hole.

Calling on Mandira he squeezed out more details. The windows weren't just dark – they were hollow, empty of glass. A vast tarpaulin hung down the tower's nearside wall. Upon it, in pale letters taller than a man, Ben read: *McLeod Demolitions*. Below this: *Sunday 6 April*. He tried to remember what today was. All he knew was that in less than a week the Easter holidays would be over. As if he didn't have enough to worry about.

'Hey,' Kevin nudged him. 'Look sharp.'

Ben glanced around.

'Where's–?' His heart stuttered. Fisher was nowhere to be seen. Yet Ben had only looked away for a moment. His Mau whiskers should have jangled like tripwires if any foot had taken a step. But… nothing.

Kevin shushed him. 'He's around, okay? Watching and listening. Here.' He handed out folded sheets of paper. 'Martin drew these for us. One each. I'll explain the job inside.'

They crossed the square of flagstones to a fence topped with barbed wire and signs saying *DANGER. KEEP OUT.* Over they went. The tower's main doors had been removed. The lobby wall bore two ragged holes where the lifts should have been. It looked as if everything had been ripped out: radiators, light fittings, even the banister of the stairwell that they climbed in single file. Ben saw doorways with no doors, empty window frames, scars in the walls where the plumbing had once been. Up they tramped, floor after floor, pausing for breath on the fourteenth landing. He gazed down the stairwell, into the darkness that rose below them. Was Fisher lurking in that gloom, following just out of sight, or did he wait for them somewhere higher up? The air smelled musty.

At floor seventeen Kevin called a halt. Jeep and Antonia unfolded their sheets of paper and Ben did the same. He saw sketches like an architect's blueprints, roughly drawn in biro without a ruler and yet with an artist's hand. They showed a floor plan and a side-on view (elevation, that was the word) of a tall building.

'Can't make it out,' Jeep grumbled. Kevin lent him the glow of a phone.

'Are these drawings of this tower?' Ben whispered.

'No, it's Buckingham Palace, innit,' said Antonia.

Jeep snorted. 'So much for bringing him along.'

'He's useful,' said Kevin. 'See how he didn't need the light?'

'Yeah. Doesn't that worry you?'

'The Ferret said to bring him, so we bring him.'

Kevin told them what to do. It sounded simple enough. Simple and baffling.

'Me and Jeep'll do the top half. Toni, you're with Ben. Start on the tenth floor.'

'Why her?' said Jeep. 'I want to keep an eye on him.'

'Relax. Martin already is.'

Ben hid his unease behind a cool cat's blink.

'Meet us in the lobby at four a.m. sharp,' said Kevin. 'You've got forty-eight minutes.'

Descending the stairs with Antonia, Ben noticed more interesting details. Shreds of gaffer tape, a toolbox on one of the landings, a tea mug with dregs still wet inside. Workmen had been here recently.

'I think they're going to knock this building down,' he whispered.

'Says who?'

'Says the sign outside, for one.'

'Maybe they are, maybe they aren't.'

He didn't press the point. Their task was puzzling him.

'Remind me what we're doing?'

'You *are* a bit dumb.' Antonia rustled her sheet of paper. 'We look for little round holes in the walls, count them, and mark where they are on these building plans.'

'And?'

Antonia shrugged.

'He wants us to count mouse holes?' said Ben.

'You can argue with the Ferret. Me, I'm gonna start looking.'

She crept across the tenth floor landing to a doorless doorway. With no better ideas, Ben followed. He fingered the crater where a light switch had been and suddenly his mind teemed with images: cosy flats, burbling tellies, cheap sofas, children's toys on the floor. Noisy neighbours, nosey ones. Friends saying hi on the stairs that vandals had spray-painted. Twenty storeys, eighty little worlds, each one called Home by somebody. Now the carpeted floors had been flayed to raw concrete and the wind gusted through the tower's bones.

A search of all four flats revealed no obvious holes at all, but on the floor below they found lots. It was as if sections of wall had been nibbled by giant woodworm, their jaws an inch wide. These woodworm could count, too, for nearly all the holes came in sets of three. They seemed to prefer the taste of the outside walls and the stout columns near the stairwell, for the thinner partitions between the rooms had few holes or none. Antonia took her pencil and circled zones on the building plans.

'Two hundred and thirty-three holes on this floor,' she said.

The eighth floor was another barren one. Ben grew restless.

'We've got twenty minutes left. We should take a floor each.'

Antonia stiffened. 'Dunno about that.'

'You'll be all right,' said Ben. 'This place is empty.'

'I ain't scared, idiot!' When the echo had died she whispered, 'Go on, then. You do six. But if I shout you better come running.'

Ben took off down the stairs. All he really wanted

was space to think. A quick survey of the sixth floor revealed no holes here either. The fourth, however, was riddled with them. Why? Were they to weaken the building so that cranes could bash it to bits? Now he thought of it, Thomas had mentioned drilling holes. But in a tunnel, not a tower block...

A faint sound needled him. Like a rat squeaking, only regular, insistent. It was coming from the farthest flat on this floor. He stalked across the landing and peeped through the doorway. Two eyes in a dark face widened in fright.

'Antonia? You made me jump –' Wait. That wasn't Antonia. This person was shorter. And a boy. Ben gasped.

'*Daniel?*'

'Ben! In here.'

Ben bit his tongue before he swore the place down. He followed Daniel through a stripped hallway and noticed something silver in his fist.

'You were blowing Tiffany's dog whistle!'

'Cat whistle,' Daniel grinned. 'Come on. We know you haven't got much time.'

'We?'

'He means me,' said a familiar voice. Ben rushed into the largest room.

'Evening, Mr Gallagher.' Geoff was squatting in the Sitting Cat pose, smiling beneath his white war-paint.

With an effort Ben managed not to hug him. His voice quavered. 'It's good to see you.'

'And you.'

Cecile, huddled beneath the empty window, waved.

'How did you know I'd be here?' asked Ben.

'Did you think you were on your own?' said Geoff. 'You were never alone. Ever since you got yourself captured, I've been making sure you were safe.'

'You followed me?'

'Not exactly. I tracked you. With the Oshtian Compass.'

'I– I thought you couldn't use that on me.'

'I couldn't before.' Geoff beckoned him to sit at his side. 'Relax. You've earned it. Yes, my Oshtian Compass can lock on to you now. I've known you long enough and, well. I like you. You're a great kid. Sort of remind me of me, when I was young. And I'm not such a bad bloke, am I?'

'Course not.'

'Don't worry,' said Geoff. 'It doesn't mean we're engaged or anything.'

Ben laughed through his nose to stay quiet. 'So you didn't need Tiffany's help this time.'

'No. Luckily.'

Ben heard the arch note in his voice.

'She's gone somewhere, hasn't she?'

'Mm-hm.' Geoff nodded. 'And taken Yusuf and Susie with her. Don't suppose she told you where?'

'She might be trying to find Mrs Powell.'

'Thought so. All that badgering me about the Compass. I should have put my foot down.'

'Because we need her here?'

'Yes. And because she's wasting her time,' said Geoff. 'To reach someone across great distance, you need to be close to them. Really close. If I couldn't find Felicity – me, her lifelong friend – how could Tiffany expect to? She knew her, what, six months? Arrogant kid.'

'She only wanted to get help,' ventured Cecile.

'No doubt,' said Geoff. 'She thinks I'm not up to the job. Well, I know a man who is.'

Ben felt the weight of Geoff's hand on his shoulder. It was suddenly hard to speak.

'What's the matter?' said Geoff.

'You came to ask me what I've found out.'

'And to check you're okay,' said Cecile.

'I haven't found out anything.' Ben stared at the floor. 'I can't. I've tried.'

'You're scared,' said Geoff. 'I know. You've done more than I had any right to ask. Please forgive me. I made you my cat's paw.'

'Cat's paw?'

'Tool, it means,' said Geoff. 'Agent. Someone who does my dirty work for me. Etcetera. I never really thought you'd go through with it. You've done me proud.'

'Even though I can't tell you anything useful?'

'Oh, you've told me quite a bit by leading me here.'

'I wish I knew what.'

'They're going to blow this tower up. Not tonight,' Geoff added, seeing Daniel's expression. 'This coming Sunday. Crowds will gather to watch it fall down. Now you tell me. Why does a mad ferret-man visit a place like this?'

'He told us to find the holes in the walls.'

Geoff nodded. 'Those holes are where the demolition crew will pack the explosives. Someone wants to know where they are in advance.'

'Fisher's going to steal the dynamite–!' A hand clamped over Daniel's mouth.

'I think the folks down in Chelsea didn't hear that.' Geoff cautiously let Daniel go. 'Yeah. Sherlock here is right. Soon each of those holes will have a small charge inside it. If you dug out all those little bits and put them together,' he paused, 'you'd have one big bomb.'

Ben's flesh crawled. 'Why would Fisher need a bomb?'

'Good point,' said Geoff. 'He's mad, and a killer, but a terrorist? Hardly. We're missing something.'

'The police can find that out,' said Cecile. 'Or whoever it is we report terrorists to.'

'Send the plods after Fisher?' said Geoff. 'That's like trying to swat a flea with a cricket bat. He'd disappear before they got near him, and I'd lose him all over again. No, we bide our time, keep watching, and stay under his radar.'

'We ain't letting him build a bomb, Geoff!'

'No, Cecile, we ain't.' Geoff made a calm-down gesture. 'Keep your fur on. If he is coming back for the dynamite, he'll have to wait till it's in place. Which won't be till Saturday at the earliest.'

'How do you know all this cool stuff?' asked Daniel.

'I was a soldier of misfortune,' said Geoff.

'Huh?'

'Spent a year in the army,' Geoff explained. 'One of those daft things. I was pretty messed up in my head after I lost touch with Felicity. Still, I learned a fair bit–' He broke off. 'Hear that?'

Silence set in, till Geoff broke it again.

'Maybe nothing.'

Daniel hugged himself. 'I ought to get home. Before my mum finds out the lump in my bed isn't me.' Cecile nodded fervently. Ben felt a thought creeping up on him, half-formed. Maybe his spying hadn't been a total waste.

'Geoff,' he murmured. 'You said we might be missing something? Well, there are these two kids at the Hermitage. They were doing a job for Fisher. Using a drill. They mentioned Embankment station –'

'Hush.' Geoff turned his head so sharply it blurred. 'Ben?'

'Yes?'

'How many polecats came in with you?'

'Three. But I don't know where–'

'Keep still, all of you. Do not move.'

Two gleams vanished as Geoff's eyes closed.

'Four sets of footsteps,' he whispered. 'He's here.'

The smell that Ben had been trying to ignore came to choke him. A musty reek.

'Who?' mouthed Cecile.

Ben was gagging. 'Can't you smell it?'

'No,' said Daniel.

'That's him,' said Geoff. 'He's close. Below us.'

Seeming to float on all fours he stole into the

apartment's hallway. Ben followed just as stealthily, wincing at the noise his friends made behind him. Nearing the threshold that would have been the front door, Geoff made a fierce gesture: zipping his mouth shut. Ben sank to his belly on the dusty concrete to peer through the crook of Geoff's arm. At the stairwell's elbow a wiry spectre paused, then spidered into the apartment across the landing.

Daniel poked him in the back. He wanted a better view. Ben gave him a glare to curdle milk.

Fisher was hunting them. The knowledge settled on Ben like six feet of earth. He could smell Fisher, so Fisher would certainly smell him. Geoff had said that the young Martin Fisher could sniff out a coin in a dark room. Nor was that the worst of it. If he had tracked Ben to this floor, he might detect another familiar scent.

Geoff must have shared his fears.

'On my signal, go for the stairs.' His whisper barely stirred the air. 'So long as he's looking in the other flats–' He clammed up as the tall shape reappeared in a doorway.

They were trapped. What now? Would they have to fight their way out? It was four against one. One of their four was Geoff White. Then Ben remembered the other polecats. If they appeared it would be four on four. In his mind he squared up Daniel against the likes of Jeep. That was not happening.

Fisher roved the landing, sniffing the air. Ben felt a nudge and saw Geoff drawing in the dust with his thumb. Letters and symbols appeared like an equation:

IF I → MF = U RUN

Ben solved it and his stomach clenched. *If I attack Martin Fisher then you run.* He watched as Geoff traced beside it: OK?

Geoff would cover their escape. He would battle Fisher so that they could get away. Well, Daniel and Cecile could. Ben wasn't clear what he was meant to do. Return to Kevin and hope to maintain his cover? Slink away and go back home to Dad or Mum? Both these options boiled down to one thing: leaving Geoff, deserting him, abandoning him here.

Fisher made a strangled whining noise. Geoff tapped the floor-marks impatiently. *OK?*

Ben nodded, sick inside. This could end only one way. Fisher had learned mustel-id at Geoff's own hands. He was younger, bigger, stronger than Geoff. He burned inside with murderous hate, and he hated the White Cat worst of all. Ben stole a glance at his teacher's face, shiny with sweat, wondering if he would see it again.

I'm not such a bad bloke, am I?

No. Not at all.

You're a great kid. You remind me of me, when I was young.

Except that Geoff would have stayed to fight by his master's side. Ben was convinced of that. Part of him wished for the courage to stay, while a darker part, the scaredy-cat, whispered that it would do no good, that he would only get in the way and die for nothing.

Any moment now Fisher would be upon them. He would see Geoff and Geoff would have to attack. But what if–?

What if he saw someone else?

Wriggling on his stomach, Ben squirmed into the doorway and stood up. The dead silence behind him, he knew, was Geoff trying not to gasp in amazement. Ben stepped out onto the landing as Fisher approached.

'I've finished this floor.' He unfolded the sheet of paper from his pocket, guessed a number and wrote it down. 'Two hundred and sixty holes.'

Fisher looked at him.

'Toni – Antonia – might be on the next floor up. We're doing different ones to save time. I can call her down if you want.' Ben was gabbling. Anything beat silence.

'I smell him,' said Fisher.

Ben ran out of words.

'The traitor,' said Fisher. 'The one who left me. Why do I smell the White Cat?'

'It's me.' Ben gulped. He prepared to receive the blow that would snap his neck. 'You're smelling him on me. I was Geoff White's pupil. Remember? Maybe it's… rubbed off.'

It was gobbledegook. Yet Fisher did not scream. Rather he gazed down almost tenderly, the tattoos on his face like giant teardrops. He bent till he was nuzzling Ben's sleeve, while Ben fought not to flinch. Fisher drew a deep breath.

'Yes.' He sniffed again. 'The mark of him is on you.

Not good.'

'It'll fade,' said Ben. 'I'll stay with you and it'll fade.'

'Yes. We will be rid of him.' Fisher held him tight. 'You must be washed. Washed clean.'

What happened then made his insides heave. Fisher bent over his arm and gave it a long lick, rasping his tongue from the wrist up to the shoulder. He did it again before turning to the other arm, then to the flesh of Ben's hands, licking them front and back, while Ben shut his eyes, knowing that if he shuddered then both he and his friends would be finished. Just before the cry escaped him, Fisher stopped.

'Better?'

Ben nodded. The stony eyes gleamed on. He said, 'Yes. Better.'

He wiped his hand behind his back. Still Fisher awaited something more. Could it be…?

'Thank you,' said Ben.

Fisher cocked his head. Then he gave a dazzling smile, which Ben felt horribly sure had been copied, muscle by muscle, from a photograph in a glossy magazine.

'You're welcome,' said Martin Fisher.

BEAST OF THE MOORS

Tiffany lay on Susie's bed reading something out of Mrs Powell's bookcase. It was a fat historical novel that wouldn't let her past page five. The cottage's wonky rafters creaked in the sunshine. She was, to her surprise, still here.

Yesterday morning, after the others surfaced, Mrs Powell had offered them a lift in her Land Rover to fetch their stuff from the hostel. The lonely grey building was closer than Tiffany had thought. After checking out, she supposed they would now head for Exeter station, and London, with a twinge of sadness at leaving so soon. She was delighted, if surprised, when Mrs Powell spun the wheel and drove home along the jolting stony trails.

'Smell that heather!' Susie's whole top half leaned out of the bedroom window. 'Come for a hike?'

Hike was her new word for *walk*. Something odd had happened in the last twenty-four hours. Susie, who used to shudder at the country air, was now stuffing her face with it.

'Another one?' Tiffany wiggled her blistered bare feet.

'Indoors on such a lovely day.' Susie sounded like

someone's mum. 'See you later then.'

Tiffany curled against the pillows, sucking one set of toes. She heard the creak of the front door and Susie singing to herself, dwindling into the woods. Sun dapples on the wall danced with the breeze. No wonder they had stayed here a second night. Time passed like sleep in this place, and for long moments it slipped her mind why she had come here in the first place. It was all too easy to relax and feel that things could take care of themselves for a while.

She closed her eyes, savouring the previous day. Mrs Powell had introduced them to her friends. The woods behind the cottage hid a series of clearings, each separately fenced with wire mesh. Though smaller than the enclosure they had entered on Monday night, these were generous compared with the pens at London Zoo – and after the hellish cages of the cats' former lives, they must have been heaven.

'Charlie and Jane.' Mrs Powell pointed out a pair of sunbathing lynxes. The larger lolled its head to notice them, his face framed in mutton-chop sideburns like a Victorian gentleman. All he needed was a top hat, thought Tiffany, but then he would have covered those gorgeous ears, tapering to smoky wisps.

Yusuf would have stared until sunset had Mrs Powell not coughed meaningfully. They moved on to a pen containing three ocelots. Marvellously, Mrs Powell fetched one out, draped over her shoulder. It looked so much like a spotted housecat that Tiffany, stroking its neck, imagined that she had simply got smaller. In a clipped patch on its flank she saw a puckered oval scar, but this was the only sign of what an evil man had once done.

It was feeding time. Yusuf insisted on helping, tossing gobbets of meat to far-flung bushes and boulders to avoid causing ocelot squabbles. In a bigger enclosure a solitary tawny cat stalked imaginary prey. Susie asked, was it a lioness? Mrs Powell said 'Puma,' and Yusuf said 'Cougar,' and even the puma-or-cougar looked round, shocked to see Mrs Powell laughing. The next pen was the largest of all.

Tiffany approached the fence as if it were high voltage. She was awfully afraid. Her legs still ached after their flight from the jaguar, yet she had no fear of *it* anymore. Rather, she feared that she would look through the wire and see something hateful and ugly. Was this cat ruined for her forever? And then the leaves rustled and her mouth fell open.

'Cubs!' she cried. 'Mrs Powell, how did you keep that a secret? Your jaguar's had babies!'

'Four weeks old,' said Mrs Powell. 'Now you know why Frieda was so tetchy.'

It would almost be worth the risk to run in there, pick up those cubs and cuddle them. Almost. There were three, fluffy as toys, their spots smudgy as if they'd been playing with crayons. The nearest cub lolloped after a grasshopper, while the others pounced on their mother's twitchy tail.

Frieda looked worn out.

'Don't suppose she gets much help from the daddy,' said Yusuf.

'Absent.'

'You re-homed him?'

'No. I only ever had one jaguar.'

Susie drummed her fingers, as if to say she was tired of riddles.

'Before Christmas,' said Mrs Powell, 'Frieda escaped. For weeks she wandered the moors.'

'People must have seen her!' Tiffany broke in. 'My brother found reports. It's what put us onto Dartmoor in the first place.'

'Perhaps. Anyway, I tracked her down and – with great difficulty – led her back here. Not long after that she started getting, well, fat. And now I have four jaguars.'

'Are you saying,' Yusuf said slowly, 'that somewhere out there, on the moors where we've been walking…'

'Flippin' heck!' said Susie.

Mrs Powell shrugged. 'I'm only mildly surprised. There have always been stories of odd beasts round here. Exotic pets that escaped years ago. Don't worry, I doubt they eat ramblers. Walking boots are hard to chew.'

Tiffany laughed to make sure that was a joke.

'Good job you came along when you did,' she said. 'Or you'd have been flossing me out of Frieda's teeth. If you hadn't scared her with that starting-pistol…'

'Starting-pistol?' Mrs Powell frowned. 'Oh, I see. No, that wasn't a gun. It was this.'

A noise split the air. Tiffany, Susie and Yusuf flinched. The jaguar raised her hackles and her cubs scampered.

'That was *ptah*,' said Mrs Powell. Only now did Tiffany understand that the astonishing sound had come from her mouth. 'Some call it the pashki stun-gun. That's what cats are really doing when we say that they're spitting. What they spit is a blast of sound. *Ptah* can freeze an enemy in its tracks. It may buy you a few seconds.'

She demonstrated again, her features screwing up in a scary snarl before the bolt of noise came like a dent popped out of metal. Tiffany felt as well as heard it, a physical impact. Rufus often did a similar thing, usually when she was holding a worming tablet. She tried it herself.

'Yuck!' Susie wiped phlegm from her jeans. Yusuf burst out laughing.

'Blend Parda with Kelotaukhon,' Mrs Powell advised, 'and keep practising.'

Tiffany, giggling, wiped her mouth. She watched the cubs stalk and chase and wrestle.

'Shame they don't have a dad,' she said. 'Couldn't you have tracked him down?'

'Who's to say I'd find the right one?'

'Risky,' Yusuf agreed. 'Another male would kill any cubs that aren't his own.'

Tiffany made a face. 'Why does nature have to be so…'

'Inhuman?' said Mrs Powell.

'Icky, I was going to say.'

The largest cub cuffed at the head of the smallest,

with club-like paws that foreboded how big it would grow. Tiffany winced again.

'He'll claw his little sister's eyes out.'

'Brother. Actually that's not as dangerous as it looks. They won't use their claws on each other.'

'Never?'

'Instinct,' said Mrs Powell. 'Cubs of the same litter fight with their claws sheathed. Domestic kittens are the same.' She curled up her own fingers to demonstrate. 'One of nature's nicer tricks. The bond between them is so strong, I doubt they could scratch each other if they tried.'

Now Tiffany, curled upon Susie's bed with the unread book on her knees, heard these words replaying in her head. Oh, of course! That time when she sneaked into the Hermitage. Ben, on a reflex, had struck at her with his Mau claws, and she'd suffered not a scratch. At the time she had dismissed it as mere luck. Now it made sense. Were the two of them like the jaguar cubs? Protected from each other's claws because of something between them? Some special link or force, perhaps the very same one that drew the needle of the Oshtian Compass.

She sat up as if a bucket of water had tipped over her. Oh no! What day was it? What was she doing here, sprawled in a guest room drowsing to birdsong? With a rush of guilt, Tiffany realised something. She had been so consumed with her wish to try and find Mrs Powell again, and so overjoyed with the miracle of actually succeeding, that she had let herself lose sight of her most important reason for doing it. Tiffany bounced off the mattress, flung the book aside and thundered down the stairs.

'Ben needs your help.'

She found her teacher at the kitchen table tinkering with the radio.

'Whoever christened this contraption a wireless?' Mrs Powell murmured. 'I can see enough wires from here.'

Jim trilled a greeting and butted Tiffany's calves, rubbing at her jeans as if she were a balloon he wanted to stick to the wall.

'Mrs Powell,' she said, 'I'm sorry. I've let everyone down.'

'Hmm?'

Tiffany repeated the whole story: the polecats, the fears she had for Ben. Maybe the other night she hadn't made it clear. Only when she had trailed into silence did Mrs Powell speak.

'You want me to go back with you.'

'Yes!'

'You think Geoff's bitten off more than he can chew.'

'Maybe. I just want all the help we can get.'

Mrs Powell rolled a screwdriver back and forth on the tabletop.

'Geoffrey wouldn't accept my help.'

'Why? I thought you were friends.'

Mrs Powell said nothing. She rattled the screwdriver to and fro. Tiffany reached out and pinned it to the table.

'Tell me.'

'I need to fix this.'

'Fix it while you tell me.'

Mrs Powell plucked out one of the radio's vital organs.

'All right. Pass me that wire-stripper. Geoffrey and I...' she squinted at her work. 'You know most of the story, I take it. He was my first pupil and then, when he returned from his training abroad, my associate. A useful chap to have around. I've never known such a fighter. Claws that could splinter pine doors. He could pick locks with the damn things. We made a formidable pair. He had the brawn, I had–' She chuckled. 'We both had brains, of course. So what if he respected mine more.'

Tiffany watched her unravel an endless wire coil. Where was this leading?

'We were colleagues,' said Mrs Powell. 'From Asia and the Far East to London's East End. Comrades. Friends.' She paused. 'Just friends. But when you are alone in a wide, wide world, with only one constant companion, well. Things happen. Like they happened with Frieda.'

Jim rustled between the chairlegs, playing with a curl of cut wire.

'We were travelling through China when I realised I was pregnant. I didn't tell Geoffrey. I had decided what to do. I'd messed up motherhood once before, as you know. I saw no sense in trying again.'

'But–' said Tiffany.

'I invented an excuse to hurry back to England, where I had a termination.'

'You got rid of the baby?'

'It wasn't a baby at that stage,' Mrs Powell snapped. 'I don't have to justify my decision. It would have been unfair on any child to have us two as parents.'

'Why?'

'And it would have tied me to Geoffrey too much. Besides, I was a lot older than him. In my mid-forties, though I dare say I didn't look it.'

'That's not too old to have a baby.'

'It was for me.' Mrs Powell held her gaze but blinked first. 'And I had more reasons.'

So much for not justifying her decision, thought Tiffany.

'You might not think it,' said Mrs Powell, 'but Geoff, he's got a temper on him. He was always too hot-headed, too much ruled by his feelings. On two occasions I had to intervene to stop him killing the poachers we had apprehended. He'd beat the daylights out of them, and all the time he'd be yelling that they deserved it for what they'd done. I'm not sure I'd have wanted that man to be the father of my child.'

It didn't sound much like the Geoff that Tiffany knew. 'So you just…?'

Mrs Powell nodded. She started to wind up the wire coil. 'I never said a word to Geoffrey. Unfortunately, his Mau was sharper than I realised. He'd sensed that

I was carrying his… that I was pregnant. And when I had it sorted out, he knew that too.'

'What happened?'

'Not much.' Mrs Powell shrugged. 'Nothing was said openly. But the frost set in. He and I saw less of each other. We met only occasionally, and then… then we didn't.'

She pushed aside Jim, who was sitting on the radio's detached rear casing.

'So that's why Geoff didn't want me to look for you.'

'Whatever ties I had with him, they withered long ago,' said Mrs Powell. 'We couldn't work together now. It was Geoffrey's decision to take on this Martin Fisher. He must deal with the consequences.'

'But what about–'

'It's up to him,' Mrs Powell repeated. 'And you, of course. There's always you, Tiffany.'

Tiffany drew breath to protest. Then the radio crackled and began to sing a Take That song. Mrs Powell tapped it. 'A-ha. Good as new.'

PEST CONTROL

Ten hours' sleep out of forty-eight was too little for a teenager and nothing like enough for a cat. Ben was knackered. He could almost feel grumpy claws scratching in his head as something tried to curl up in there. Another broken night. He only hoped he could get upstairs without waking anyone else.

The sleepers were quiet tonight, the moans of their night-terrors just a background gurgle. He Eth-walked down the line of them, still in his pyjamas, the platform chilling his bare toes. In the escalator hall he eyed the door to Fisher's private lair beneath the stairs, before placing his feet on the steps one at a time, five seconds apart, all the way to the top. Up in the ticket hall he dared to reread the scrap of paper in his fist.

Last night, as they parted, Geoff must have slipped this note into his back pocket. *Tomorrow. Surface.* That was all. No time, no explanation of 'surface' – Ben guessed he meant the industrial estate built on top of the Hermitage. Ben found the ladder and climbed to the trapdoor. Undoing the slide-bolts he eased it open. The night air ruffled his hair.

After the blacked-out passages below, the streetlights made it seem bright as day. Even so, it was hard to see far. Mist wrapped the ground in a smooth white sheet. The boxy edges of buildings blurred into more mysterious shapes, like canyons or ravines. A glow tinted the fog and he heard a car swish along Hermitage Road. He was straining for other sounds when he caught a scent: something between dried herbs and after-dinner mints.

He roved about and the smell grew stronger. Catnip. He'd guessed right. It led him through the misty maze until, on a wall of ribbed steel, he saw a mark. A white paw print. He sniffed the scented paint and his catras dreamily sparkled.

A shape dropped to the ground. He glimpsed half a face, blanched like a naked skull, and believed for an instant that it was a demon come to slay him. But it was only Geoff, wearing his usual white cat face-print.

'Better late than never.'

'G- Geoff.' A cold sweat seeped into Ben's pyjama top, already clammy from the mist.

'Crikey, this is a dull place to wait. Next time I'm bringing my Sudoku.' Geoff touched his shoulder. 'Hey. You're shivering. I've got some tea.' He produced a Thermos and poured out a few dribbles. It was lukewarm but Ben gulped it gratefully.

'Thanks, Ben,' said Geoff. 'For last night. Never imagined in a million years that you'd do that. I appreciate it.'

He finished the tea. 'That's okay.'

'You were telling me something, weren't you? Before Fisher came along. You mentioned Embankment station.'

'It was the only thing I found out,' said Ben. 'These two kids, Thomas and Hannah. They had to do some work for Fisher. It was near Embankment and they used a drill. That's all I know.'

Geoff unfolded a map of the London Underground. 'See here. See where Embankment is.'

Ben knew the map like the lines of his palm. He saw nothing odd.

'On the bank of the Thames.' Geoff spoke in urgent whispers. 'The tunnel from there to Waterloo runs right under the river.'

'I don't get you.'

'Yes you do. You just don't want to know it. Because it's too horrible.' Geoff stopped whispering. In a casual voice he said, 'Those kids were drilling holes in the tunnel roof. Fisher will steal the explosives from the tower block and pack them into those holes.'

'But–'

'If he succeeds, the blast will rip the tunnel open, right up to the riverbed.'

'*Why?*'

'Because.' Geoff shrugged. 'It's how he is. Fisher can't bear to be with human beings. Perhaps they remind him that he is one himself. It's a pattern. He endures other people for a time, then he snaps. Now he lives in a seething nest of them. For him it's like sitting on an ant hill. And what do you do with an ant hill? You pour a kettle of water on it until all the little ants are washed away.'

Ben couldn't speak. He was trying to imagine what kind of mind could see people as no more than ants.

'That's the thing about Martin. He's not evil. He's criminally insane.' Geoff sighed. 'Give me evil any day.'

'What would happen ? The tunnel would flood?'

'Every tunnel would. For miles and miles.'

Ben shook his head. 'No. You're wrong. Fisher lives underground. He'd flood the Hermitage too.'

'Good point. So I did some homework.'

'Homework?'

'Research. See, I thought to myself: aren't there safeguards against this kind of thing? Turns out there are. In World War Two, they feared a bomb might do this very thing: breach the Thames and flood the Tube system. So they built sets of floodgates, centrally controlled.'

Ben noticed that Geoff hadn't relaxed.

'Then I dug up the history of the Hermitage station. There's a reason it never got finished. They built that line during the Cold War, when the big threat was a nuclear attack. In those circumstances, the floodgate controls at Leicester Square might be destroyed. So they needed a backup. More than a backup – an override.'

Ben saw it now: the row of mysterious doors in the escalator hall. *Danger. High Voltage. Private.*

'They installed it at Hermitage,' said Geoff. 'Far enough from the centre to be safe. From there, you can order any of the floodgates on the

Underground to close. Or, if you so wish, to open.'

Ben sucked the empty plastic cup.

'If the tunnel between Waterloo and Embankment is broken,' said Geoff, 'the water's got nowhere to go but up. The surge would reach Tottenham Court Road in four minutes. Because of all the interchanges, the river in those first minutes is already pouring down six other lines, filling every station along the way. In twenty minutes Zone One is under water. Thirty thousand people there at rush hour. How would you get them out? You couldn't.'

Ben's head was full of freezing grey floods. Why did he have to be the one to know all this? What had it to do with him? Mum and Dad paid their taxes so that other people could do the worrying.

'But,' Ben clutched at a hope, 'we've found out in time. Haven't we?'

'Yeah. Thanks to you.'

'You've told the police?'

'It's not a job for them.'

'MI5?'

Geoff shook his head.

'You haven't told *anyone*?'

'Who could I convince quickly enough?' asked Geoff. 'And if I did, do you think even the SAS could be sure to capture Fisher? They'd storm into the Hermitage and find an empty cave. The only people who can stop this happening–'

'Is not us!' Ben couldn't help shouting. 'It's too much. I'm not taking the blame when we mess this up!'

'Ben, calm down. You're right about one thing.

We have the advantage now. So we can't waste it. We know what Fisher's planning. We have a chance.'

'Yeah. We get the police to close the Tube.'

'What then? Fisher disappears. Ben, it took me eight years to hunt him down. Who's to say what he'll do next time, when we're not there to stop him?'

Ben bit his lip. Not being there sounded fine to him.

'But now,' said Geoff, 'we can stop him once and for all. Before he gets anywhere near that tunnel.'

'How?'

'Simple. Fisher has to work to a timetable. His first task is getting hold of that dynamite. The demolition is scheduled for Sunday morning, so the crew won't finish installing it until Saturday. That gives Fisher one opportunity.'

'Saturday night?'

'Right. He'll be at the tower. And so will I.' Geoff flexed his fingers. 'It's what I've been waiting for. I need to catch him out of his comfort zone. Underground, he'd slaughter me. He'd be on home turf and I'd be off my game – you know how drained you feel down there? That's your Mau body, it hates being cooped up. But if I can confront him in that tower, a high place…'

'You could beat him?'

'We'll see.' Geoff set his jaw.

Ben's insides felt funny, worse than they did before exams. Geoff would be facing Fisher one-on-one. That was bad enough, and it wasn't even true.

'But Fisher won't be alone, will he?'

'You see my problem,' said Geoff. 'Counting you – that's if you remember to switch sides, Ben – there's still only four of us Cat Kin. Everyone else is off on holiday.'

'I think Olly's back from Paris tomorrow.'

'Hurrah, we're saved.' Geoff rolled his eyes. 'The polecats, Ben, count 'em. We're outnumbered four to one, now that Tiffany and co. have done a runner.'

'Try calling her in the morning,' said Ben. 'Wherever she is, she could get home by Saturday.'

'You do it. She'll listen to you.'

'Okay. I'll try.'

'Don't try. Do it. Now go, quickly. And Ben–'

Ben turned back, already struggling to distinguish Geoff from the foggy shadows.

'We never know our luck. So if by some miracle Tiffany has managed to track down Felicity Powell, then…'

'Yes?'

'Then tell her, for Isis's sake, to bring her back here. We need all the help we can get.'

Tiffany picked at a half-hearted cheese sandwich. No proper lunch had materialised today. She guessed Mrs Powell was avoiding her. Maybe one of these kitchen cupboards would surrender some biscuits…

Her phone buzzed: unknown caller.

'Hello?'

'Tiffany? It's Ben. Where are you?'

'Ben!' She unleashed a flood of questions.

'No, Tiffany, I can't talk long, they'll hear. Tell me quick. Did you find her?'

'Find who? Oh, Mrs Powell. I suppose I have.'

'Right, bring her back with you.'

Right? That was all he had to say? He might at least pretend to sound impressed. But already he was rabbiting on. She listened, annoyed. Then astonished. Finally, appalled.

'Ben. That *can't* be true. It *can't* be.'

It was true. She could hear it in his voice. With the phone crammed against her ear, she cursed herself for being so far away.

'Okay.' She tried to sound reassuring. 'Don't worry. We'll help.'

Minutes later she was running through the trees, stumbling on roots in her haste. A red scent on the breeze suggested that some of the residents, at least, had been served lunch. She came to the fence of the jaguar pound.

'Do you think she'd let me have a go?' Yusuf was saying.

'No,' said Susie. 'And nor will I.'

Frieda and her cubs were red to their whiskers, rending great clubs of flesh and bone that might have been a freshly butchered deer. A crimson haunch in a velvety pelt had become the bloody rope in a cub tug of war. Beyond them strolled Mrs

Powell, strewing more meat in the undergrowth. Tiffany called her name.

'Later. It's feeding time.'

'Mrs Powell, this is important!'

'You're in a queue behind four jaguars,' Yusuf pointed out.

'Mrs Powell!' Tiffany shouted. 'You must come. You have to. Because he does want to see you now! He really does!'

'Who does?' asked Susie.

It was no good. The distance and the trees made it too easy for Mrs Powell to feign deafness. Tiffany lost patience. She pushed through the gate and strode across the clearing, stepping so suddenly in front of Mrs Powell that she almost got an intestine in the face.

'Please talk to me.'

'Tiffany, in the name of Anubis–' Mrs Powell turned pale. Tiffany realised she was inside the enclosure with the jaguars less than two bounds away. Yusuf and Susie stared aghast through the wire. Oh well, too late to run. Tiffany relayed what Ben had told her, doing it in one breath.

'So you see.' She gasped for air. 'Things have changed. A lot.'

Mrs Powell nodded.

'Shall we?' She indicated the other side of the fence and Tiffany was way ahead of her. Once healthy amounts of chain link stood between them and the jaguars, she filled in the others on what was happening in London, making sure Mrs Powell heard every word.

'Well,' said Yusuf, 'that sucks.'

'It sounds like a job for the counter-terrorist police,' said Susie.

'Oh, like they never mess up,' said Yusuf.

'Susie's right,' said Mrs Powell. 'This is hardly my line of work. Plus, I'm retired.'

'You've got to come,' said Tiffany. 'Geoff wants you to. And Ben *needs* you to.'

'Tiffany.' Mrs Powell drew her to one side. 'It's admirable that you came all this way just to get help for Ben.'

'It wasn't just–' She stopped, sensing a trap.

'Why did you come?'

'To help Ben! But I also came because...' Tiffany looked Mrs Powell in the face. 'I missed you. Because we never really said goodbye.'

'No, we didn't.' Mrs Powell's hand rested on her arm. 'I was sorry for that. And I have been glad to see you. Still, I wonder.'

'What?'

'Was it not also a good excuse?'

Tiffany didn't understand.

'An excuse,' said Mrs Powell. 'To seek me out. It must be good to have someone else to guide you. To tell you what to do, what to think. So much easier than making your own choices, blaming yourself when they are wrong–'

'That's not how it is!'

'Who leads the Cat Kin now?' Mrs Powell demanded. 'Not Geoffrey. He'll move on once you've sorted out his mess for him, mark my words. Not Ben, for all his exceptional talent. And not me. You lead the Cat Kin now, Tiffany. Or else no-one does.'

'Me?' said Tiffany. 'Look! Mum sews my name in the collars of my T-shirts!'

'Then don't,' said Mrs Powell. 'Use pashki as a way to keep fit. Or give it up. Or else follow it to whatever dangerous place it leads you. But do not sit forever at my feet.'

Tiffany searched her face, feeling the green eyes becoming cold and distant. And the rage rose in her.

'Don't give me that–' she cried, '–that high and mighty wisdom! Pretending you're teaching me some big final lesson!'

'It's the truth.'

'The truth? Or a good excuse?'

Her teacher's face tightened.

'You're a coward,' said Tiffany. 'That's the real reason. You're afraid to see Geoff again. Because then you might have to say sorry.'

The green eyes flashed. 'I have done nothing to apologise for.'

'No? Then why haven't you spoken to him since before I was born?'

Mrs Powell turned from her. 'Think what you will. I am not returning to London. When you're older, you'll understand.'

She walked back towards the jaguar enclosure.

'You do not say things like that!' Tiffany screamed.

'Go and help your friends,' said Mrs Powell.

'You will manage without me.'

'Come on, Tiffs.' Yusuf touched her shoulder. 'Better pack our bags. I'll check the train times.'

'Mrs Powell!' Tiffany shouted. 'If anything happens to Ben, or to Geoff, or to anyone else, I'm holding you responsible! I'll never forgive you, Felicity!'

Tiffany was used to thinking of cats as graceful, powerful and mysterious. It came as a shock to be reminded that they could also be breathtakingly selfish.

FORGIVE AND FORGET

'…and they let us drink wine at dinnertimes, which was hilarious, but the Mona Lisa was a massive let-down, you can't even get close because of the bullet-proof glass.' In the shade of the chapel's threshold Olly scrolled through the photos on his phone while the others craned their necks to see. '…and the Eiffel Tower, or *la Tour Eiffel* as we say in France, it's twice as big as you think it'll be, though I was quite glad Tiffany wasn't there – I bet you'd have gone Eth-walking along the girders.'

'Good trip, then?' Tiffany glanced at Yusuf and Susie. Oh no, was she wearing that same fixed smile?

Olly, who like them had arrived back in London this very afternoon, looked happily exhausted. Tiffany just felt exhausted. Mum and Dad, of course, had wanted to know all about Paris, and if not for Stuart (who knew the truth, and fed her morsels of information in the questions he had prepared) she would have given herself away. They were miffed when Tiffany insisted on going to her pashki class as normal, rather than staying in to talk to them.

'Some of that French arrogance has rubbed off on you,' was Mum's opinion.

Geoff arrived late to the chapel, scruffier than ever and squinting from lack of sleep. He greeted Tiffany with a nod as if she'd never been away.

'Er. We're back,' she stammered.

'Mm. Wondered where you'd got to.'

'Sorry.'

'So,' said Geoff. 'Did you succeed?'

'What do you mean?'

'You know.'

'Do I?' Tiffany sighed. 'I found her. She's alive. Alive and well and living on Dartmoor.'

'And?'

'And she's not coming.'

Geoff's eyes widened. 'You *saw* her?'

'Yes. Stayed at her house.'

'And you explained what's going on? Ben told you that?'

'Everything. She knows. About Fisher. The tunnel bomb. Everything.'

'But she's not coming.' Geoff fell silent. He walked to the end of the nave and stood with his back turned. For a moment he could have been a priest. Then he raised his head to the rose window and a yell bounced off the stone.

'*Damn it!*'

She couldn't have put it better herself.

Yusuf let out his breath. 'What now?'

Tiffany rubbed at her mouth. Now, no doubt, she would trudge off home and bury herself under a duvet. Then she noticed Cecile looking at her. Daniel was looking at her. Olly was still perusing photos on his phone, but Susie was looking at her, and all of them had drifted closer. Yusuf stood expectantly. He was genuinely asking what they should do. Asking *her*.

'What now?' she replied. She paused. The duvet plan disintegrated. 'It's simple, isn't it? We do what needs to be done.'

'What needs to be done,' Cecile echoed, flatly.

'Sorry, I'm lagging a bit here.' Olly put his phone away. 'I'm still not clear about… about what that is.'

'Geoff?' said Tiffany.

He swivelled to face them.

'The night after tomorrow, Martin Fisher's going back to that tower block. So am I. And one way or another it will end there.'

An early owl trilled in the silence.

'And, um,' said Olly, 'where are *we* at this point?'

'That's not for me to say,' said Geoff. 'Though I expect Ben will be there. He hasn't a choice, you see. Fisher's sure to bring him. Along with twenty-odd polecats.'

'If Ben has no alternative,' said Tiffany, 'then neither do we. We'll be there too, Olly. Does that answer your question?'

'Ri-ight. So, is that a *you* "we", or a *we* "we"?'

'You look like you need one,' Daniel sniggered.

'It means all six of us.'

'Plus Geoff and Ben, makes eight,' said Yusuf. 'Facing what, twenty? Twenty-five? Full marks for ambition.'

'Are you saying we have to fight this gang?' asked Cecile.

Susie shrieked with laughter. 'Yeah right, we're fighters.'

'I'm a graphic designer,' said Olly.

The chattering grew. She was losing them. Tiffany moved into the doorway, blocking the shaft of light, so that they all had to turn to look at her in the sudden gloom.

'I'm not a fighter either,' she said. 'But if I have to, I'll fight. Everyone find a mat and get into pairs. Cecile, you're with me. It's time for some pashki practice.'

The first noises came to him in dawn dreams: the roar of the sea in a conch shell, rising in waves, receding. Then a hush before the singing of the rails, ushering in the rush and the roar again. All morning it repeated, every three, four, five minutes, as it would all afternoon and deep into the night. Ben had grown used to the trains that howled through Platform 1, but he could no longer ignore them. He heard them as he knew Martin Fisher must hear them, feeling every wave of noise tighten Fisher's madness another notch.

'A house on Mayfair, please,' said Thomas.

Ben passed him a green block. Hannah rolled the dice and drew a Chance card: *Get out of jail free.*

At least his two friends seemed to have forgiven him. Terrified of upsetting them again, even by accident, he was careful not to ask any more questions or mention anything unusual. So careful, in fact, that he had managed to buy up the full set of red streets before he noticed that their game of Monopoly was being played with real banknotes. Thomas, who played like the devil, was kneeling on about two grand of cash, and had just snapped up the last of the Utilities when Kevin called them all for mustel-id training.

'Don't we get a day off today?' whined Dean, at the games console.

'Why? There's nothing special about today. Routine is important.'

After the workout Kevin, who seemed restless, went to knock on Fisher's door. While the weary polecats sprawled on the floor of the escalator hall, Ben sneaked upstairs to a corner where he had found a pocket of mobile phone reception. Tonight was the night. He had to be ready for the worst. Maybe he had enough credit left to hear two voices first.

He dialled Dad's number and tried to sound light-hearted. 'Hi Dad, it's only me, just thought I'd–'

'*Ben!*'

He hated that falling feeling.

'Ben, are you there? Is that you? Ben, where the hell–?'

Though he knew deep down that it was pointless now, he started to say, 'But I'm at Mum's.'

'Your mum rang me, she rang *me*, Ben, to ask when I would kindly let her see you again. And I was set to ask her the same thing. She thought you were staying at my place! What have you been telling her? She's called police, social services, the works… Two weeks, Ben! Two whole weeks! Where, where…?'

A hopeless silence.

'Sorry. It's hard to explain,' Ben mumbled.

'She thinks you're missing. You – you *are* missing! Ben, you haven't run away or anything daft?'

'*One minute remaining*,' said a robotic woman's voice.

'Tell me, son. You haven't run away from home?'

'Yes,' said Ben. It seemed easiest. He turned the phone off.

'Mouse purrs?' Olly frowned.

'Mau spurs,' corrected Geoff. 'The short auxiliary whiskers on the back of a cat's forelegs. Useful in combat. They let you feel the attacks you can't see coming, and help you block and strike. It's like having extra eyes in your hands.'

Tiffany practised, invoking the usual alloy of Ptep and Mandira for whiskers, trying to channel the sensation to her wrists instead. Geoff moved on to watch Yusuf and Daniel sparring. Susie mediated in the Sphinx crouch and Cecile was curled up in a corner.

They're never going to want to do a pashki routine

again, thought Tiffany. Her own limbs ached in agreement, trembly with fatigue. They had spent all Friday at this, going through the rudiments inside the chapel before running assault courses through the cemetery woods. Now it was nearing Saturday lunchtime and the only sign of sustenance was the carrier bag of hot cross buns that Olly had thoughtfully brought.

Between each draining bout of exercise they rested, using the Omu meditation as Cecile was doing now. In this state, which was like an ultra-deep sleep, the Mau body could recoup its strength. Cecile's hands jerked and her face twitched as the lessons she had learned replayed in her mind, were perfected and set in stone. She looked dead to the world, yet if anyone were to call her name she could be instantly wide awake.

Most of all they worked on Ten Hooks, pashki's fighting system. Under Geoff's tuition they saw how the stylish kicks and slashes could become more than mere display.

'You never said you'd learned jafri zafri,' Geoff exclaimed, as Tiffany tried one of the hardest attacks, a flying, flailing spin.

'I got it off the internet,' she confessed. 'Still not sure if I'm doing it right.'

'You're not, but I'm the one to show you. This thing is my baby.'

'You invented it?' said Daniel.

'I did. And Felicity Powell named it. Jafri zafri. Geoffrey's Affray.'

'Geoffrey's Affray!' cried Yusuf. 'See, I told you it wasn't Arabic.'

Geoff demonstrated, seeming to hang in the air before exploding in a flash of hands and feet.

'I created that after watching my cat Claudius fight three rats at once. Felicity told me that no-one had designed a new Ten Hooks strike since Kati Singh in 1953.' He went quiet. Then: 'Tiffany, how hard did you try? Really? To make her come back?'

'Hard!' she protested. 'I was practically on my knees.'

'Then I'll go myself,' said Geoff. 'You can tell me how to get to her place.'

'I don't know,' said Tiffany. 'It's funny. Her house felt like it was lost on the moors. I'm not sure I could find it again.' A thought struck her. 'Anyway, that's silly. Fisher's going to the tower tonight, right? We'd never get to Devon and back in time.'

Geoff looked dumbstruck, as if this simple fact hadn't occurred to him.

'Particularly with the trains the way they are,' somebody said.

Tiffany whirled. That had not been Susie's voice, nor Cecile's. And that wasn't the shadow of a tree trunk in the doorway.

'Hello, Geoffrey,' said Mrs Powell.

Geoff stood like a man squirted with a trick flower,

the expression on his face ready to go either way. Then he chuckled. He laughed aloud as Mrs Powell stepped out of silhouette and came inside.

'I never hear you coming!' he said.

'Interesting choice of studio,' said Mrs Powell. 'Most gothic. Chilly in winter, I should imagine.'

Tiffany felt dizzy, full of white light. She clenched her fists in triumph. Cecile boggled, then gave a dazzling, crescent moon of a smile.

'Geoff looks as if he's seen a ghost,' said Daniel.

'Hello, Geoffrey,' Mrs Powell said again. 'You are going to say hello?'

'Felicity,' said Geoff. 'Stone me. Felicity Powell. How long is it? Where have you been wandering?'

'No more wandering,' said Mrs Powell. 'I found a home. Stillness is nice. You should try it.'

'No doubt I will.'

There came a lull, the sort of pause that Tiffany recognised as awkward.

'I heard you weren't coming,' said Geoff.

'Did you.'

'Why change your mind?'

'Curiosity.' Mrs Powell shrugged. 'So. I gather you're looking for an extra set of claws. Something about impending doom. Prevention of.'

'I could use some help, yeah.'

'But otherwise it's been quiet?'

Geoff gave a puzzled frown.

'All these years, I hear nothing,' said Mrs Powell. 'This is the first time you've asked for my help.'

Geoff shook his head. 'I tried to find you, lots

of times. But I couldn't. It was–' He broke off. 'It was tough.'

'You wanted to see me again?'

'Yes.'

'Friends once more? Forgive and forget, is that it?'

Tiffany saw the other Cat Kin looking on, with puzzled frowns, wondering what these two were talking about. Later she would have to try and explain it to them. Geoff's fingers combed his messy hair. A sunbeam through a high window disappeared as the angle of the Earth minutely moved.

'I can never forget,' he said. 'It hurt, you know. For a bloke like me, growing up without family... you were the first person who gave a damn. I can't forget that. And I can't forget how great it felt when I thought I was going to have a son. I knew he'd be a son, don't ask me how. And you his mother.'

'Geoffrey–'

'I heard the world telling me I mattered. For the first time, I really mattered. I would be, like, *so important* to this kid. And to you. No-one could tell me I was worthless.' Geoff stared at the floor. 'And then, when I realised that you'd, well, that you'd done what you'd done, and that there wasn't any child to be born, not anymore, well... I can't forget that either.'

He lifted his eyes as if they weighed too much and looked at Mrs Powell.

'But I can forgive,' he said. 'I've learned a lot since. Both good and bad. And I understand now what I didn't then.'

He crossed the gap between them.

'I can never forget, but I can forgive. And we went through so much together, didn't we?'

'So very much,' said Felicity Powell.

They're going to hug, Tiffany thought. But no. Geoff leaned as if to kiss Mrs Powell, and then, instead of kissing, they rubbed their heads together, lightly, hair against cheek, cheek against hair. It struck Tiffany as utterly un-human and at the same time entirely natural.

'Geoffrey,' Mrs Powell mumbled into his shoulder, 'Geoff, I'm so sorry.'

'No. Sshh. It's all right.'

They pulled apart. Mrs Powell was smiling, blinking tears away.

'Well then.' She cleared her throat, businesslike. 'You'd best get me up to speed.'

Tiffany crouched amid the uppermost leaves of the cemetery's tallest poplar tree, pitching in the breeze. The chapel reared below her from its gloomy glade, the steeple's sharp finger pointed at the evening star. Beneath her the lower treetops reached all the way to the bus-clogged High Street of Stoke Newington, trickling with slow lights. The city grew into the pink sky. Officially she was sleeping over at Susie's, while her parents moaned that they saw nothing of her these days.

After a strategy meeting with Mrs Powell, Geoff set off for Tottenham alone. He wanted to study the layout of the derelict tower block and get a feel for the territory around it. He would then find the best place to watch and wait until the others joined him later. That way, he said, they could get a few hours' rest.

By the cemetery gates stood a street lamp, blood red, as if a drop of the draining sunset had been left behind in a slender metal chalice. Paler streetlights gleamed in the dusk like endless chains of cats' eyes.

Tiffany's eyes closed. The rocking of the branches soothed her spiky nerves and she napped.

SHOCK TROOPS

It had the air of a school trip. The escalator hall was full of hyped-up kids, dressed alike and carrying bags, clumped into groups that jostled, joked and goofed around to ease the tension. Any minute now, Ben felt, they'd board a coach that would whisk them off to the Chiltern hills or the Eden Project, and he'd join the scramble for the back row of seats. No coach came. Even the last tube train of the night had long since whispered into oblivion.

'You're in Team One,' Kevin told him. Team One turned their bandanas into polecat bandit masks. Their leader issued from his lair beneath the escalators, killing the holiday mood stone dead.

Fisher led them to the surface exit and out across the rooftops. Jeep, Antonia and Ben retraced their journey of Tuesday night, joined this time by Alec, Gary, Dean and two others whose names Ben had never learned. Everyone else was in Team Two, led by Kevin on a longer, easier route through the deserted back streets.

Standing at the end of Griffin Road, the doomed tower block took a slice out of the night. Tall wire fences around it skimmed the edge of communal gardens belonging to neighbouring blocks. There in the thickets of trees and potted shrubs the two teams of polecats regrouped, whispering together while the half Moon toppled slowly across the sky.

What were they waiting for? Ben's watch crawled towards 3am. The lurking polecats yawned and nervously relieved themselves behind bushes. Ben shivered, glad of the extra layer he had put on beneath his combat gear. He heard a whine of impatience.

'Off we go!' hissed Martin Fisher.

Kevin shook his head. 'That police car's still there. Checking up on the place. Last night he left at three o'clock.'

Ben peered and saw the vehicle, aglow beneath a streetlight on the tower's south side. He could make out the two officers inside, a man and a woman. Fisher grizzled like a hungry child.

'Off we go.'

'Wait. They'll be gone in a minute.'

'Sick of waiting. I will kill them.'

'No,' said Kevin. 'If they don't report back–'

Fisher seized Kevin's neck and shook him like a rattle.

'No? No?' Spittle flew from Fisher's teeth. '*NO?*'

Kevin's eyes bulged and he plucked at the throttling hand. He might as well have tried to bend an iron bar. Giving up, he groped at Fisher's tunic, feeling inside it, as his fellow polecats shrank back in fright. Ben, the last one standing his ground, caught Kevin's frantic stare. Then he was catching something else.

A scrap of cloth.

Not just a scrap, though. It had shape. A ragged shirt-shape. With sudden, bottomless horror Ben knew exactly what he was holding, and what Kevin wanted him to do with it.

'Martin!' he called. 'Here.'

Ben waved the rag in his face. Kevin fell coughing onto the grass as Fisher released him. In a change so sudden that it was almost more frightening than his rage, Fisher took the scrap of rag tenderly in both hands and cuddled it to his cheek. He whined softly. Things stayed that way for a while.

The comfort rag. The rag that had belonged to the boy in the shed. Of all the hideous details in Geoff's tale, that had been the hardest to forget. Ben watched Fisher cuddle it to his whiskery chin. And he knew that, if he were to peek inside that frayed fold which had once been a shirt collar, he might see a label that read *2–3 years*.

Kevin climbed to his feet.

'Thanks–' His voice, in shreds, honked strangely. Mistaking Ben's stunned look, he explained, 'That thing, it's just something he likes. Worth–' he coughed, 'worth remembering.'

Ben's mind was at snapping point. *Something he likes*. All his terrible life Fisher had kept it, this moth-eaten scrap. Did he even know why? Ben couldn't guess, he was terrified to try, but an idea haunted him anyway. Perhaps Fisher kept it because, as threadbare as it was, it *was* a thread, a thread that led back, through the mazes of cruelty and loneliness, to some other place and time where even memory failed, a place of warmth perhaps, of light, of childish laughter.

Fisher's whines dwindled into silence. He folded the rag, stowed it back inside the breast of his mink-fur tunic and snuffled at the wind.

'There is no police now.' Moonlight turned his eyes metal. '*Off we go.*'

The tower block had been refitted with doors, bolted ones plated with *Danger* signs. The polecats swarmed in through ground floor windows, Fisher ripping away the covering boards.

The lobby was unrecognisable. Ben crept after Kevin through an eerie grotto, wreathed with what looked like giant cobwebs. Not fond of spiders, he flinched. Then he got a better look and his mild heebie-jeebies turned to dread. The webby strands were cables, sprouting in clusters from every wall, twining round the pillars, rooting into tumours of polythene and black tape. He didn't need to understand any of this stuff to know it was bad.

'What are these wires?' Antonia whispered.

'Not wires,' said Jeep. 'It's shock tube. Detonating cord. Sort of like a fuse, only it works–' he snapped his fingers, 'that quick.'

'Why so many of them?' asked Ben. Jeep's contempt showed through his mask.

'The explosive isn't in one place, is it? It's distributed

around the whole building. There's shock tubes running to hundreds of charges on each of the blast floors. They all link back to the main detonator.'

Ben trod very carefully.

'Chicken! Look, he's afraid of setting it off.' Jeep sneered. 'Only the detonator can do that. Even a flame won't – see?'

He raised his cigarette lighter towards one of the cables. Kevin caught his wrist. 'Jeep! We believe you.'

'Polecats.' Fisher's whisper brought silence. He stood in the hollow where the lift should have been, tall as a spectre, arms half-aloft as if he was reading an invisible newspaper.

'Polecats. When I was in chains I found a stone. I broke the chains. I burned the one who kept me caged. Then other people came, but they caged me too. I burned the ones who kept me caged. Now they cage you inside your very own home with their trains and their noise and their stink. But this time we cannot burn them, or break our chains with a stone. I have found another way.'

He threw back his head and screamed. It was the scream of a child being murdered. The lift shafts hollered back until Ben feared the tower might fall at the sound of it.

'Find it,' cried Fisher. 'Bring me what I need. Dig it from the walls and bring it to me.' As his troops poured past him he added, unnecessarily, 'It looks like raw bread. Don't eat it.'

In his strikingly artistic hand Fisher had drawn new sheets of instructions, with the charge-loaded walls now marked in yellow highlighter. Kevin, ever the organiser, split the gang into yet more groups to tackle each of the blast floors. Squad A, which included Ben, was assigned to the highest. Squad D would scavenge the explosives on the ground floor while the others pillaged the storeys in between. Following Jeep up the stairs, Ben looked around for Thomas and Hannah. Both were in Squad B. Floor nine.

Barking orders ridiculously, Jeep led his squad to the fifteenth floor and into the first apartment. City lights twinkled in empty window frames, otherwise it was as black as a coal mine. Gary and Antonia stumbled ahead into a room that Ben guessed had once been a kitchen. The wall with the window was creepered with cables that grew from silver roots, planted in oozing foam. His team-mates got busy with pliers, screwdrivers and Swiss Army knives, digging into the holes. Soon Antonia was dropping putty-like lumps into her bag.

Gary tossed his dreadlocks. 'Get a move on.'

Ben started chipping with his screwdriver, filling his bag with chunks of plaster which he hoped would fool them for now. Where was Geoff? Was he even coming? What if they finished the job before he got here? Then, as if in answer, a warm light kindled inside him. Yes. Geoff was out there somewhere. He was close by. Ben's Oshtis catra pulsed again and he was sure – could it be? – that he sensed someone else too. Tiffany? His tiredness melted away.

Pretending to finish this wall he entered the shell of

the old living room. There he found Jeep, apparently messing around. Jeep had cut loose a snake of cable, still attached to its silver cylinder.

'What are you doing?'

'Don't talk. Work.'

'Aren't you s'posed to help?' Antonia asked. 'We're getting blisters here.'

'Yeah, stop skiving,' said Gary.

'Check it out,' said Jeep. 'See what shock tube can do.' He tied the cord into a crude loop. 'You, Ben. Gimme your hand.'

Ben folded his arms.

'Spoilsport.' Jeep crossed to the window, where roosting pigeons huddled out of the wind. Instantly he had one flapping by the neck, while its friends clattered into the night. He twisted its wings one after the other and the bird stopped flapping. Shrill cries gurgled from its beak and it bobbed its head crazily back and forth, as if trying to catch Ben's eye. Did its stupid bird brain hold out a glimmer of hope? Whatever was happening, Ben would let it happen. He was going to stand here and watch it happen.

Jeep looped the shock tube around its plump body and took up the end with the silver cylinder attached.

'What you doing?' Antonia demanded.

'All right,' said Jeep to himself. 'Couple of these beauties left.'

He produced one of his bangers and pushed it deep inside the silver cylinder. He twiddled the firework's blue touch-paper. Out came his lighter.

'Jeep, don't.' That was as far as Gary got. Jeep lit

the banger and dropped the loop of shock tube. The pigeon struggled. What happened next was too fast for even Ben to follow. He supposed the banger went off first. Yet between the bang and its echo came a whip-crack, the cord gave a twitch and the air was full of feathers. Then the loop was empty. An odd smell tainted the air, like roast chicken on Bonfire Night. The shock tube itself looked undamaged, but of the pigeon there was no sign.

Jeep whooped in delight.

'Did you see that?' he crowed. 'Watch the birdie! I'm going to zap something else.'

He looked at Ben. Ben stepped backwards. Then Jeep was slammed into the wall and pinned by something tall, red-haired and furious.

'What–' Kevin panted, 'what did you just do?'

'Nothing! Just seeing if a banger could set off a blasting cap. Like it said in my *Guns and Ammo* magazine.'

'No more magazines!' Kevin bellowed. 'No more till you behave! Got that?'

'But Kevin–'

'That's final. You could've blown us up. Be glad it was me that caught you.'

Jeep continued to protest while Gary and Antonia got back to work. Ben saw his chance. He slipped round the corner, then ran across the landing and down the stairs to the ninth floor. He knew what to do. His friends were out there, Geoff, Tiffany and probably the other Cat Kin too. They would be waiting to strike. But Geoff was counting on him to make their job easier.

He found Thomas and Hannah in a room by themselves, bickering over the best way to extract plastic explosive from a borehole.

'...barbeque tongs would be the most efficient implement...'

'What we have is a knife, a screwdriver and pliers–'

'Can I interrupt?' said Ben.

Hannah flicked the hair from her eyes.

'You're not meant to be in this team,' said Thomas.

'No,' said Ben. 'And neither are you. None of us are meant to be here. Are we?' He grabbed hold of them. '*Are we?*'

'Leave us alone,' said Hannah, but weakly.

Ben took a deep breath. This was such a risk.

'You remember that guy who came to get me before? Fisher calls him the White Cat. He's the only person Fisher's afraid of. And he's here now. He's outside.'

Thomas's eyes widened. 'Then we have to tell–'

'*Think!*' Ben shook him. 'Look in your bag. What's in there? What's it for?'

Thomas shrugged.

'You know Fisher's plan,' hissed Ben. 'You helped him drill underneath the Thames. Put two and two together!'

'It don't matter what we think,' said Hannah. 'You got to do as he says.'

'If we refused,' said Thomas, 'it would happen regardless. Only we'd be dead.'

'Got no choice,' sniffed Hannah.

Ben wrung the cloth of Thomas's jacket in frustration. His fingers ripped the seams of the grey urban camouflage and he had one final, foolish idea. Oh well – he'd tried everything else.

'Yes you have.' Summoning his Mau claws he gripped his own jacket and tore it open down the middle. Underneath was no red Superman letter 'S', but a pale green pattern of whiskers on black. It would have to do.

'The White Cat will stop Fisher. But he needs my help. And I need you.'

At last, hope in their eyes. Ben tore at the rest of his polecat gear, casting it off, feeling the freedom of his pashki kit by bouncing on his toes. From his toolbag he retrieved the object he had hidden for so long among his bedclothes. Inking up the cat face-print he pressed the tabby markings onto his skin.

'Tomorrow you'll see your families again. If you help me tonight.'

'Um,' said Hannah.

'You can't expect us to make a decision so quickly–'

'*Yes or no?*'

'Yes,' said Thomas and Hannah together.

'Let's go.' Ben mounted the stairs.

'Shouldn't we be heading down?' asked Thomas.

'No. Up.'

'But Kevin's up there,' exclaimed Hannah.

Ben set his jaw. 'Yes.'

Kevin stopped on the stairs between the deserted twelfth and eleventh floors. A black-clad figure had occupied the landing below him. Its face was whorled with peculiar patterns.

'Who's there?'

'It's okay. It's me.'

'Ben?' Kevin frowned. Hannah and Thomas moved in the shadows. 'And the Dozy Twins? What is this?'

'Your voice sounds rough,' said Ben. 'Does it hurt?'

'Why don't you do the talking, then?'

'Does Fisher strangle you a lot?'

'Get to the point.'

'We're not doing this,' said Ben. 'We are not going to drown thousands of people.'

'Who said anything about that?'

'You helped, didn't you?' Ben advanced up the stairs. 'You helped him plan it. Only now you're not sure. You try to forget it, but it's in your head. All the time. You make yourself not think about it, but I know…' Ben stopped two steps below him. 'I *know* you dream about it.'

Kevin looked down with sad eyes.

'Jeep was right about you.'

'I'm not your enemy,' said Ben. 'I came to help. You don't have to stay with Fisher.'

'Don't I?'

'You can leave him tonight. He won't be able to stop you.'

'Why's that?'

Ben had given enough away. He said nothing.

'You don't understand,' said Kevin. 'Martin could

slaughter us all in a minute. But he doesn't. Which means he must love us. He doesn't kill us because he loves us. And I'm telling you, Ben, before I met Martin Fisher, I had no idea what that felt like.'

His eyes flickered dreamily upwards.

'You're as mad as he is,' said Ben.

'Now, Jeep.'

A plucking noise, as if the tension in the air had snapped. No human eye could have seen the feathered bolt on its way to plunge into Ben's chest. But feline senses pierced the darkness equally well. His sight and his hearing formed one searchlight beam, tracing the arrow's flight as a needle of fire, and his Mau body grabbed his muscles like an electric shock, twisting him out of harm's way. He saw Jeep, one flight of steps above, peering down the stock of his miniature crossbow.

One movement flowed into the next and Ben's dodge became a leap. Quite how he did it he was hazy himself; all he remembered was kicking out against opposite walls and bounding vertically up the stairwell, over the heads of Kevin and Jeep to gain the upper landing. Catching his breath he remembered something Tiffany had told him: a cat always looks down on danger.

Jeep wore the expression of a tennis player served an ace. He folded his crossbow and flicked out the blade of his knife.

'Try not to kill him,' said Kevin, drawing his own.

Both were squinting. How well did their training let them see in this faint light? Ben was sure now that his reflexes were faster. And even if they proved stronger than him, he knew something they didn't: behind and below them, lurking in the gloom, Thomas and Hannah stood ready to help. Although they wouldn't be his first choice as warriors, Ben had seen their mustel-id skills and reckoned them handy enough. If they could only catch a spark of courage...

'Okay, I'll try not to,' Ben replied.

He let Jeep and Kevin advance to the top of the flight, where the landing opened up to give him more space to move. And then, like a whirlwind, he moved.

CAT VERSUS POLECAT

Crowned with watery halos, the streetlights stood guarding the dark tower. Cold signals shivered through her Mau whiskers as the dew descended. Crossly she refused Olly's offer of chewing gum, then changed her mind and took it.

'Do you think they're in there?' said Daniel.

'I can hear them,' Tiffany replied.

Yusuf fidgeted on top of a post box. 'Remind me what we're waiting for?'

'For them to thin out,' said Geoff. 'The explosive is spread across four separate floors. To save time they'll put a team on each floor. There shouldn't be more than six in any team.'

'Whereas there are eight of us,' said Mrs Powell.

'So we can take them one group at a time,' said Geoff.

The two pashki masters crouched in the shadow of a van, so much like hunting cats that Tiffany rubbed her eyes to make sure. Geoff's face was marble in its ghostly cat-paint, and with his hair tied back he looked sharp and lean, a warrior once more. Mrs Powell's prowl suit bore the grey and black patterns that recalled her cat Jim's dappled coat, while her vivid face-print was the brand of the ebony mould she had once left behind at her London flat. She'd been touched to discover that Tiffany had kept it safe, in case they ever should meet again.

Tiffany felt Cecile tremble. 'What's the matter?'

'N-nothing.'

'It's okay to be afraid.'

'I'm not.' Cecile gulped. 'It's not the polecats. Not really. It's just that– that place. The tower. It feels... deadly.'

'Buildings packed with dynamite often do,' said Olly.

'It can't go off, though,' said Daniel. 'Right?'

'Not without a massive electric charge to its detonator,' said Geoff. 'No chance of that. The building's own power will have been cut off months ago. Nothing can happen till the demolition crew come in the morning, by which time –'

Tiffany heard no more. Her stomach cramped, her Oshtis catra burning red.

Mrs Powell turned. 'Tiffany?'

'Ben,' she gasped. 'It's him, I know it. In there.'

'What about him?' Susie spat her gum out in alarm.

Tiffany fell to one knee. 'No. It's terrible. Make it stop.'

'Let go,' said Mrs Powell. 'Tiffany, let it go. Or it will drain your strength.' Grasping Tiffany's shoulders she made a purring noise from the depths of her larynx. Tiffany felt the soothing vibrations drill into her bones and found she could breathe more easily.

'Ready?' said Mrs Powell.

Impulsively Tiffany held out her hand, like a paw in its fingerless leather glove. The Cat Kin reached out and touched it.

'I heed no words nor walls,' she murmured. Hesitantly the group joined in:

'*Through darkness I walk in day*

And I do not fear the tyrant.'

'Let's go,' said Geoff.

Dropping in behind him they scaled the tower's security fence. Spreading out in a ripple of darkness they came on, stealing across the plain of paving stones as stealthy and swift as a killer tide.

'Remember.' Mrs Powell's whisper reached their ears. 'We are the hunters. They are the prey. Although they outnumber us, with pashki we outmatch them. Mustel-id is a crude weapon, a feeble imitation.'

'I can't really say I agree–'

'Sorry, Geoffrey, it is. Mustel-id is effective, in its way, but brutal. And full of gaping holes. If we pile on the pressure, we will see their clumsy armoury fall to bits.'

They were too close now for Geoff to argue back. At his signal they climbed the wall, their Mau claws finding cracks in the concrete. Empty first-floor windows offered a way in. Geoff halted them with an upraised palm, then made a cat-ears sign with his fingers: *Listen*. From below came an exotic brew of sounds: voices, taps and clinks. He sniffed.

'Can't smell Fisher. He must be on a higher floor. Still up for the plan, Felicity?'

'You know me, Geoffrey. Humane.'

'What's the plan?' hissed Olly in Tiffany's ear.

'You'll get the hang of it,' said Mrs Powell.

'The hang of *what?*' pleaded Susie.

'Scaring the willies out of them.' Geoff spun a coin. 'Heads it is. You get the stairs.'

He dived into a lift shaft. Mrs Powell was already bounding down the staircase. Tiffany sprang after her and the Cat Kin followed. Down hurtled Daniel, above him Susie, angled on the air in a poise beyond most human gymnasts. Yusuf leapt five steps at a time. Tiffany glimpsed the shade of Cecile, near-invisible around the whites of her eyes, and Olly's normally friendly face twisted in a tiger snarl. Down they came like the wrath of Pasht, the scorching desert wind, and the roar of their approach was the deafening roar of silence.

Touching down on the ground floor a beat behind her teacher, Tiffany found her eyes tangled in the jungle of cords and cables. Then her Mau senses got to work, breaking down the blast-floor's landscape into passages, escape routes, dangers and mystery zones, scrubbing out the parts that didn't matter. Any moving object seemed to glow in the dark, the faster the brighter, leaving sparkler trails. Brightest of all burned the three figures rushing from behind a square pillar, their faces masked in black.

Ptah. The noise detonated in the polecats' faces, stopping them two strides from Mrs Powell. Their knives and screwdrivers stabbed the air. A growl came from the lift shafts.

'Good evening, vermin. The White Cat is here. I eat weasels alive, and I need my five a day.'

The masked figures whirled and collided. Outnumbered in front and spooked from behind, they clawed past one another in their dash to escape. But Geoff and Mrs Powell had scared them rather too well. In their confusion they ran to the main door, forgetting it was shut fast. Tiffany, leading her friends in pursuit, realised too late that she had cornered them in the lobby. The trio, two boys and a fair-haired girl, rounded on her.

'We don't want to–' That was as far as she got. With a screaming war-cry the polecats charged. Yusuf tackled the biggest to the ground and Olly piled on top of him. The girl leaped over the scrum, only to be grabbed by a sudden Mrs Powell. The remaining boy slashed wildly with a knife until Tiffany kicked it flying and the others brought him down. Pinned on the floor by a dozen knees and elbows, all three polecats thrashed like rats in traps.

'Look out,' cried Geoff. Two more of the gang burst from a hidden corner and ran full-pelt for the stairs. 'Don't let them warn the others!'

Tiffany wrested free of the pile-up and gave chase. Geoff caught the first quickly, whipping the feet from under him. Tiffany blocked the exit to the stairwell moments before the second boy reached it. He was a hulking teen with a smudge of moustache beneath his huge protruding nose. He glared through his mask at this slender girl who seemed to think she could stop him.

Even as Tiffany braced herself, her mind was elsewhere. Ben needed her, she knew it. Every moment she wasted here, she was not helping him. She hardly saw the screwdriver that slashed at her face – she flinched not a millisecond too soon.

'Made ya blink!' the boy snarled, raising his blade to strike.

Tiffany's jaw clenched, fear lodging as a lump in her throat. A lump, a copper-gold blend of catras, a bullet of energy… *Ptah.* It wasn't quite the thunderclap that Mrs Powell had mustered, but it caught her attacker smack between the eyes. He looked as if he'd walked into a glass door – or, as her dad might have said, like you could knock him down with a feather. She stepped forward and, experimentally, pushed him over.

Which felt worst? His battered bones, his face squashed against the concrete floor, or his arms twisted behind his back to be tied up yet again? None of them beat the feeling of being so badly let down.

'This is for the rips in my jacket,' said Jeep, pulling at a knot till Ben yelped in pain. '*This* one is for breaking my knife, *this* is for the cut on my ear, and *this* is because I hate you.'

'Do some for me.' Kevin scowled, flexing his scratched hand.

'And for us,' chirped Thomas and Hannah together.

Jeep eyed them. 'Right.'

If they had offered the slightest help, Ben was sure he could have won the fight. If they had merely sat by and watched, he would still have had a chance, for neither Jeep nor Kevin could match his agility in an open space. But Hannah and Thomas had watched only until Kevin saw them and yelled. From that moment Ben was fighting four, and the end was swift and inevitable. The bruise that hurt most of all was where Thomas had kicked him on the shin.

He lay face down, his tongue exploring a broken tooth. A draft made him shiver. His captors had stopped talking and he sensed clear space around him. Kevin's trainers nervously scuffed the dust as a new footstep settled. Ben tensed – was it Geoff, come to save him? Then a musty smell stung his nostrils.

'Kevin. Tell me about this.'

'He attacked us. Said he had to stop you. It's okay now.'

'Why?' Fisher spoke in an incredulous whisper. 'I never did him any harm.'

'Maybe he's some kind of spy.'

'I know! I know!' Thomas piped up. 'He's working for the White Cat. He told us everything. The White Cat's coming here tonight to try–'

'–to try and stop us,' Hannah chimed in, 'and he sent Ben, and Ben tried to make us obey him but we wouldn't, but the White Cat's coming anyway and–'

'The White Cat. Geoff… *Geoff*… *GEOFF*.' Fisher gnashed the words, groping at the rag stuffed inside his tunic. 'I understand you, Martin. I can help you, Martin. I won't ever leave you, Martin. Trust me. *Gaaaaaaaarggh!*' His fist crashed into the wall. As Fisher's gangling height swooped down at him, Ben tried to curl up. Hands hooked into the loops of his bonds and hoisted him up level with the stony eyes.

'He is coming here? Don't fib. Don't fib. He is coming here?'

With the last of his courage Ben shook his head.

'He is,' cried Hannah. 'He told us.'

Ben hit the floor like a sack of china. Through ringing ears he heard Kevin say: 'I'll get them ready to leave.'

'No leaving!' Fisher breathed deeply through his nose. 'He is here. I want him.'

'Ex-cell-ent.' Jeep unfolded his pocket crossbow. Kevin drew his knife.

'Let's go.'

Fisher seized Kevin's red hair.

'He is not alone. He has other cat-people. You must be cunning. Bait them.'

'M-Martin, I don't under–'

'They are hunters,' said Fisher. 'Hunters chase. Don't try to fight him. Lure him to me.'

Kevin stumbled free, rubbing his scalp. Fisher stretched a hand towards Thomas and Hannah.

'Bring the cat-boy.'

Stumbling between them towards the stairs, Ben blinked at the cords that bound his arms, legs and chest. Where, in this stripped building, had they found so much rope? He fingered its plastic texture and felt as if a sword had gone through him. This stuff wasn't rope. Jeep had tied him up with shock tube.

PLAN B

'Snappy little devils, aren't they?' Through a torn window board Geoff cheerily waved off the five polecat kids fleeing down Griffin Road into the night. 'Good job, everyone.'

'Messy, I thought.' Mrs Powell stretched as if to ease backache.

'She's a sourpuss. Pay no attention.'

'We were lucky, Geoffrey. If they had got upstairs they'd have warned their master.'

'Lucky I'm lucky, then.' Geoff had a final nose around. 'Okay. This floor's clear. Let's do the fourth.'

'Same plan?' asked Yusuf.

'You bet. Get above the polecats, then rush them so fast they don't know what's hit 'em. Break them up, flush 'em down to the exit. Simple.'

'Simple can mean daft, of course.'

'See what I used to put up with?'

Prickly as pincushions, thought Tiffany, amused. It was like her and Ben multiplied by ten. Geoff and Mrs Powell must have had some famous quarrels in their years of working together. On the other hand, they seemed able to communicate with barely a word. Was it telepathy, or merely that they knew each other so well? She saw it happen on the third floor landing.

Geoff said, 'Best if we–?' Mrs Powell merely glanced at the window. To that fleeting gesture, Geoff replied, 'Then I'll take–' and Mrs Powell said, 'And Tiffany, you come with me.'

The confused Cat Kin followed Geoff to the lift shafts, except for Tiffany who climbed after Mrs Powell out of the window to cling to the tower's sheer cliff face. This was hell on the fingers until Mrs Powell led her to an easier way up. A vast tarpaulin hung down the building's flank, made of a glossy fabric that clung easily to their Mau claws. Looking up, Tiffany saw a surreal sight: tomorrow's date in huge white letters. *Sunday 6 April.* Hang on a mo. It was early morning already. It was today.

'We climb to the fifth floor,' Mrs Powell whispered down. 'The others will attack from the lifts. A pincer movement. Oldest trick in the,' she missed a beat, 'book.'

'What's wrong?' asked Tiffany.

A headshake. 'Nothing I can put my finger on.'

They slipped inside through another empty frame. Mrs Powell held up a hand. 'I'll let you get your breath back.'

Tiffany was grateful, though she noticed Mrs Powell still panting after she herself had stopped.

'You *are* all right?'

'Twinges.' Mrs Powell grimaced, flexed her right shoulder. 'Don't nag. I'm over sixty. And I don't recover from gunshot wounds as well as I used to.

Ready now?'

'Yes.'

Once again they swooped down the stairs. On the blast floors Tiffany could see better, for the darkness was diluted by the wads of pale padding that wrapped many walls. She swept the landing with ears and eyes. Empty. Then a figure rushed her and she arched into a Ten Hooks defensive stance. She caught the glint of Daniel's glasses.

'Oi!' she cried. 'No hitting! It's us.'

Daniel swerved round her, skidding backwards on his toes as he turned. 'Whoa. Sorry. Any luck back there?'

'What's that mean?'

Cecile appeared with Olly in a doorway.

'Find anyone, Dan?'

Daniel shook his head. 'Nah. It's like the *Mary Rose* up here.'

'The *Mary Celeste*,' said Mrs Powell. 'You mean it's deserted?'

Three more approaching shades turned into Susie, Yusuf and Geoff.

'Zip,' said Geoff. 'I smell um but I no see um. Just tools on the floor. Must have left in a hurry.'

'They ran away?' Olly said hopefully.

'Not down,' said Yusuf. 'We'd have seen them. They must have retreated up the stairs.'

'Perhaps,' said Mrs Powell, 'they heard someone coming.'

Geoff bristled. 'They never heard me. Nor my team. Whereas I heard you two talking–'

Tiffany cut in.

'You stay here and argue over who they heard. I'm going to catch them before they reach their friends. They've still got five floors to climb.'

The others stared. Mrs Powell smiled. 'Listen to that girl.' Then she was off, springing up the stairs in enormous bounds as if thirty of her years had melted away. Tiffany barely saw which way she went and even Geoff seemed hard-pressed to keep up. They took a scrambling corner on the seventh-floor landing and Cecile gave a cry, pointing upwards. Loose flakes of darkness – human shapes diving out of sight.

'Got 'em,' panted Geoff. 'End of the road.'

At the next break in the stairs he crouched.

'They're on this floor, I'm sure–'

The air zinged. A blur crossed the corner of Tiffany's eye and Mrs Powell spun past her, one arm cutting like a propeller. The zinging sound broke with a crack and two bits of stick fell to the floor.

'Watch out,' cried Mrs Powell.

Geoff looked stunned. He picked up the sharp end of the crossbow bolt she had chopped in half, in mid-flight, on its way to his heart.

Mrs Powell prodded him. 'Over there!'

Tiffany saw a figure with tattooed arms, leaning from the lift shaft aiming a weapon. Another hiss punctured the air and Geoff's hand swept before his face. Suddenly an arrow was clasped in his fist. With lazy menace he advanced, twiddling the crossbow bolt through his fingers. Yet another bolt flew – *whack*, he caught that one too.

'*Do that again!*' he bellowed. 'I dare you.'

The shooter ducked back into the lift shaft. Geoff lunged across the landing, only to be swept aside by the torrent of polecats that poured without warning from the second shaft.

Mrs Powell uttered a piercing howl. Many times Tiffany had woken to that sound when Rufus, patrolling among the chimney pots, sent warning to his rivals to steer clear of him, and even through layers of snug duvet it turned her nerves to tinkling icicles. Here, in this stark tower, it was electrifying. The time for stealth was over, it cried. This was war.

The Cat Kin sprang like scalded cats. Tiffany watched herself as if from high above, flying in an arc, into the belly of the many-headed beast that rushed to meet them. Dreamily she thought *We're going to fight*, and felt no fear, no emotion at all, just a huge *rightness* as the hours of practice and the wild force of Mau took over, and she was back in her body. Hands grabbed and knives whickered, all missing as she rebounded off invisible walls. Lashing down at her attackers with double-strikes, four claw jabs and a volley of sharp kicks, she felt as if she was doing the triple-jump over the tops of their heads.

But the polecats came on. Forced to give ground in the face of their ferocity, she grasped a straw of wisdom that maybe saved her life. Cats were great warriors, but they weren't soldiers. They were the air force. They fought like planes, striking from on high, lightning fast and untouchable. Comprehending the Ten Hooks dance as never before, she watched in fascination as her body became a whip and her leg a ball and chain, chopping her charging foe in mid-leap while twirling herself aloft, like a lethal version of the ballerina she'd once wished she could be.

She felt the air shake from an impact nearby. Three masked figures reeled into three walls before Geoff's falling feet touched on the floor. Tiffany knew it now by sight: jafri zafri, Geoffrey's Affray, delivered by the maestro himself. He tipped her a wink.

With that the polecat assault ran out of steam. In seconds they changed from a ravening mob to a bunch of unsettled teens. A tall boy with red hair was the first to flee. This broke the gang's nerve and they scattered, some to the stairwell, some to the lift shafts. Most fled downwards but a handful seemed determined to reach their comrades on the floors above.

'Stop them!' Yusuf, his eyes white with battle fever, went charging with Daniel up the stairs.

'Wait,' called Mrs Powell, but Susie, Olly and Cecile were already in pursuit.

'We can catch them,' Susie cried, and was gone.

'*Stop this instant!*' Mrs Powell heaved a sigh. 'I know, I'll talk to this wall here.'

'Never fear, I'll head them off.' Geoff climbed into the lift shaft. 'You stay on the stairs.'

Tiffany looked to Mrs Powell for a lead. All she got was an unreadable frown.

'Mrs Powell? Do we go after them?'

The brow stayed wrinkled.

'Are you all right? It's not your injury, is it–?' Tiffany touched her. Mrs Powell twitched, as if waking up.

'Oh. Tiffany.'

'Mrs–?' She was getting worried. 'We still on the same page?'

'You go.' Mrs Powell was suddenly brisk. 'I need to check something.'

'Check what?'

'A feeling. Probably nothing. I'll join you in a minute. Now go. Chop-chop. You're the only one I can trust to keep those silly kittens in line.'

'But Mrs Powell!'

'I said you're in charge, Miss Maine. I trust that's not a problem?' She stepped into the lift that wasn't there. When Tiffany stared down the empty shaft, her teacher was gone.

'Thanks a bunch.' She ran for the stairs.

Ben recognised this feeling. He'd been placed centre stage. Being in the spotlight never normally bothered him, for at heart he was a show-off, usually first to volunteer for the school play. But if ever there was an excuse for stage fright, this was it.

Fisher had dumped him by the concrete rail where the rooftop met the sheer drop. The tower's roof was a flat, black yard, surrounding a central brick cabin that he guessed might have once held the water tanks. Anyone climbing to the top of the stairs would emerge from the cabin door and see Ben, trussed with explosive shock tube.

Standing guard over him were Thomas and Hannah. Hannah held the end of the cord, tipped with a silver blasting cap and the last of Jeep's bangers. Thomas held Jeep's cigarette lighter. Every so often he tested it, striking a flame that veered wildly in the wind.

'Would you mind?' Ben jerked his head.

'Oh. Sorry.' Thomas moved so that the lighter wasn't so close to Hannah's fuse.

'Hannah,' Ben hissed. 'Do you know what'll happen if he lights that?'

She looked away.

Ben knew. At least, he could guess. In a slipknot of shock tube a pigeon had popped like a feathered balloon. The same cord was looped a dozen times around his body.

Close overhead rolled earthy clods of cloud. Through the rail he could see the city of London, traced in lights and looking, to his sleep-starved brain, like a pinball table on standby. The bulbous Gherkin tower and its skinnier sisters could be the deflectors. The bonus multiplier was St Paul's cathedral. Soon the sun's shiny coin would slide through the horizon and it would all blaze into life… Oh no, please, he couldn't die. Not if his final thoughts were going to be about pinball.

What were Mum and Dad doing right now?

Wandering around their separate homes, too distraught to go near their beds? In sudden horror he found he'd forgotten what they looked like. When he tried to picture their faces he saw two terrifying egg-like blanks.

His tongue kept revisiting his agonising tooth, and his eyes kept returning to Fisher. Every time he saw the same still shadow, crouched atop the corner of the roof.

A pounding headache competed with the cracked tooth. What exactly was concussion? He wriggled to scratch an itch on his back and noticed that his bonds felt looser. It struck him that the smooth shock tube was quite bad at holding knots. He blew out all his breath and fidgeted some more. One knot unravelled.

'Stop doing that.' Fisher was there beside him. Ben forgot how to breathe.

'I count sixteen knots,' said Fisher. 'If any more come undone, Thomas will light you.'

'Certainly, yes,' said Thomas.

Ben's lungs stayed empty.

'I can hear your mind speaking,' said Fisher. 'It is speaking, isn't it? Thomas won't do it. Thomas is my friend. He won't let the cords crush me. I can hear your mind, Ben. And it fibs.'

His chest began to pound.

'He will do it. Hannah will do it. They pray to me for the chance to do it.'

'Please, Martin.' His guards spoke together. 'Please let us do it.'

'Hush.' Fisher sniffed the air. He cocked his head and his huge bony hands clenched into fists. He emitted a chainsaw growl.

'He is coming.'

Ben breathed, like a drowning man pulled into the air.

'Yusuf?'

Tiffany tiptoed through the ninth floor. Her feet picked their way between discarded tools.

'Cecile?'

She pushed aside cables that dangled in her face, edging round corners packed with padding. Harsh drafts blew through every room, rinsing away the polecats' scent.

'Susie? Geoff?'

Her Mau whiskers buzzed. Vibrations swarmed towards her through the air and floor. Fast feet, lots of them, rushing ever closer on a wave of raucous voices. She had to escape.

'Here!' someone hissed. Geoff's face in a window made her jump.

'Climb out, quick.'

Geoff was clinging to the glossy banner that cloaked the outer wall, framed by the white D of *Demolition*. She swung herself out to join him as polecats stormed past the room where she'd been hiding.

'That was a narrow squeak.' He touched her shoulder. 'You okay?'

She nodded. The banner billowed in the wind, making the gleaming city sway.

Geoff looked anxious. 'Where's Felicity?'

'Oh, don't ask. Did you catch the others?'

He thinned his lips.

'Well? Did you?'

'They had the hunting frenzy. Nothing I could do. When a cat's chasing prey you can't just shout *stop*.'

'But–' Her hands slipped. She desperately scrabbled. Geoff grabbed the scruff of her pashki kit.

'Whoa. Your claws can't cope with all this hanging around. Let's find a safer spot.'

Heart ka-chunking, Tiffany tried to re-summon her Mau claws. She used them so often she forgot they weren't real, weren't solid, but just a spooky sort of energy at the fingertips. Closing her eyes she flicked through the rainbow of catras in turn, Ptep, Mandira, Kelotaukhon, Parda, Oshtis and Ailur, until the skin tingled beneath her nails. Geoff was right – she couldn't sustain such concentration much longer than ten seconds. She stared at him in awe: he'd been climbing on his own claws for minutes.

'Here's comfy enough.' He helped her to the nearest balcony and she fell into it with relief. He sat on the edge dangling his feet.

'I didn't count on losing everyone like that,' he said. 'We're a bit stuffed.'

'Why?'

'I can't face Fisher and his gang alone.'

'But you're not. Alone, I mean.'

'Nor am I keen on watching Fisher gut you.'

Tiffany felt sick. Geoff cracked his knuckles.

'We may need Plan B.'

'Plan B?'

'We find our friends,' said Geoff. 'We round them up. Get out of the tower and leave Fisher here.'

Tiffany thought her ears must be full of wax.

'We leave?'

Geoff's mouth twisted as if tasting something bad.

'Need to tell you. I didn't before. Not even Felicity. Knew she'd disapprove.'

Tiffany waited.

'I explained, didn't I, how this tower's rigged up. There's a detonator. But it needs an electric charge to set it off.' The blue eyes never blinked. 'I'm handy enough with electrics. Before you got here, I ran my own cable to a lamp post outside. Years ago I found that you can tap the electricity–'

'I know, Mrs Powell told me. Geoff, what are you saying?'

'I'm saying that if we get our friends out, I can plug my cable into the detonator. And the tower implodes with Fisher inside it.'

Her hands went to her mouth.

'His kids would be buried with him, of course,' Geoff mused. 'That's why I'm reluctant.'

'Geoff, we couldn't.'

'If it's my last chance to stop Fisher, I will. Better a few children killed here than thirty thousand dead under London.'

She had no answer to that. A hard core of ruthlessness lurked inside Geoff White that she'd never felt from Mrs Powell. Maybe, in such terrible times, that was what you needed. Someone who was prepared to kill in order to stop his enemy.

'But haven't Fisher's kids been taking the dynamite out?' she said.

'Only a fraction of it. There's more than two thousand charges and most are still in place. The tower might not fall as cleanly as it would have, but it's gonna fall.'

She listened, aghast. So this was where pashki had led her. This was what it meant to live the life her teachers had chosen. A life red in tooth and claw.

'Let's find our team,' said Geoff.

They entered an apartment through the balcony doorway. Geoff led her up to the fifteenth floor, stalking through the undergrowth of explosive cords. They found no-one.

'Don't like this.' Geoff hurried her to the window. They resumed their climb up the outside wall, using the great banner as a scramble-net. Passing each window Tiffany peered in and softly called. Every apartment rang empty. The tower's summit came within arm's reach. Geoff eased himself up to peer across the roof.

'*Set.*' He spoke the word savagely, like a curse – one of the Ancient Egyptian oaths that he and Mrs Powell sometimes used. Tiffany joined him at the concrete guardrail, ready to see the worst – or so she thought.

The rooftop was infested with black masks. Surely the entire polecat gang was gathered here. She even recognised some whom she had chased from the building herself. Had they only pretended to flee? Knots of polecats shuffled past the central cabin, manhandling heavy burdens – *struggling* burdens. A voice shouted feebly, sounding like Susie's. Tiffany saw a face with a tortoiseshell print: Cecile, hanging limp between her four captors. A writhing Yusuf was thrown to the deck and held down.

She choked on her words. 'They got them.'

Her horror mounted as she counted her friends. There was Daniel. Olly. Susie with a bleeding nose. Who was missing?

'Ben's not there!'

Her spirits nearly rose. Then Geoff shifted out of her line of sight.

Ben sat hunched against the adjacent guardrail, flanked by three polecats. They had tied him up with some rubbery rope. Her Oshtis catra throbbed with dread.

The wind threw a shout.

'White Cat! Where is the White Cat?'

She looked at Geoff. Was that sadness in his eyes?

'I know you are here!' The cry seemed to circle them. 'Geoff, I can smell you. You are listening. Listen to this.'

She saw him then: gangling, powerful, moving as if made out of scissors. Tiffany bit her thumb. So that was Martin Fisher. She couldn't let herself be scared of him. For Ben's sake, she couldn't.

'I have your boy here,' Fisher called. 'Come out. I will let him live.'

'Geoff–' that was Ben, '–don't listen to him!'

'Jeep.'

The largest of Ben's guards struck a flame from a lighter.

'Your boy will be broken in pieces,' Fisher yelled. 'Will you leave him as you left me?'

'What's he saying?' Tiffany moaned. 'What are they doing to him?'

'Come to me,' cried Fisher. 'Take his place. Or hide and watch him die.'

That was all the information she needed. They were going to kill Ben, *kill* him. Where was Mrs Powell when they needed her? In the name of Anubis, where was she?

'I've got to stop this.' Tiffany reached up to the guard rail. Geoff pulled her back.

'Sorry, sweetie. It's not your time yet.'

Tiffany met his gaze with a horrible *déjà vu*. Once before she had watched a friend cut down in front of her. Could she bear to see it happen again? Geoff bit his lip.

'This one's mine.'

DON'T LET GO

When Ben saw Geoff vault up onto the roof, in his mind he shouted *Run, save yourself*. But his mouth wouldn't say it. His mouth belonged to someone who was too afraid to die. He was a coward, a treacherous coward. Geoff strolled nearer, crossing the square gravel plain. *Run, save yourself*. No, it wasn't in him. Overcome with shame he couldn't bear to look at Geoff, and yet he could not wrench his gaze away from his last hope.

'Hi, Martin. Long time and all that.'

'A long time,' said Fisher. 'A long time. Come along–' He cocked his head, looming towards Geoff. He was so much taller. 'You come to save him. That means. He means more to you than I did.'

Geoff shrugged. 'He's not a deranged killer.'

Fisher struck him across the face. Geoff went sprawling. Jeep chuckled in Ben's ear. Thomas and Hannah, pale-faced, watched. The other Cat Kin, pinned down by polecats, looked on with defeated eyes.

'Not so fast as you were.' Fisher pulled Geoff to his feet and studied his face almost lovingly. Geoff's lower lip was swelling. Fisher threw him down again. 'Now you are mine. Not his. Mine.'

'Stop,' Ben croaked.

'I will drink your blood as the ferret drinks the rabbit's. I will make myself a rattle from your teeth and your skull. We will be together, Geoff, you and I. You will never leave me again.'

Another cracking blow to the head. Geoff didn't try to defend himself.

'Please, Geoff!' Ben cried. 'Don't let him–'

'You interrupt again,' Jeep hissed, 'and bang.' The flame of his lighter lapped thirstily towards the fuse that he now held in his own fist. 'Remember the pigeon.'

'Martin.' Geoff startled everyone by slipping out of reach. 'Before you kill me, you let Ben go.'

'Let him go? No. He will live. He will live with me. They will all live with me and become like me.'

'And everyone else has to die?'

'They betrayed me. You all betrayed me.'

'And the thousands of innocents you plan to drown? Did they betray you too?'

'They are human beings,' said Fisher. He advanced on Geoff, who backed away in circles. The polecats tracked his every movement, a score of heads swivelling together. Ben fumbled at the knots behind his back.

'So you kill half of London. What then?' Geoff waved his hand at Fisher's followers. 'What happens when you've got no humans left to kill? If I was in your gang I'd be getting *really* worried. What happens when you notice that they're human too?

What happens when you look in the mirror, Martin?'

Fisher lunged. This time Geoff was too slow. He went down.

'Martin!' Ben knew his own voice, but had no idea what it would say. 'Martin, do you think they ever gave up?'

'Huh?' Jeep seemed too puzzled to silence him.

'When do you think they gave up hope?' Ben worked another knot loose. 'Martin, your parents. Your real, human parents. The ones who lost you as a child. When do you think they gave up?'

Fisher shook his head as if a gnat had buzzed him. Ben noticed how very still Thomas and Hannah were standing.

'Did they forget they had a child?' Ben yelled.

Jeep rattled the shock tube. 'Shut your yap.'

'Or do you think,' Ben plunged on, glancing at Thomas, sensing Hannah's shifting feet, 'do you think they're still out there somewhere? Wondering what happened to you?'

'Last warning!' Jeep's lighter flamed.

Ben yelled, '*Do they still dream that you come home?*'

Jeep lit the banger's blue touch-paper. He staggered and fell to one knee. Thomas had chopped him, hard, in the neck. Hannah darted forward and plucked the banger, spewing sparks, out of the blasting cap and flung it away. *Bang*. Jeep roared and his knife flashed. It never reached its target. Ben slipped free of the slack cords and let his inner wildcat take over. His hand jabbed twice, a leopard's crushing paw, and even before his enemy had crumpled to the floor Ben was spinning clear, scanning the rooftop for Geoff.

But the Geoff he knew was gone. In his place was something terrible. Some furious white-masked human beast that carved the air with shredding blows, piling into Martin Fisher like a natural disaster. Fisher reeled backwards. And there, leaping the guardrail at the edge of the roof, was Tiffany, a sleek black missile aimed straight at the polecats. The vanquished Cat Kin suddenly showed they were not so vanquished after all. Yusuf lashed out at the two pinning him down. Daniel squirmed free of Gary and Dean. And as Kevin arose to crush this alarming rebellion, Tiffany hurtled into him and bowled him off his feet.

For a whole second Ben did not know which way he would go. If Tiffany was fighting Kevin she would need his help. But now Geoff's ferocious onslaught had burned itself out. Fisher was back on the attack, his bloodied face all snarl, his mink tunic flapping where Mau claws had ripped it to ribbons. To go in that direction was to run into a fire. But sometimes someone came along who could make you do just that. He hadn't come this far to let Geoff stand alone.

At full sprint down a residential street, Ben could trigger speed cameras (a trick he sometimes played on his French teacher's car). He crossed the rooftop in a flash. In that instant a savage kick sent Geoff rolling away. Ben felt his hair stand stiff as a brush and he found, to his horror, that instead of leaping on Fisher's blind side he was skidding to a halt right under his nose. The long fingers sought Ben's throat.

He had noticed before how the moments before certain death could last – well, a lifetime. And with a lifetime to think, he could have some very bright ideas. Ben knew what to do. He dived under Fisher's hands, reached through the rips in the mink tunic and plucked out the rag that was nestling within.

Tiffany thought she'd have a chance against the big red-haired youth, so long as she could keep dodging. She feinted and kicked to put him off balance, then scissored with both hands in a Ratbane Lunge. Her mistake. He ensnared her arm in the crook of his elbow and she knew she was in trouble. Not only was the chief polecat well trained, he was taller, heavier and strong enough to fling her down with brutal force. She hit the gravel and lay there, stunned, waiting for the killing blow. It never came. Tiffany peered up through her flickering eyelids. The gang leader stood over her, statue-still. She craned her neck to follow his gaze.

Geoff was huddled in the corner, clutching his ribs. There was Ben, there was Fisher, they were face to face. Ben was backing off, moving like a bullfighter, brandishing a cloth that wriggled in the wind. Such a scrappy thing it was, she might never have noticed it, but for its effect on Martin Fisher. He was spellbound. Tentatively, fearfully, he inched towards it, as a man in the desert dying of thirst might approach a mirage. Yet his eyes blazed at Ben, lasers of hate.

Ben said something. Tiffany couldn't catch it. Slowly Fisher reached for the rag. Then he seized Ben by the neck and yanked him off his feet. Tiffany heard choking. The rag fluttered. Ben seemed desperate to give it to Fisher, waving it in his face, but Fisher was murderous, blind. The rag slipped from Ben's fingers. A gust of wind snatched it aloft and off the edge of the roof.

Martin Fisher hurled himself after the scrap of cloth. With arms flung out like useless wings he clawed at the wind, screaming like a fisher no more but like a child in despair. His red-haired henchman stood frozen in shock as he plummeted out of view. Tiffany scrambled to the guard rail. Fisher's falling shape was the size of a raven… a blackbird… a beetle. His scream sank to a low moan, ending in a sound she had never heard before and hoped never to hear again, for she guessed it was a human body hitting distant paving slabs.

Someone made a strangled noise, halfway between a sob and a laugh. The chief polecat had joined her at the rail. Together they watched the ownerless rag circle downwards. With another cry the tall boy broke away and ran stumbling for the stairs.

Tiffany was still groggy from her battle. It had all happened so fast. Something troubled her, something was wrong. When she realised what it was, her heart fell through her bones. When Fisher had leaped off the building he'd been holding onto Ben.

'Ben!' she screamed. And again. And again. There was only blackness below. She was gathering her breath for a wail of grief when she caught one short, strained word:

'Here.'

She leaned over the edge, sharpening her night-sight. A human shape hung by its fingertips from a balcony wall, three floors below.

'Ben!' she yelled again, joyfully. He didn't answer, nor did he move. His fingers, she saw, had grabbed at bare concrete. It amazed her that his Mau claws worked on it at all. One thing, though, was certain: they wouldn't work for long.

'Geoff!' she shrieked. 'Geoff, help!'

'I'm here.' Geoff bent over the rail. The bristles on his face were crusted with blood but he seemed in one piece. He took in Ben's plight at a glance.

'Can't get to him from here. Down the stairs.'

Between them and the cabin lay the scrum of polecats and Cat Kin, apparently fossilised in mid-brawl.

'You lot!' Geoff roared. 'Clear off!'

The polecat gang scrambled for their lives. Tiffany charged through them before the Cat Kin could get to their feet. She took the stairs in suicidal leaps, knowing already that she was too late. Ben would fall. He would fall and at this height he would break upon the stones, whether he landed on his feet or not. Her own Mau claws never lasted this long, even on soft stuff like wood.

Ben's were no better. Already he had used up his ten seconds... twenty... twenty-five...

He did not move. He did not breathe. Apart from gasping that one word, *Here*, he made no sound. He did not even think. All his strength, all his being, was pouring into one thing alone.

Ptep – Mandira – Kelotaukhon – Parda – Oshtis – Ailur.

Blue, green, copper, gold, crimson, indigo. The cat's eyes flashed in the blackness of his mind, the wheel of catras, spinning. The wheel was a generator, charging up his Mau body with the force it needed to make physical claws. He didn't feel the ache in his shoulder muscles, the knives of cramp in his fingers. He just kept that wheel turning.

Ptep – Mandira – Kelotaukhon – Parda – Oshtis – Ailur.

A gust of wind made him gently swing. His hands were numb as clay. Copper, gold, crimson, then the wheel of colours juddered. What– what next? His Mau claws boiled away. The concrete skinned his finger pads as he slipped down with a scream.

And then he was dangling. His wrist was clamped in a wrinkled hand. A matching hand joined it and one tremendous tug lifted him up and over the side of the balcony. Flat on his back Ben stared up at a familiar face, too shattered to realise that he had been saved.

'Hello, Ben,' said Mrs Powell. 'You look pleased to see me for a change.'

THE EYE OF RA

I strike quicker than the serpent
even in sleep am I watchful
I am called the Eye of Ra.
From 'Song of Pasht', Spell 9, Akhotep, c. 1580 BC
Translation: Matthew Toy.

The sight of those two on the balcony would stay with Tiffany always. Ben's face was classic, but then, it would be. He hadn't seen Mrs Powell for over six months, and now this.

'About time you showed up!' said Tiffany. Joy had made her cheeky. 'You picked a fine time to slope off for a nap.'

Mrs Powell stayed poker-faced. 'I was where I needed to be. You seemed to manage well enough without me. As I suggested you would.'

'Oh, hang on a sec!' Putting her pupils to the test was one thing, but risking their lives just to make a point... she wouldn't do that? Tiffany spluttered and eventually said, 'But you would have helped, right? If we'd really been in danger?'

Even as she asked the question, she remembered Mrs Powell's Mau garden, with its Eth-walking posts like spears. Put a foot wrong there and you might be skewered.

Ben gave a shaky laugh. 'Do you hear me complaining?'

Tiffany helped him up off his knees. He sucked at his grazed fingers and gave her a strange look. Then his old mischievous grin flashed out. It amazed her, like some fragile ornament left intact after an earthquake.

'I see you tracked her down.'

'Yes.'

'Nice one.'

'Thanks.'

'No, really. That was not bad.' And he hugged her. It was almost as if he'd lost his balance and had to lean on her a moment, for he stepped back just as quickly and examined his grazed hands. But a hug it definitely was.

The sky behind him was lighter, showing up his split lip and a cut on his temple. 'You're hurt.'

'Hadn't noticed.' He tried another smile and winced. 'Look's like someone's been hitting you too. Where is he? I'll kill him.'

'He's gone,' Daniel called. 'They're all gone.'

Susie and Cecile appeared in the hollow hall.

'They've skedaddled, one and all,' crowed Susie. 'We scared them out of their mangy skins.'

'We didn't scare them,' said Ben. 'It's because they're not scared anymore. They only stayed together 'cos they were terrified of Fisher. Now he's gone.' He rubbed his eyes and yawned. 'Let them go.'

'And we should be gone,' said Mrs Powell. 'Before daybreak.'

Cecile beamed. 'Hallelujah.'

Tiffany said, 'I'll round up the troops.'

Seeing Ben safe had made everyone a bit wild. Yusuf and Geoff had rushed back to chase the polecats from the roof, and Olly, of all people, was so fired-up that he'd joined in. Searching for them up the stairs, Tiffany met Geoff hurrying down. He had cleaned the blood off his face and seemed to have recovered from his duel.

'Hey, well done,' he said.

'Oh,' she shrugged. 'I didn't do much.' She paused. 'Geoff. I'm sorry.'

'Sorry? What for?'

'All that stuff before. I didn't much like it when you took over the class. And it stopped me liking you.'

'It's okay. I've had worse.'

'Well anyway.' She was blushing. 'I hope you stick around. Stay with us a bit. You will stay, won't you? You're a great teacher.'

'Aw.' Geoff waved her away. 'You're forgetting about the real hero.'

'I know. Ben was incredible. The way he –'

'I'm talking about you,' said Geoff. 'You did what I could never have done. You found Felicity and brought her back to me. Thank you.'

'You mean that?'

'I do.' Geoff moved past her, seeming fidgety. 'What a night. Nearly over though.'

'Nearly?'

'Some of those polecats ran off with their bags of explosive. I doubt they'll do much with it now, but I'd better catch them just to be safe.'

Exhausted as she was, Tiffany said, 'I'll come.'

'No need,' said Geoff. 'You get some rest. I'll see you tomorrow. Today. Ah, whatever.'

He was gone. Tiffany mounted the stairs to the roof. It was deserted now and, in this space before dawn, as silent as London could be. Nothing stirred between here and the clouds, except for the flicker of two cast-off polecat bandanas, dancing in the wind. One side of the sky had a polished look, with a light band on the black horizon that reminded her of cream on coffee. Mm, coffee would be nice.

She headed back down. 'Yusuf? Olly?' On the seventeenth floor she met the others. 'Is Olly with you?'

'Na,' said Daniel. 'Did you check up there?'

'I reckon they'll be down in the lobby,' said Susie.

'Ssshh!' Cecile's head flicked round. Mrs Powell pushed past, crossing into the next apartment. They trailed after her, mystified. A pained sound, a sigh or a groan, drew Tiffany to the farthest room. Mrs Powell was kneeling by two bodies. Olly lay curled up, bleeding from his head. Yusuf sprawled with his left leg at a sickening angle. Susie squealed.

'What happened?' cried Tiffany.

Mrs Powell checked that both were breathing. She adjusted Yusuf's head and he gurgled. The other Cat Kin crowded round. Olly moaned.

Mrs Powell bent over him and a purr rumbled in her chest. He opened his eyes.

'No! Please–'

'Ssh. You're safe.' Mrs Powell purred some more and Olly's breathing steadied.

'It's okay, Ol.' Ben touched his arm. 'Can you talk?'

Olly began to shake as if very cold. At first his teeth juddered too much. Then he murmured, 'It was him.'

The chill entered Tiffany's heart. She saw Ben pale under his cat-paint. *It was him.* Martin Fisher had survived, somehow he'd survived, he had fallen twenty storeys and still he lived. They were fools to think he'd die that easily. And now he was in this building, hunting them down, and Geoff wasn't here to protect them anymore.

Olly seemed to read the fear in her face. He tried to sit up.

'No, no,' he gasped. 'Not Fisher. It wasn't Fisher.'

A quiet voice spoke.

'Felicity.'

Mrs Powell sprang up. Tiffany ran with her to the window. Far below stood a man beneath a lamp post. At his feet lay two cables. He stooped and picked them up. One of them was orange with a stout shiny muzzle.

'Hi,' said Geoff. Even seventeen floors below, his voice was crystal clear. 'Felicity, you remember how I told you I can never forget, but I can forgive? I said I can, Felicity. I never said I do.'

Ben laughed dutifully. This was clearly some private joke he was too sleepy and sore to get. Did Tiffany get it? Her face was a puzzle. She was about to laugh… or cry… or scream… or be sick. But why? Mrs Powell seemed as baffled as him.

'Geoffrey? I don't understand. What are you doing?'

'Ask your little lap-cat. Ask her what these wires are.'

'It's…' Tiffany's lip was red where she'd bitten it, she was shaking her head. She blurted, 'Geoff said he ran a cable from a lamp post. That he could plug into the detonator. To blow up this tower and stop Fisher. But– but–'

'Spot on,' said Geoff. 'And I'm hardly going to let my handiwork go to waste. *Am I, Felicity*?' These words were a shout of rage.

Mrs Powell whispered.

'Tiffany. You and the others help these two downstairs. Get out of the building. I'll keep him talking.'

'We can't–' Tiffany began.

'Oh, you'll keep me talking. Great plan. You stupid woman, you think I can't hear you? Anyone tries to leave…' Geoff motioned with the two cables as if to join them together.

'Stop!' cried Ben. His mind was collapsing. 'What is this? Can't anyone tell me what's going on?'

Geoff lowered the cables. 'Ah, of course.

No-one's told you, have they, Ben? What a pity. To you, she's still the flawless, fabulous teacher of ancient wisdom. Not someone who'd kill an unborn child. *My* child.'

'You arrogant fool,' said Mrs Powell. 'You think it was easy for me?'

'He was *my son!*' Geoff roared. '*Mine!* And you murdered him!'

'Keep your voice down. People are sleeping.'

'I'm glad you find it funny. Since you enjoy killing children, look around you. Your adoring pupils will die now and it will be your fault. You'll be buried together under tonnes of rubble, their eyes will be the last thing you see, the last thing you hear will be their screams, as they *curse* you, *hating* you, as you die knowing what you've done. *Do you hate her, kids? Do you hate her now?*'

'Go to hell,' sobbed Tiffany.

Olly was pushing at Daniel and Cecile. 'Please. Get away. Leave me.'

'Are you speaking for Yusuf too?' snapped Mrs Powell. 'Your friends are taking you out of here. *At once.*'

'But–' cried Tiffany.

'Do as I say!'

'You'll never reach the door,' said Geoff. He lifted the cable that ran from the lamp post. He lifted the orange cord that coiled towards the tower. Ben couldn't move from the window. His understanding grew like a thorn, tearing him inside. This was not just some silly mistake.

'Geoff. Please. This isn't you. I know it's not.'

'I'm sorry, Ben,' said Geoff. 'For you, I am.'

'You stopped Fisher. We helped you. You saved my life. You wouldn't do this, you can't.'

'I'm sorry you got caught up in this, Ben. Thanks for your help.'

Geoff plugged the two cables together.

Somewhere a bird twittered. Nothing else happened.

He pulled the leads apart and reconnected them. Still nothing happened.

Mrs Powell called down. 'Technical problems?'

Geoff blinked hard at the tower block as if he couldn't believe it was still there. He stared up and around. For the first time he noticed – Ben noticed – they all noticed – that the street light trailing the electric cable wasn't actually lit.

'What the–?'

'Oh dear,' said Mrs Powell. 'Is that one broken? Maybe you could phone the Council.'

'*Set!*' Geoff cursed.

'Isn't *sabotage* a lovely word?'

'She broke it.' Tiffany's face shone with wonder. 'That's what she was doing, all that time. She found his trap and she broke it!'

'Mrs Powell, you rock!' cried Daniel.

Far below Geoff whirled to and fro, as if trying to guess how quickly he could wire the connected cords to another street light. The stupidity of it struck him almost at once and he flung the useless cable to the ground.

'Fine. You missed your chance of a quick death,

Felicity. I'll do this the old fashioned way.'

He ran towards the tower. His light steps skittered across the paving stones, fading to silence before rising again, echoing in the stairwell.

'He's coming up,' said Cecile.

'I've changed my mind, get us out of here,' groaned Olly.

'They will,' said Mrs Powell. 'Everyone, ready. You take Olly and Yusuf when I say.'

Tiffany clutched at her. 'What about you?'

Mrs Powell gently extracted herself and pulled Ben alongside. Ben felt her green eyes searching inside him.

'Now you listen. As you've never listened before. From this moment on, when I speak, you *must* obey. You really must. Trust me now, if you never trust anyone again.'

'Aren't you coming with us?' Tiffany pleaded.

'No, and here's why,' said Mrs Powell. The footsteps on the stairs were now very close. 'Geoff isn't content just to kill me. He could have done that already. No, he wants me to watch you die first. *That's* his real revenge.'

'I won't let you face him alone.'

'You have to, Tiffany. As long as we stay together we are all in mortal danger. Me, you, your friends. But if we can stay apart, he won't kill me. He couldn't bear to. Killing only me would be failure. Tiffany, to keep me safe, you *must* desert me.'

'We understand,' said Ben. He turned Tiffany towards him by the shoulder. 'You always told me to trust her. And you're always right.'

A shout sent a buzzing echo through the walls.

'*Felicity!*'

'I can give you one chance,' said Mrs Powell.

Ben and Tiffany bore up Yusuf under the arms. His head lolled. He whimpered in pain as Susie tried to support his broken leg. Daniel and Cecile helped Olly to stand.

Geoff blocked the doorway. He glared at Mrs Powell.

'You knew.'

'No. I suspected.'

'How?'

'When I saved you from that arrow. You were surprised.'

'That's all?'

'Not quite.' Mrs Powell glanced from Geoff to Tiffany and back again. 'Love and hate can look so similar, until you see them side by side.'

'Nice. I'll scratch that on your gravestone.' He shifted his weight into Arch on Guard.

'Geoff,' said Mrs Powell, 'hear me. Even now you and I could be friends. Unlike you I can forgive. And I do. But if you move again to harm me or my children, then I swear by Ra I will kill you.'

The hairs rose on Ben's neck. It was coming. Geoff peered around the room in mock fright.

'And your trained attack panthers are... where, exactly?'

He stepped forward.

Ptah. The noise cracked out. Geoff blinked and

Mrs Powell was on him. Her fists rammed into his chest and drove him away from the exit.

'Go,' she cried.

Terrified that Tiffany might not obey, Ben heaved his heavy burden forward, leaving her no choice but to help him drag Yusuf to the stairs. Olly managed to stumble along between Daniel and Cecile, but Yusuf gasped and cried out with every jolting step. His sweat mingled into Ben's already soaked pashki kit.

'What is she doing, fighting him?' Susie wailed. 'She can't fight him!'

'We'll get these two out,' panted Ben. 'And then. I'll go. Help.'

'No.' Tiffany spoke through clenched teeth. 'She told us. You heard. If he catches us with her, she's dead.'

Yusuf's weight was nearly breaking his back. Ben focused on that, trying to blot out the noises from above. Something was being hit over and over. Walls shuddered. Snarls, curses and half-human shrieks blurred into one banshee howl. A war, that's what it sounded like – a war of giant cats. And a war that could have only one winner. Even if she'd been in the prime of her life, Mrs Powell was no match for Geoff White. Her long years of learning counted for nothing. It didn't matter that she had the sinews of a tennis racket, that old age hadn't dulled her speed nor rusted her iron strength. Geoff had everything she had and more, reinforced by the mind of a warrior and razor claws.

The first dawn light peeped through the fifth floor landing window, making Ben's shadow loom over him accusingly. A terrible cry floated down, a woman's scream of pain. Tiffany flung Yusuf's arm onto Cecile's shoulder.

'Stuff this!'

'No,' Ben protested, 'you said… she told us to–'

'Since when do we do as we're told?' Tiffany doubled back, tearing up the staircase. Ben pushed his half of Yusuf towards Daniel.

'Call an ambulance.' He threw himself after Tiffany, taking the first flight in one bound. Sparing a final glance down at his friends he saw their eyes cast up at him in horror. He hesitated. 'Better make it two.'

Catras Ailur, Parda and Ptep cracked together, powering him to top speed, yet still he was trailing when he reached the seventeenth floor. His ears immediately told him that the battle had moved higher. He yelled Tiffany's name and heard her shout.

'The roof!'

Ben burst from the rooftop cabin into the wind. The sky was brighter, the torn clouds catching fire, and fairy chains of streetlights broke as more of their number went dark with the dawn. Colours seeped from the darkness as from ink on wet paper.

A screech of agony paralysed him. He saw Mrs Powell fall against the guard rail, Geoff pouncing to pin her down, drawing back his right hand with the fingers wickedly hooked. Tiffany crashed into him from behind.

'Get off her!'

Mrs Powell gave a cry of dismay.

'No, Tiffany! Get away. You can't be here. You can't–'

Tiffany hung round Geoff's neck like a lioness.

'Get off her! *Get off.*'

Her claws scrabbled for his eyes. Geoff threw his weight backwards, crushing her under him, breaking her hold. He flipped over and dealt three slashing blows before Ben could reach him. In fury Ben clawed at the man who minutes ago had been his friend. Geoff hardly flinched, batting him away. Then Mrs Powell was up again, grappling his arms, and there was Tiffany counter-attacking, her eyes crazed and bloodshot.

'Ben,' Mrs Powell gasped. She was trying to get Geoff in some kind of neck-lock. 'Tiffany. Leave me. I'm begging–'

The world somersaulted. Ben felt as if an axe had chopped him in the windpipe. He lay on his back, ashy clouds afloat above him. They were pretty, edged with pink in the light leaking over the horizon. Sounds wallowed through the haze, scuffles, choking cries. Some sort of fight close by. Something important. With a jolt he came back to himself. Tasting blood he swallowed. It felt like gulping down a fragment of flint.

'Ben.' The weak voice was Tiffany's. She lay by the rail at the roof's edge. He crawled to her side.

'Are you– oh, no.' Her sleeves were cut to ribbons. 'You're bleeding.'

'You're bleedin' right.' She giggled unnervingly.

That didn't sound good. Losing all this blood must be making her faint. With desperate resourcefulness he clawed off the sleeves of his own pashki kit and tied them as bandages around Tiffany's arm.

'Er. Keep pressure on it.' That was what they said on TV.

By the muffled screams and snarls he guessed the fight had moved back inside the cabin. Ben breathed a silent thank-you to Mrs Powell – she must have driven Geoff away from them while they lay helpless. Probably with the last of her strength. Ben wept tears of despair.

'We were beating him. It was three on one. What happened?'

'Jafri zafri.' Tiffany chuckled again. 'Should have seen that coming.'

Maybe they should. But now Ben grasped the terrible truth. Secret weapon or no secret weapon, Geoff was a foe beyond them. He had weapons at his fingertips they could barely imagine, and what did they have? Compared to him they were defenceless. They were kittens before a cat.

'Tiffany, I'll– I'll get you to a hospital. Hang on.'

'Oh. Yuck.' She seemed to notice how gravely she was wounded. 'Whoops. Still, at least he didn't hurt you.'

'What do you mean? He nearly broke my neck.'

'No scratches, though. Look.'

Ben examined his bare arms. No, this couldn't be right. There were the bruises from his earlier battles, but where were the slashes from Geoff's claws?

He checked his torso, his face.

'That's impossible. I was fighting him.' It seemed unfair to have no proof. 'He was clawing at me.'

'He can't have missed every time. Unless…' Tiffany sat upright. 'Ben! That must be it. The claws. Kittens and cubs. Oh. He's fallen for you.'

'You should lie down, Tiffany.'

'Ben, listen to me. Between you and Geoff… There's something. It's like love.'

'Hold on. The ambulance is coming.'

'I'm bleeding, Ben, I'm not mad!' She caught her breath, her eyes rolling unsteadily. 'Trying to… explain. Ben, even if he always meant to betray us, he still got close to you. Really close. Close like brothers. Like cats from the same litter.'

'Meaning what?'

'Meaning… Ben, you won't know this, it's one of those cat things, but brother-or-sister kittens, no matter how much they look like they're fighting…'

She was mistaken, however. Ben did know, he must have heard or read it somewhere, a useless scrap of cat folklore he had thought no more about. Before she could finish telling him, he was on his feet and running. It was true, it *had* to be, for still he could feel himself drawn to Geoff, as if by a rope that bound them together.

He reached the far side of the cabin to see Geoff in the doorway, flinging Mrs Powell to the floor. There was no more fight left in her. She lay at the top of the stairs, barely struggling as, clasping her hair with one hand, Geoff raised the other over her neck.

His fingertips twitched and the air faintly sang. A snarl twisted his lips.

'Remember that day we met, Felicity? You should have let me steal your handbag.'

Down came his claws. Ben didn't think. He dived through the doorway and thrust his palm between Geoff's fingertips and Mrs Powell's bared throat.

It hurt. But it was the stab of hard fingers, not the agony of hooks tearing his flesh. Geoff gave a strange whinny of astonishment. He had the look of one who throws a brick at a window only to have it bounce back. Frozen in his crouch at the top of the stairs he could only mouth 'How?'

'Look,' said Ben. He scratched gently at Geoff's arm. The skin bore just the pink marks of fingernails. 'You did that. Because I trusted you. Because I needed you. Because you needed me too, I suppose. It wasn't all lies, was it? You'd kill me along with the others, yeah, but you were ready to cry about it afterwards. We know it. And our Mau bodies know it. Which is why they won't hurt each other, no matter how much we try. How about that, Geoff? We're like family. Your claws don't work on me, and mine don't work on you.'

'Ben…' Geoff's blue eyes glistened in wonder.

'Which means I have to do *this*.'

It wasn't a pashki move – it was a football one, the kind used to take penalties. All the grief Ben felt inside him went into that kick. Geoff caught it on the bridge of his nose and plunged backwards down the stairs. The banisters had been ripped out when the tower was prepared for demolition, so there was nothing to stop Geoff pitching sideways off the steps and falling, with a yell, into darkness.

Ben knelt by Mrs Powell. A frail old lady mugged and left for dead could have looked no worse than she did. Her face-print had been lost inside a mask of bruises and blood, the grey hair on her head torn up in clumps. From her eyelids, not a flicker. Geoff had killed her after all. Ben's throat closed. He clasped her cold, wrinkled hand in both of his.

'Mrs Powell. No.'

Her eyes snapped open and she sat bolt upright.

'Ben! You're not still here?'

'Y-yes.'

Not so much as a thank-you. But then that was typical of your average cat.

'Ben Gallagher, get this through your head!' She was hissing in his face. 'That streetlamp he was trying to use. It isn't really broken.'

Somewhere deep in his exhausted brain, alarm bells started to ring.

'It's not broken,' Mrs Powell repeated. 'I just reversed its relay switch. I rigged it so it would light by day instead of night. *Do you understand?*'

No – wait – yes, he did. Streetlamps were light-sensitive, he knew that much. Most were primed to switch on automatically at dusk. But not, she was telling him, not this one. *This* one would light at dawn.

Which was now.

Colour bled into the sky. His shadow cowered

on the cabin wall.

'That detonator. He never unplugged it.'

'Ra is rising,' said Mrs Powell.

The stairwell howled with a cry of rage, of astonishment, of mortal fear.

'Felicity!' Geoff was on the staircase only two floors below them, racing up the steps towards them five or six at a time. 'Felicity, what have you done?'

Mrs Powell looked at Ben.

'Save her,' she said.

She leaped at Geoff as he reached the final flight. Ben heard a noise like a lion-tamer's whip. Mrs Powell locked her arms round Geoff and they fell, tumbling, down into the stairwell's folded depths. Another noise punched through the soles of Ben's feet, a roll of drum beats rising to a blow that seemed to smash his toes into his teeth.

He ran. Out of the cabin, onto the roof, into a blaze of sunlight – the very light, he knew, that had ignited the streetlamp and triggered the explosives in the tower. The boom reverberated from the buildings all around, billowing up in clouds of startled birds. Then the birds appeared to freeze in the sky, flapping as slowly as newborn butterflies, as Ben's Mau body found its magical top gear.

With the speed of a terrified cat he sprinted across the roof, which had begun to yield underfoot, its hard paving cracking as if thawing in the sun. His stomach lurched into his chest and he realised he was falling, falling as he ran, dropping with the tower's walls, its stairs, its floors, its bones. Concrete and steel crashed and folded into one another, shattering under their own weight as they crumpled unstoppably towards the ground. With his trainers barely brushing the disintegrating rooftop, Ben flung himself towards the far guard rail where Tiffany was staggering to her feet. There was time to do only one thing, to shout one word above the roar like thunder. He hooked his right arm under her left and gave it everything he had.

'*JUMP!*'

A giant fist slammed him in the back, a wind so thick with grit that it felt solid. Roiling waves of dust engulfed them both. He could see nothing, not Tiffany, not himself. Was he still in the air or had he already hit the ground? He hit the ground. It crumpled his legs under him and tore Tiffany from his grip. Curling into a ball of pain he rolled and rolled until the crashing in his ears died away.

He looked up. A fog of golden brown had hidden the world. Trace by trace shapes appeared. Wire fencing. Rows of lamp posts. A peak like a rugged pyramid. It looked to be steaming in the morning sun, yellow dust venting from the fissures of its slopes.

'Tiffany?' He tried to stand. Just as he was panicking, he saw her. She was clambering on the pyramid, tearing at the rubble with blood-caked hands. His strength spent, he could only crawl towards her over the painful rockeries of concrete and mangled steel. Dust parched his mouth and stung water from his eyes.

'Tiffany, don't.'

She didn't look at him. She strained to lift a grey slab that five men couldn't have moved. She searched for other rubble to dig. There was plenty.

'Tiffany, you're hurt. Stop it.'

'No!' she cried. 'No, no, you can't.' She raked out clumps of plaster and screed. 'You can't. You can't do this to me. I won't let you. Not again. Not again.'

'Tiffany, stop. Please stop.' He reached her. With arms wrapped around her he tried to pull her from the feeble hole. 'Stop.'

She sank upon the rubble as if onto a bed. Down a ragged slab ran a stream of tears, making muddy rivulets in the dust. He sat beside her. He had nothing left, not an atom of strength, not a word in his head that might comfort her. He could barely remember his own name. All had boiled down to a faint, tingling sound. At first he supposed that the deafening implosion had set off a ringing in his ears. Then he managed to place it. In the communal gardens across the way, where the sun had just alighted, the birds were singing in the trees.

PINS AND NEEDLES

Ben woke up. He'd had the strangest dream.

The bedroom walls were sunlight. He lay warm under the duvet.

In his dream he'd been at home. Mum and Dad were there. That was all. That was his dream. It was the most extraordinary thing.

This looked like his bedroom. One of his bedrooms. Where had it come from? Through the window was a morning sky. He found the glass of water he somehow knew was on the bedside table. The door opened and Mum came in, wearing her dressing gown.

'Mum! What are you doing here?'

'That's the third time you've asked me that.'

Was it? His memory was like a jigsaw puzzle box. He rummaged. Getting Tiffany to A&E at Homerton hospital. Then a gap. Beating at the door of Dad's flat. A gobsmacked Dad, a wailing Mum. Falling against them. Being carried to his room, undressed and put to bed. Sleepy glimpses of Mum at his bedside, then Dad, later both of them... unless those parts were dreams.

'Don't tell me he's finally awake.' It was Dad,

with a cup of hot tea.

'Finally?'

'You've slept a whole day and night, Benny. Guess you were tired.'

'Uh. Yes.'

Dad laughed as if this was the best joke ever. Mum's eyes twinkled like sugar dissolving.

'Oh, young man, you are in so much trouble!'

Ben lay back on the pillow and shut his eyes.

'Not any more.'

There came a twenty-fifth hour of sleep, then a huge breakfast in bed. After this Mum ordered him to get dressed and help with the washing up. He dried every teaspoon and then offered to help clean the kitchen, even though the slightest movement made him ache.

Mum and Dad were furious with him, but their fury took the form of delight. Both kept demanding where he had been, then saying, before he could answer, that it didn't matter, he was home now. When he did finally get a word in, he said he'd slept in a tube station with some other runaways. It was hard to tell if they heard. He was home, that was all they cared.

Midway through fish and chips the following evening, he plucked up his courage.

'How long are you staying, Mum?'

'Why? You bored of me already?'

'No, I thought… your job.'

'I can get up earlier and go by train. Till I find one locally.'

'Locally – ?' He took a gulp of Coke, which almost fizzed out of his nose as he realised what she was saying. 'You don't have to, you know. Not if it's, you know, difficult. Not just for me.'

'What are you blithering about?'

'I mean,' said Ben, getting hot, 'you two don't have to pretend to get back together. It's all right. I won't run away again. I promise.'

His parents stared at him. Dad chuckled.

'Don't flatter yourself, Benny. It's not only for you. Is it, Lucy?'

'Ben,' said Mum. 'When we worked out what had happened – that you'd run away – it was the worst thing. Worse than having our home knocked down. It was awful and no-one could make it better. No-one could understand. Except your father. There was one person in the whole world who I could talk to about it, who wanted you back as badly as me, and who might get me through it. And he did.'

'No, *she* did,' said Dad. 'You were the strong one, Lucy.'

'So,' Ben tried to get his head round it. 'You're not pretending.'

'Don't think we are,' said Dad.

'Then we're all living here now? Mum as well?'

'In this dump? I think not.' Lucy Gallagher snorted. 'Which reminds me, Ray. That pinball machine in the living room…'

The next day he went back to school. Few remarked on his absence before the holidays, though he had to think quickly when Miss Bird, his form teacher, asked if his tonsillitis was better. Walking home he took the turning that led to Tiffany's house. He braced himself and rang the doorbell.

'Oh,' said Peter Maine. A rat on the porch would have got a more welcoming look.

'Is Tiffany around?'

'No. And she can't be disturbed.'

Tiffany's voice called down. 'Let him in.'

'See here.' Mr Maine came out onto the step. 'I think it's best if you stay away. Don't you?'

'I said let him in, Dad.'

Mr Maine's face quivered. Taking that as a yes, Ben slipped inside and upstairs.

Tiffany was in bed. Had been, Ben guessed, for several days. The sheets had the look of mixed cement starting to set. He sat near her feet.

'I see your dad's still my number-one fan.'

'Sorry. He'll be worse than ever now.'

'He doesn't know–?'

'All they know is that something's happened. Something awful. Some reason why I won't stop crying.' She gave a choking laugh. 'It's obvious. They think you're my boyfriend.'

'Ha. Funny.'

'And that you've dumped me. And now you've come to upset me even more. Maybe you should leave by the window.'

'Thanks for the tip.' He sat where he was. She was clutching an elderly teddy bear, which he pretended not to notice. A queasy thought crept up on him.

'What about your arms? The claw wounds? Your parents must have seen them, they must have.'

'No,' said Tiffany. 'Long sleeves. Sulking in my room. I'm good at secrets.'

'But the doctor…'

'He won't tell. He didn't even ask me how I got them. He just stitched up every cut, one after the other. Then he asked if I was unhappy.' Tiffany shrugged. 'I said no.'

'Do they hurt still?'

'I don't notice.' Her face lost all its shape. Tears sluiced down her cheeks. 'Ben. I can't feel this way. I can't bear it.'

Ben said nothing. What could he say?

'I'm giving it up. Pashki. I'm giving it up. I won't ever do it again.'

'Okay.' Now he couldn't even reach for her hand. 'Okay.'

'It was me,' Tiffany whimpered. 'I killed her.'

'No.'

'I did. I tracked her down. I did exactly what he wanted me to do. I should have seen it. He couldn't find her himself because he didn't–' she shuddered from deep inside, 'he didn't love her.'

Ben twisted a corner of her bed sheet.

'If it wasn't for me,' Tiffany whispered, 'she'd still be alive.'

'It was Geoff,' Ben burst out. 'He didn't have to connect that detonator, did he? And she didn't have to stay and fight him. But she did. To save us.'

'I helped Geoff to get her.'

'He used you,' said Ben. 'It's not your fault.'

'It is. I wanted her back. I wanted to find her so badly.'

'Yes. *You* wanted to.' Ben found he was holding her hand. 'You'd have done it anyway. No-one could have stopped you. That's how it works. We know that.'

She stared into space. Her head wobbled, a nod maybe.

'That's the other worst thing. The Oshtian Compass. I thought it would stop, now she's gone. But it's still there. In here.' She pressed Ben's fingers into her stomach below her ribs. 'I can feel its needle sort of… spinning. Going crazy. Trying to point to something that isn't there.' Abruptly she pushed him away. 'Oh, what's the use. You never really liked her.'

'I've dreamt about her every night since,' Ben confessed. 'Her face. Over and over. Telling me to go and help you instead of her. It was the last thing she said. I–' He broke off. He always awoke from that dream on a pillow wet against his cheek.

'Sorry,' said Tiffany. 'Didn't mean it.' She gave an exhausted sigh.

'The weirdest thing,' said Ben. 'I even miss *him*. Geoff. Even though I know what he was. I miss the person I thought he was. I remember someone who felt like, oh, like he was a friend. Who did some good things.' He looked to Tiffany, exasperated. 'Was he ever real? Was any of it real?'

She turned her head to face the wall.

'I don't miss him.'

She made Ben leave before her parents kicked up a fuss. Weary bedsprings creaked underneath her. Her stitched wounds itched, raging hot. Farmers were burning stubble on her arms. Rufus came to lie on her duvet, purring as if he had swallowed a live dove. Her hand lay upon his back. The digits of her clock tiptoed from 5:20 to 6:20. At twenty-eight minutes past seven came a knock at the door.

'Go away.'

The door opened.

'No, Stuart. Go away.'

'I need to rest first. I'm practising walking with these.' Stuart had been prescribed a new pair of KAFOs to brace his legs, as he was outgrowing his old ones. 'Doctor Bijlani says to try short distances first. It's a short distance to your room.'

'What do you want?'

'I could use some help with the PM.'

'PM? Prime Minister?'

'Paranormal Map. It needs some adjustments.'

Oh, if it would get rid of him. She rolled herself out of bed. Crossing the landing behind her brother's ponderous steps she felt hollow and light, transparent from weeping. Up on Stuart's wall was the map of the British Isles, speckled with coloured dots.

'Need more pins pushing in?'

'Actually,' said Stuart, slumping into his chair, 'I need you to take some out. Down there.'

In the shaded patch that was London she saw a cluster of green pins. Nine of them.

'I thought green ones were sightings of the Loch Ness Monster?'

'They used to be. But under the old system I had too many greens left over. So now they represent people with supernatural cat skills.'

'What,' she asked, suspicious, 'am I doing with them?'

'Well.' Stuart pushed up his arms to make a shrug. 'It's not accurate anymore, is it?'

'In what sense?'

'You're giving up your pashki. Which means the others will probably give up too.'

'I told you not to spy on me.'

'I forgot. Anyway, you see the problem. I need you to take all the green pins out. I can't do it myself.' He lifted a book on UFOs off the arm of his chair and used both hands to guide it to his bedside table. 'I don't have the strength to pull a pin out of a notice board.'

Oh, she saw what this was about. It was a nice try. It wouldn't work.

'Fine, I'll do it. They're gone.'

She plucked out the first pin fiercely. That was easy.

The second was harder, for it was stuck in very deep. On the third, her bloodless fingers couldn't get a grip. She tugged. She tugged some more. The pin wobbled like a loose tooth. She resolved to do the others first and come back to that one. All at once her hand went heavy.

'Forget it! I'm not in the mood for your silly games.'

She stormed from his room and flopped back into bed. Then she felt suddenly hungry and had to nip downstairs for a bowl of corn flakes.

At the weekend Ben called on Olly. Apart from an egg-sized lump on his head he seemed in good spirits, and his parents had virtually ignored his curious injuries. 'In the Sanders family,' he explained, 'we have accidents. Dad says I take after Clumsy Uncle Bob.' Olly had heard from Yusuf, whose leg, to the despair of his football coach, was in plaster. They talked for a while in Olly's bedroom about all that had happened. Ben had hoped that talking might help. It didn't seem to.

The tower that had blown up too soon became a local news sensation. A week later the story went national, when the diggers clearing the rubble uncovered the pulverised remains of two people. Ben couldn't bear it, switching off whenever the report came on.

On Monday, trudging home from school in the drizzle, a flutter in a rubbish bin made him stop. He fished out a sodden page of newspaper and scanned it, wondering what had caught his eye. Then he saw the second story. *Soap star's son 'returns from the dead'*. He read it and reread it to make doubly sure. The details were few. Tony Sherwood, better known as teacher Keith Grogan in *Eastenders*… his son, missing since the age of ten…tearful reunion… A photo of Tony Sherwood's character but not his son.

Ben folded the wet newspaper into his schoolbag. He no longer noticed the rain. Thomas had made it home. Ben did something he hadn't done for years – he jumped in a puddle. Mum would moan about his trousers and even that would feel good. He paused before the next puddle. There was still Hannah. What about her? In his heart, he knew that she too would be all right. Either Thomas's family would help her or, more likely, she herself had already plucked up the courage to ask someone where Cambridge was, and had found her way back to the house she'd once left to go shopping with her mum. Here was her finger, reaching for the doorbell.

Ben didn't jump in the second puddle, though, because his phone rang. It was Tiffany.

'I'll tell you what else I'm glad to see the back of,' she snapped.

Ben got the impression that he'd missed the first half of this argument.

'Er, what?'

'Hiring that crummy church hall,' said Tiffany. 'Week after week. It was always me who had to phone the warden, and then squeeze the money out of you lot. At least that's the end of that.'

'But what about–' Ben was going to mention the cemetery chapel, then remembered that this had been Geoff's idea. 'What if we did start classes again? I could do all that stuff.'

'You? You'd forget after two weeks.'

'Okay then,' said Ben. 'How about this week and next week?'

'Dunno.'

'All you have to do is turn up. I'll book the hall and everyone will be there. Guaranteed.'

'Yusuf's got a broken leg.'

'Exactly. No more football practice.'

'Hadn't thought of that.'

'And Olly will not be late.'

'Ha. I'll believe that when I see it.'

'You've got to be there to see it,' Ben pointed out. 'There's just one thing.'

'What's that?'

'Don't forget to bring your three pounds.'

At last, she laughed.

Ben relished his new role of club secretary for about five minutes, after which it made him want to climb the walls as he tried to fit it in with school, homework, the arcade, and spending as much time as he could with Mum and Dad. It amazed him that Tiffany hadn't complained about it more. In that first lesson the Cat Kin mostly just talked, but it felt right to be meeting again. Olly spent much of the second class decorating Yusuf's cast with graffiti. Still, Ben had lasted his two weeks, and then he managed a third.

It was Wednesday lunchtime. Tired of sandwiches he left the school grounds in search of proper junk food. He bought a Cornish pasty from the shop on the corner. When he came out he saw a cat. It was sitting, amusingly, on the warm leather of a motorcycle seat. It swivelled its head to look at him.

'Jim?'

Ben was proud to admit that usually he couldn't tell one cat from another. But this cat, Mrs Powell's cat, he could have picked out of a line-up. The frosty coat ingrained with black, the bewitching olivine eyes. But Jim should still be in Dartmoor, shouldn't he? Two hundred miles from here.

'Jim!' It *was* him. Ben went and stroked his head. He got a mild electric shock, which he was used to, and in return Jim took a corner of his Cornish pasty. He looked half-starved.

How could this cat be here? There was only one explanation. When his owner never came home, Jim had started to wander. And his homing instinct – his Oshtian Compass – had guided him off the moors, through the fields, lanes, villages and towns, all the way back to east London, his old home. He was trying to find the flat he had shared with Mrs Powell. A wave of pity caught Ben off guard. He wished he could tell this animal that his journey had been in vain, that his old home wouldn't have him back, and that his friend was dead.

Abruptly Jim sprang from the motorbike's seat and onto a garden wall. Ben made up his mind. He couldn't let this orphan roam the city streets. Back at home he had a real family now. What better way to make it complete?

'Puss-puss!' he said. 'C'mon, Jim. Come with me.'

Jim turned his stare upon him. For a moment gratitude glinted in those gemstone eyes. Then his tail swished and he trotted along the wall – the wrong way.

'Jim!' Ben called. 'Here, kitty. Cornish pasty! Nice pasty!'

The cat glanced back and gave a funny sort of blink. Almost, unless Ben imagined it, a wink. Then in one bound Jim crossed to a fence, flowed over it and dropped out of sight.

Ben ran behind the terrace and saw an empty alley. He called Jim's name, over and over, until he felt like a twit and stopped. He bit into the remains of his lunch.

That had looked like a cat who knew precisely where he was going.

Ben chewed, brushing away crumbs, while one car passed after another. He ought to tell Tiffany. What, though, could he tell her? It might not mean very much.

Fingering his phone, he saw the time. Afternoon classes would start in fifteen minutes and he still had homework to finish. Ben tossed the pasty wrapper into a rubbish bin and hurried back to school.

THE END

STRIDENT

The Cat Kin

ISBN 978-1-905537-16-7 (paperback, RRP £6.99)

Everyone who came to the strange gym class was looking for something else. What they found was the mysterious Mrs Powell and Pashki, a lost art from an age when cats were worshipped as gods.

Ben and Tiffany wonder: who is their eccentric old teacher? What does she really want with them? And why are they suddenly able to see in the dark?

Meanwhile, in London's gloomy streets, human vermin are stirring. Ben and Tiffany may soon be glad of their new gifts. But against men whose cunning is matched only by their unspeakable cruelty, will even nine lives be enough?

The Sons of Rissouli

ISBN 978-1-905537-21-1 (paperback, RRP £6.99)

When Danny goes to live with his cool Uncle Angus, he knows life will never be the same again. But he doesn't expect to be catapulted into a world of guns, explosions and high-speed chases.

After they uncover a top-secret, highly illegal operation to ship arms out of the country, Danny and Angus race to North Africa to investigate. As they pursue the bloodthirsty Sons of Rissouli across country the stakes get higher, and Danny is thrown into dangers he could never have imagined.

He'll have to be tough enough to survive in the brutal furnace of the desert. But when another life is at stake, will he have the guts to risk his own?

There's no doubt about it. It's going to be an adventure...

Bree McCready And The Flame of Irenus

ISBN 978-1-905537-17-4 (paperback, RRP £6.99)

Eight months after her death-defying escape from Castle Zarcalat, Bree McCready thinks she's seen the last of the half-heart locket and the dangerous magical book that goes with it...until Honey's kid sister Mimi disappears. Suddenly, the locket and the book plunge Bree, Sandy and Honey into a world divided by the mysterious Flame of Irenus. Burning in a secret part of the castle, some think the Flame is the source of peace and light. Others say it brings bloodshed and must be extinguished.

Faced with a bone-crunching race against time to rescue Mimi and find the hidden chamber, Bree must rely on her friends more than ever. But a new boy at school has caught her eye and brought unexpected jealousy...She saved the world once before. Saving her friendships might not be as easy.

The explosive sequel to Bree McCready and the Half-Heart Locket is packed with action, secrets and heartbreak.

The Comet's Child

ISBN 978-1-905537-12-9 (paperback, RRP £7.99)

For as long as anyone can remember there have been rumours about the return of a chosen one. When Fin discovers the prophecies point to him he is scared, at first. He resolves to learn the truth about his origins and uncover the secrets surrounding his birth; only then can he embrace his true destiny.

The journey ahead is exciting and full of danger, but others must stop him before he learns the truth…